A SLAYING AT THE SKI LODGE

ELLIE ALEXANDER

Storm
PUBLISHING

Previously published in 2016 as *Slayed on the Slopes* by Kate Dyer-Seeley by Kensington Publishing Corp.

Ebook ISBN: 978-1-83700-147-7
Paperback ISBN: 978-1-83700-149-1

Cover design: Dawn Adams
Cover images: Dawn Adams

Published by Storm Publishing.
For further information, visit:
www.stormpublishing.co

ALSO BY ELLIE ALEXANDER

Meg Reed Investigates

A Murder on the Mountain

A Body at the Beach

A Body at Boot Camp

Revenge on the Rocks

A Secret Bookcase Mystery

The Body in the Bookstore

A Murder at the Movies

Death at the Dinner Party

A Holiday Homicide

A Victim at Valentine's

A Body at the Book Fair

For Vintage Books. The first bookstore signing I did was with Vintage Books. The staff and booksellers were such champions of the series and me, and we had our own adventures all across the PNW! They happily and eagerly brought boxes and boxes of lovely books to events and gave me so much early insight into the bookselling side of publishing. They've just celebrated fifty years in business, and here's to fifty more!

ONE

THE SILCOX HUT, TIMBERLINE, OREGON.
ELEVATION 7,000 FEET

You're an idiot, Meg.

Yep, that was pretty much the first thing that came to mind as I frantically scanned the frozen sky.

Why didn't I trust my intuition? If I ever bothered to stop and listen to Gam's oh-so-wise advice, I'd never get myself into these situations. But what did I do instead? Forged on, ignoring that nagging voice in my head.

What I couldn't ignore now was the howl of the wind and the pounding in my forehead.

At 7,000 feet above sea level, where the air began to thin, I couldn't seem to fill my chest. My breath came in shallow, wheezing spurts and felt as thick as the snow beneath my feet. My head throbbed from the lack of oxygen, and my fingers burned with cold. Seventeen inches of new snow had fallen since the blizzard hit yesterday, and it didn't look like Mother Nature intended to let up anytime soon.

For some strange reason I thought I could hear the faint sounds of Frank Sinatra's crooning voice singing words about kissing goodbye humming on the wind. Message received. If I didn't find my way back to the Silcox Hut—fast—I'd be kissing *my life* goodbye. I couldn't be hearing music up at this elevation, could I? Was I losing it? How long did hypothermia take to set in?

Pausing in the knee-deep snow, I searched the sky for any clue that might lead me in the direction of the Silcox Hut and safety. Nothing but blinding white greeted me. I couldn't tell how much snow was actually falling and how much was being hurled back up into the air by the deafening wind.

Yet there it was again. The swell of big band music teased my ears.

Guide me back, Frank, I thought as I used all the energy I could muster to free my tingling feet from the snow and trudge toward the sound of the music.

Thank God I'd worn my fur-lined snow boots, because even with two pairs of thick wool socks I was losing feeling in my toes. My fingers were another story. The super-cute cashmere fingerless gloves seemed like an excellent fashion statement a couple days ago, but in terms of function, not so much.

I kicked my foot free from the powder and took a step forward. It was getting hard to stay upright. Icy flakes pelted my face. I sank deeper in the snow.

At this rate you're going to end up a Popsicle, Meg, I thought just as I heard a bang.

At first I thought it must be a drum—the bang of the big band reaching its crescendo. A moment later I realized I was horribly mistaken.

Lurching forward through the heavy snow, I heard another bang. This time there was no mistaking the sound—it had to be a gunshot.

I had no one to blame but myself. The assignment at the Silcox Hut was my idea. Two days before, while on my way to

Government Camp, Oregon, there was no sign of the storm that had been battering the mountain ever since.

The languid late November sun warmed the interior of the car as I stuffed the cargo area with ski boots, snowshoes, my winter parka, and a suitcase before setting off. I was looking forward to this assignment.

After my disastrous initial assignment last spring for *Northwest Extreme*, the award-winning adventure magazine where I was currently a staff writer, I had vowed to hone my almost non-existent outdoor skills. And hone I did. I had spent the better chunk of my summer training with the Crag Rats, Oregon's oldest volunteer mountain rescue team.

Thanks to the Crag Rats' expert guidance and steadfast patience, I gained some creditability with the team at *Northwest Extreme*. Don't get me wrong. I wasn't planning to bungee jump off a bridge or scale Everest anytime soon, but I could hold my own on a day hike now. Plus, the Crag Rats schooled me on all their lingo and gear. It was like a summer-long immersion camp.

I emerged from my outdoor intensive training more confident and with the equivalent of a bachelor's degree in extreme adventure. Hopefully I'd be able to apply what I learned from the Crag Rats to my writing. I knew that Greg, my editor and distractingly gorgeous boss, was thrilled that I'd invested the time in training.

Fortunately my Crag Rat friends were generous in reporting my progress to Greg. I think I won them over with batches of my grandmother's—Gam's—orange dreamsicle cookies and my determination to ask unexpected questions. The Crag Rats convinced Greg that I could hold my own with any thrill-seeker or professional athlete that he might task me with interviewing. Okay, so maybe that was a stretch of the truth, but I wasn't worried. I figured any future blemishes in my outdoor prowess could be glossed over by my ability to wield a paper and a pen. Or keyboard.

That's why I was an idiot.

I was the one who approached Greg about writing a feature on a new high-altitude guiding team—the Ridge Rangers. In fairness, I didn't have an inkling of worry that things might not go according to plan.

"Got a minute?" I asked as I peered into Greg's office earlier that month. The rising sun cast a pinkish glow on the wall of windows behind his desk and illuminated the Willamette River outside that divided my hometown, Portland, in half. *Northwest Extreme*'s headquarters were in a funky industrial space right on the river with huge windows and shared open spaces with cozy couches and plush writing chairs. The break room was always stocked with the latest energy bars or running goo, and in the warmer months Greg often hosted outdoor gatherings— happy hour and dinners for the entire team. It was far from a corporate vibe.

I liked to arrive before the rest of the staff in the morning. It gave me time to pull together my thoughts before the office started to buzz with people facing the frenzy of deadlines.

"Hey, Meg, you're here early." Greg waved me in. "Come on in. What's up?"

I thought I'd recovered from my crush on him. The distraction of my intensive training over the summer almost did it. But at the sight of his scruffy stubble and tanned forearms, I had to stop myself from swooning. Having a crush on your boss was a bad, bad idea.

One glance around his office revealed that our photography department wasn't immune to Greg's natural good looks and charm either. Covers of *Northwest Extreme* were framed on the walls. Greg's mug graced the cover of at least five. His tall, sculpted body hung from the side of cliffs and posed on summits.

"Sorry to bug you," I said, rolling a swivel chair in front of his desk. When Greg took over as editor in chief a few years before, he'd moved *Northwest Extreme* to our current refurbished warehouse on the waterfront. Mere feet from his office windows sat a multi-use path where Portlanders ran, biked, and walked in any kind of weather. We'd had a long stretch of late summer and the path was a mob scene of early-morning exercisers trying to burn calories and soak up some vitamin D before heading to work. I knew I was biased, but I adored my hometown. Even in the rainy months, the Rose City was flush with shades of green from the canopy of evergreen trees surrounding the city. Portland was the kind of place where anything goes— offbeat, artistic personalities weren't just welcome, they were the norm. Anything went, whether it was my obsession for vintage dresses or counter-culture grunge.

I adjusted the hemline of my 1950s pleated pale pink cotton dress. Despite my burgeoning outdoor skills, I couldn't give up my love of retro fashion.

"Nice dress." Greg winked. "Pink—I can always count on you for pink, Meg."

"Thanks." I held my hand on my forehead to block the glare from the water outside.

Greg glanced over his shoulder. "Is that too bright? I can close the shades." He grabbed a remote control from his desk and aimed it at the windows.

Gray shades began to lower automatically.

"No, wait. You don't have to do that. I love the sun. I just have to adjust my position. Keep them open."

"Okay, if you're sure." Greg clicked another button. The shades stopped and rose back to their original position. "How's life, Meg? I've been gone so much lately, it seems like I haven't seen you for ages."

"I know. How was Argentina? You climbed Aconcagua,

right?" No wonder his skin looked as though it had been gently toasted and buttered.

"Yep. I'm working on a feature about the seven summits. I have three left. Not a bad gig." He laughed, cracked his knuckles, and leaned even closer on his desk. "Now, what can I do for you?"

I could smell his aftershave and see the curve of the muscles in his forearms.

Stop it, Meg. I scooted back a little and crossed my legs.

Gathering my composure, I launched into my pitch. "Well, you know how the Crag Rats sort of took me under their wing this summer? They're the oldest volunteer mountain rescue group this side of the Rockies, right?"

Greg nodded.

"I learned from a few members of the team that some of them are branching off and starting a new mountaineering guiding team made up primarily of competitive snowboarders—the Ridge Rangers. They're going to lead groups of climbers up the mountain, from novices to experts. Their goal is to make sure everyone who books a trip with them summits. I think it could make a really interesting story. Readers will really connect with their tricks, skills, and a couple of them aren't so bad on the eyes." I winked.

"Oh, really? So what exactly were they *training* you on?" Greg raised his eyebrow.

Heat rose to my cheeks. "No, no, I didn't mean it like that. I just meant that we might draw in some new female readership because most of the Ridge Rangers are men—that's all." *Stop, Meg.* "The team is having their first meeting up on Mount Hood later this month and I thought I could go and do a write-up about it."

Greg leaned back in his chair. "You're too easy, Meg. You know you can never play poker. One little joke and you turn as red as those Japanese maples outside."

The maple trees lining the pathway were ablaze with color. My cheeks felt equally hot.

Greg had an uncanny ability to unnerve me no matter what.

He grabbed a pencil from a coffee cup on his desk. The cup displayed our *Northwest Extreme* tagline—KEEPING THE WEST WILD. He made a note on a blank sheet of paper, stopped and looked at me. "Yeah, I love this idea. The Ridge Rangers, right? A cover story, maybe? Oregon's wild guides on the slope. Let's do it."

"Really?" I had to sit on my hands to stop from doing a little happy dance right then and there in his office.

"Sure. So what's this meeting they're holding?"

"Hang on one sec, okay?" I scooted the chair back and sprinted out of his office. The communal area was dark and empty, aside from a few early birds like me. Everyone kept their own schedule. Greg liked his staff to have autonomy and the flexibility to be out on assignment or out for a long run at a moment's notice. I appreciated his hands-off approach to management and hoped he didn't notice that I tended to pop out for a double mocha versus for a long run.

My desk sat in the middle of the exposed brick building below high-beamed ceilings. I fumbled through a stack of file folders and found one labeled RIDGE RANGERS. I tucked it under my arm and returned to Greg's office.

"Here's everything I've gathered so far." My foot slipped out of my slide sandal and I stumbled onto his desk, spilling the file.

"You okay?" Greg smirked.

I gathered the papers together and reached down to grab my rose-colored sandal. Holding it in the air, I laughed. "Yep, just a slight wardrobe malfunction."

You're such a klutz, Meg, I thought as I slid my sandal back on and held my hand over my stomach.

I tucked my hair behind my ears. It was at a weird in-between stage. Usually I wore it short, but I'd decided I wanted to try something new going into the colder weather, so I'd been growing it out. The result was a bunch of funky blond layers that tended to flip out in all the wrong places.

Greg caught my eye and gave me an expectant look.

I turned on my most professional voice. "Right." I passed him the file. "The Ridge Rangers are hosting their inaugural training meeting before they start to take clients up the summit. They're taking over the Silcox Hut at Timberline for a long weekend of events—rescue training, boarding exhibitions, gear demos, team bonding—that sort of thing."

He thumbed through the notes I'd collected. "See, Meg, this is why I keep you around. Nice preliminary work. So when's the training?"

I grinned and relaxed my stomach muscles. "In three weeks. The weekend before Thanksgiving." Glancing out the window as a group of runners breezed past in shorts and T-shirts, I continued. "Although at this rate I'm guessing there won't be any snow on the mountain."

"Yeah, no kidding." Greg shook his head. "Such a bummer." He handed me back the folder. "The week before Thanksgiving?"

"Yep."

He paused and tapped his pencil again. "That might work out perfectly. My family has a place in Government Camp, near the lodge. I was planning to be up there that weekend anyway and I've been wanting to get the whole team together. Maybe we can do a staff meeting the day before, work on next year's editorial calendar and bond a bit. Will that work for you?"

"Uh, sure."

"Great. Let me make a couple calls and see if I can reserve the lodge. Don't say anything to the rest of the staff yet."

"Of course not." I shook my head, feeling a little beam of pride that he was looping me in first.

"If it works out, we can knock out a team retreat and a cover story. Plus, this way I'll be around to help you with the feature. I wouldn't mind taking a couple runs anyway. What do you say, Meg? We'll throw in our skis and make a weekend out of it?"

So much for autonomy. I gulped. The touch of pride quickly morphed into something resembling terror. "Sure, that sounds great."

"You ski, right?"

"Yeah. Yeah, I totally ski," I lied as I tucked the file under my arm and exited from his office.

What are you thinking, Meg? I thought as I made my way back to my desk. My last ski trip hadn't ended well. My bestie, Jill Pettygrove, was on the ski team when we were growing up. Her parents were avid skiers and Jill was shredding the slopes as soon as she took her first steps.

They invited me up to the mountain when we were in elementary school. Despite their expert training, I spent most of the weekend on my derrière. On our way home I nursed a sprained ankle and a bruised bum and vowed I'd never ski again.

Yet somehow I managed not only to rope myself into a ski trip, but a ski trip with *my boss.* My only consolation was the brilliant November sun. Its rays had penetrated through the windows on the far side of the office and warmed the back of my chair. As I booted up my laptop to begin outlining my feature on the Ridge Rangers, I was confident there was no chance I'd have to break out skis soon.

There wasn't a cloud on the horizon and the forecast called for continuing sun. In fact, the local news stations had been warning of a potential drought for the past two months.

I didn't have anything to worry about. The mountain would be bare.

Was I ever wrong.

TWO

Three weeks later, my red car, a graduation gift from Pops, was bursting with gear and equipment.

"You're sure these will stay?" I asked Jill as I struggled to tighten a pair of her old skis to the top of the car.

Jill was a good five inches taller than me. Her arms easily reached the ski rack and cinched the straps tight. "They're good. They're not going anywhere. I just hope you don't have to use them. You know the forecast is calling for snow now, right?"

I looked up at the cloudless blue sky above us. A slight breeze released a single leaf from the white birch tree in front of my apartment. "I know," I said as I dug through my purse for my sunglasses. "That means there's no way it's actually going to snow. The forecasters are always wrong. I mean, look around. The only thing I see is the sun."

"Let's hope you're right." Jill looked doubtful. "You remember what happened the last time we went skiing?"

"Uh, yeah." I pushed up my purple sunglasses (a freebie from *Northwest Extreme*) on the bridge of my nose. "Don't worry. Even if it snows, I'm not getting on those suckers." I pointed to the skis. "They're just for show."

The contents of my bulging trunk were evidence that if nothing else, I was overprepared for this assignment. In addition to Jill's skis, I'd packed snow boots, a hooded parka in a matching shade of plum, a knit pink and purple striped hat, and my favorite find of the season—fingerless gloves made from recycled cashmere sweaters. They were hand-sewn by a local seamstress and friend of Gam's. Mine were a deep shade of eggplant and embellished with tiny pastel flowers. I was focused on looking the part of an extreme sports reporter. Plus, not only would I look stylish on the slopes this weekend, but my fingers would be free to take notes. Genius, if I did say so myself.

"Anything else you need before you hit the road?" Jill asked, twisting her silky shoulder-length hair into a ponytail.

She was Grace Kelly. I was Doris Day. There was no escaping it. Jill exuded an easy elegance that I could never match. Not that it mattered. Lucky for me, Portland was a mecca for all things vintage. My style blended in with the hipsters who sought out antiques and purposely wore retro clothing. Little did they know I had a secret obsession with the 1950s. Gam said it was because I was an old soul—much wiser than my twenty-three years. I hoped she was right.

"I think I'm good," I said to Jill, reaching into the pocket of my jeans and handing her the key to my apartment. "Thanks again for letting me borrow your old skis. Here's the key. The common area is in the basement—no one ever uses it. You'll be totally alone down there, Picasso."

Jill squeezed my hand. "Thanks. And thanks again for not saying anything to Will."

Will Barrington was Jill's pretentious lawyer boyfriend. She made me promise—actually pinky swear, like we'd been doing since the third grade—that I wouldn't mention to him that she was painting. They'd been dating for a little over a year after meeting at the upscale law firm where Jill had been interning.

Don't even get me started on Will. He used a Gucci umbrella. Need I say more?

Jill's artistic talent rivaled that of any professional in the creative community of Portland, especially in the Pearl, where Jill lived. You couldn't go more than a block there without seeing an art gallery. But she was extremely protective of her work. Only a handful of people knew that she painted.

Sometimes I wanted to shake her and force her to come out of hiding, but I knew that pushing her would only make her retreat inward. Instead, I found her a space to work.

After crashing on her couch for almost a year, I had finally moved out this past summer. It was time. With Jill and our good friend Matt's help, I rented a one-bedroom apartment in a small complex in North Portland.

The sweet area boasted an eclectic mix of old bungalows, tree-lined streets, funky shops, pubs, food carts, and, of course, a coffee shop on every corner. In Portland, we took our coffee seriously. That and brunch. Brunch was obviously the most important meal of the day.

My apartment was on the ground floor with large bay windows that looked out onto the courtyard. I fell in love with it the moment I saw it. The living room was warm and cheery with scratched, yet shiny, original 1920s hardwood floors and a brick fireplace in the corner. I set up my writing desk in front of the windows, which may have been a mistake as I tended to get easily distracted by activity in the courtyard.

The kitchen was by far the best thing about the small 750-square-foot space. The walls were painted lemon yellow. There were whitewashed cabinets and butcher-block countertops, but the pièce de résistance was the rustic wooden island in the center of the room. It housed my vintage teal mixer and was usually the only spot where I ended up getting any writing done.

When I moved in, I discovered an empty common area in

the basement. It was perfect for Jill's painting, with concrete floors covered in layers of chipped paint and enough natural light from rectangular south-facing windows to allow her to work her magic on canvas.

If Jill wouldn't open up about her secret affair with art, at least she'd have a space to create.

"Did you remember to pack a dress?" Jill asked. "I'll be up on Saturday for Mike's wedding. You think you'll be able to ditch out for a couple of hours and come meet us at Timberline?"

"I'll try. I scored the cutest ivory and green taffeta dress that I'm dying to wear." The wedding Jill referenced was for our college classmate Mike. He'd been part of our group of friends since our first year and was the first one of us to take the plunge into marriage.

I rolled up my sleeves. "It's warm today."

Jill nodded in agreement but didn't look as though the heat had any effect on her. She looked casually cool in tailored black slacks and a burnt-orange silk shirt. Her outfits were understated and elegant, always making her appear much older.

Today I was wearing a pair of jeans I'd scored at the Goodwill, rolled up to midcalf, a plain ivory T-shirt, four brushed silver and gold necklaces, and flip-flops. Hopefully Mount Hood would be equally warm otherwise I'd have to stop for a costume change.

"Have a great time," Jill called as I started to steer the car away. "See you in a couple days. And, Meg, do *not* get hurt!"

"You got it." I waved out the driver's side window. If only I could have kept that promise.

THREE

Mount Hood anchored the cities of Portland and Vancouver with the Columbia River flowing from its foothills. Gam, a mystic healer, chose her condo on the banks of the river specifically for a view of the mountain. She believed the mountain held deep power and was a spiritual center.

"If you listen, you can hear the mountain call to you, Margaret," she said one afternoon when we sat on her sundrenched balcony watching sailboats float along the river. "Since the beginning of time people have made pilgrimages to the 'highest,' or mountaintops as we now call them. Their elevation above the earth pulls us closer to 'the beginning of all things.'"

I wasn't sure if it was "the beginning of all things" or the excitement of being on a new assignment, but I certainly felt the lure of the mountain as I guided my car onto the freeway and headed east.

Greg had secured a meeting space in Government Camp—elevation 4,000 feet. Or "base camp," as I'd named it. It sounded more gutsy and adventuresome.

All staff members were due by noon today. Greg planned a

team retreat. After I finished with *Northwest Extreme*, I'd head higher to Timberline Lodge and meet up with the Ridge Rangers for a weekend of interviews and observation. I did some of my best work by watching.

The city began to give way to farmhouses as I drove farther into the foothills. I breezed by Christmas tree farms where workers gathered in the fields, grooming trees for purchase in a few short weeks. Signs sprouted up on both sides of the highway directing people to hiking trails and rainbow trout fishing.

When I reached Rhododendron, a small town at the base of the mountain and the last pit stop before ascending to Government Camp, I stopped for a coffee. The tiny shop with pine-beam ceilings was empty when I pushed the door open. The scent of roasting beans and baking pastries engulfed me.

"Howdy, honey," a middle-aged barista greeted me from behind the counter. "What can I get for you this morning?"

"Can you make a mocha?"

"Sure thing. What size would you like?" she asked, pointing to a wall of paper mugs with black stamps of Mount Hood on them.

"I'll take a large, please." I wandered around the shop, leafing through postcards and homemade soy candle tins. A spinning rack near the cash register displayed a variety of ski essentials—ChapStick, mini containers of sunscreen, and hand warmers.

"Not going to need these anytime soon, huh?" I laughed and held up a package of the hand warmers.

She turned off the steam and slowly swirled milk into a cup. "You want some whip on this, honey?"

"Sure." I nodded.

"You might want to grab a couple packs of those warmers. It's supposed to get mighty wicked around here in the next couple days." She sprayed whipped cream in a mound on top of the coffee.

"Seems impossible, doesn't it? I mean it's gorgeous out there. I can't drive without these." I pointed to the sunglasses propped on my head.

"The calm before the storm." She handed me the coffee. "You want those, too?"

"Why not?" I set two packets of hand warmers on the counter. My salary at *Northwest Extreme* wasn't much as a staff writer, but it was a huge improvement from my unemployed status. Plus, the magazine offered full benefits and covered my expenses when on assignment. This coffee was on Greg.

"Be careful out there!" the barista called after me as I left the shop. "Mark my words, honey, we're going to get dumped on."

I took a sip of the hot, milky coffee. It had the perfect hint of dark chocolate without being overly sweet. Back on the road, I had to abandon my coffee to use both hands to navigate the steep, winding grade of Highway 26 that looped up the mountain. The guardrail to my right didn't look like it would do much to hold me back if...

Don't go there, Meg.

Evergreen forests towered hundreds of feet below and as far as my eyes could see. To my left, the exposed rocks of the mountainside threatened to tumble onto the road. Signs warned of falling rocks, steep grades, and sharp turns—nothing short of my worst nightmare.

My ears began to pop as the elevation increased. I could have used a trick that Pops taught me years ago, to plug my nose and swallow to relieve the pressure, but that would mean taking one hand off the wheel. No chance!

Nor did I intend to look anywhere but straight ahead. The side of the mountain literally sheared off to my right. Have I mentioned I hated heights? Yeah, I hated them.

My summer training with the Crag Rats might have honed

my outdoor skills, but they had definitely *not* cured me of my fear of heights.

A Jeep with its sunroof open moved into the left lane to pass me. I checked the dash. The outside thermometer read sixty-five degrees. Warm for this time of year, but not warm enough to have your roof half-open. Two teenagers waved at me from the backseat and flew ahead. They were out of sight by the time I made it to the next bend.

I let out a sigh of relief when I caught sight of a billboard with a snowboarder flying in the air and an arrow pointing to the turnout to Ski Bowl, America's largest night-skiing venue, a mile ahead.

The dangerous cliff disappeared and I was now level with the trunks of evergreen trees. *Thank God.* I freed my hands from their death grip on the steering wheel. *I made it.*

I steered the car off the highway and into the high mountain town of Government Camp. This was where I'd come on my one and only skiing trip with Jill as a kid. The little village boasted a coffee shop and plenty of pubs where boarders and skiers could refuel after a day on the slopes. Buildings were designed with slanted shingled and metal roofs so that the snow could slide off. The last time I'd come here with Jill, the snow was so deep it was pushed in car-high piles along the side of the road by snowplows. Today, sunlight danced on the branches of the evergreen trees. There wasn't a single flake anywhere to be found.

I found the turn for Collins Lake Resort, where Greg owned a condo and would be hosting the team. I drew in a breath as I took in the resort. New condos, each three stories high, were built to look old. Designed after a Bavarian village, each condo had two-toned brown and beige siding with red alpine roofs and balconies with picture-perfect views of the ski slopes.

Greg had a place here?

Damn, okay. This was not what I was expecting.

I had pictured a rustic family cabin tucked back in the forest, not a high-end ski chalet that made me feel like I'd just arrived in the Swiss Alps.

Finding an empty parking space nearby, I left my gear in the back of the car. I could unload it later. Greg had reserved a group of condos for the staff. I'd be bunking with two of my colleagues for the next couple of days. I grabbed my laptop bag and sucked down the last few sips of my cold coffee.

Welcome to the start of a fun week, Meg. Just think, it's almost like a vacation. My body hummed with eager anticipation. I nearly skipped toward the lodge where our meeting would take place. It was easy to spot with its huge cedar beams and a connecting outdoor pool and hot tub, which I spied through a wrought-iron fence. The mountain air felt invigorating on my face. I could smell the earthy old-growth trees and hear the rush of the creek that cut through the property.

"Yeah," I said under my breath, "a vacation."

FOUR

I slung my laptop bag over my shoulder and reveled in the clear mountain air for a moment before heading into the lodge. Inside, a giant stone wood-burning fireplace sat unused on the far side of the rustic room. A buffet of salads and juices was set up in a small kitchenette on the wall opposite the fireplace. Huge wood trusses crossed the ceiling. My coworkers sat and munched on lunch. They definitely looked like they belonged at this altitude. Most of them wore athletic gear—hiking boots, climbing shorts, and T-shirts from marathons and mud runs they'd finished.

"Meg!" Greg clapped me on the shoulder. "You made it. Grab some lunch and go find a seat. We're going to get started in a minute here." He looked at my feet. "Flip-flops? You know it's supposed to snow?"

"So I hear." My stomach rumbled as I glanced at my sparkly pink toenail polish. In my excitement to get up the mountain, I'd skipped breakfast. A gurgling sound erupted. I threw my hand on my belly to quiet it.

It didn't work.

"Sounds like you're ready for lunch." Greg chuckled. "You

better go grab something before Joe gets here. He's been climbing Hood. He'll probably finish that entire feast in one sitting."

I gave him a nervous laugh and hurried over to grab some food before my noisy stomach drew the attention of the entire room.

The food was fitting for *Northwest Extreme*. It consisted of a variety of salads—spinach with cranberries, almonds, and feta, a Greek salad with Kalamata olives, red onions, and cherry tomatoes, and a NW salad with toasted hazelnuts, fresh pears, and blue cheese. I scooped up a small helping of each, buttered a slice of organic bread, and grabbed a bottle of mango-orange juice.

A group of my friends called me over to the spot they'd saved for me near the window that looked out onto the forested trails and a creek. We chatted about our upcoming assignments and who was bunking with whom. Greg wanted us to bond, so our original plans were scrapped. He had us draw names out of a hat. I ended up with Angie, an uptight accountant. Great.

Greg started the meeting a few minutes later. He welcomed us to his "home away from home" and passed out our agendas.

My mind wandered as the ad group gave their annual report. Not that ad sales weren't important. I fully understood that without our ad revenue I'd have been out of a job and paycheck, but numbers weren't my thing.

The view from the windows made me want to lace up my kicks and get out on the trail. I'd read that the twenty-eight-acre resort housed a network of walking and snowshoeing trails. I watched as the wind stirred in the sturdy branches. As the ad team droned on, I noticed patchy clouds blanketing the sun every few minutes. Maybe we were due for a change in the weather after all.

By the time we wrapped for the afternoon, a thick wall of clouds hung overhead. I hurried in my flip-flops to grab my bags from the car and locate the chalet where I'd be staying for the next couple days, ignoring the fact that the temperature was rapidly dropping. That was normal at this elevation in the evening, right?

After dinner, Angie made it clear that it was going to be lights out in our condo. At 8:00? No thanks.

I opted for a late-evening swim, pulling on my brand-new tankini. I found it at a vintage swim shop not far from Jill's place in the Pearl. My suit was called the "Bridgette." It was a delicious shade of coral with thick, black retro straps that tied around the neck and black and white bottoms. I couldn't wait to wear it.

I walked the short distance from my chalet back to the lodge. When I entered the common room, Greg was sitting next to the fireplace in a heated conversation on his phone. He didn't notice me come in.

"Enough!" he shouted. "We've been over this a hundred times, and my answer is still no. I'm not doing that to her. I refuse."

I froze.

Greg jumped to his feet and paced in front of the fireplace. The muscles in his neck tightened. "No! You listen to me. She's been through enough. I'm done. I'm telling you, I'm done. She needs to know."

He ended the call and slammed his phone on a cedar table.

Oh, crap. What should I do?

I didn't think he'd seen me, but to make it to the pool I'd have to pass through his line of sight. I could back out the front door, but it was solid wood and iron. It would definitely make noise shutting. I didn't want Greg to think I was spying on him.

I took a timid step forward. Maybe I could slip into the attached bathroom and sauna area without him seeing me.

"Meg?" Greg's voice sounded as I scooted toward the changing area.

"Uh, hey. Hi." Dang. Caught in the act. I whipped my head around and threw my towel over my shoulder. "I'm going to jump in the pool. Swimming outside at night—it's one of my favorite things." I hoped my tone sounded casual and breezy, but I was fairly sure it didn't.

Greg eyed me from head to foot, his gaze resting on my bust just a second too long. "Cute suit."

I pulled my towel from my shoulder and covered up, feeling suddenly self-conscious. "Brr. It's chilly in here."

"Yeah," Greg sighed, and retrieved his phone from the table. "Have a nice swim." He sauntered past me and out the front doors. His gait seemed casual, but I noticed his right hand clenched his phone. What was the phone call about? Who was Greg arguing with? And who were they arguing about? He referenced a woman. Who was this mystery woman and what was Greg going to tell her?

Let it go, Meg. It's none of your business.

But I couldn't—it was the reporter in me. Pops said I was born curious.

I left my towel on a hook in the bathroom and headed outside to the pool. A four-foot cedar fence enclosed the pool space from the stately fir trees on the opposite side. It felt like finding a hidden oasis in the middle of a dense forest. The pool was heated to a balmy eighty-eight degrees year-round. No one was using it or the large hot tub this evening. I stuck a toe in the water. It felt like bathwater. Nice.

Fully submerging myself, I swam rhythmically back and forth as night ushered in. The dark cloud-covered sky felt like it was close enough that I could reach out and touch it. No stars were visible, just the glow of the moon and the hazy light from the ski slopes higher up the mountain.

Steam rose from the pool's surface as I relaxed deeper into the meditative nature of my strokes. Swimming was my sweet spot. Pops used to take me to the pool with him when I was a kid. I never had formal lessons because Pops was a fiercely patient teacher.

He'd worked as the lead investigative journalist for *The O*, Oregon's largest newspaper. I planned to follow in his footsteps, but that all changed when he died. It had been over a year since his accident. Most days I liked to pretend that he was just away on an assignment, in some far-off corner of the world where I couldn't reach him. It probably wasn't the healthiest approach to dealing with grief, but on the rare occasion when I did open myself up to the enormity of losing him, I was worried that the pain would swallow me whole like the water in the pool.

Pops used to swim every afternoon at our community pool. He said swimming was one of his secret weapons. It gave his head a chance to clear. He'd often hurry back to the office after completing an afternoon swim and finish a story he'd been working on for days in a few minutes.

Mom wanted me to be a gymnast or ballerina, but realized early on that grace and balance weren't exactly innate talents of mine. Of course that didn't stop her from constantly hounding me to be more Jill-like. "Mary Margaret Reed, why don't you take dance classes like your friends? Your hair is turning an awful shade of green from the chlorine."

"Let her be, dear," Pops would chime in. "Our Meg is *Megnificent* in the pool. You should see her breaststroke. It's a thing of beauty."

I felt *Megnificent* when Pops was around. The ache of missing him seeped into every inch of my skin. Some days it was almost more than I could bear. He wasn't just my father, he was my idol.

It was Pops who read me bedtime stories as a kid. Of course he'd always tweak the endings. "What do you say, Maggie? Do you think we can do better?" He'd remove his reading glasses and prop up our pillows. "What if the dragon isn't really a dragon? What if the dragon is..." His eyes would glimmer as he'd wait for me to fill in an alternative ending. It didn't matter what I said. Whatever I created, he celebrated.

That continued as I grew. In my later childhood he had me "work stories" with him. "Grab a pencil, Maggie. Come sit next to me." He'd push aside notebooks filled with pages of hand-written notes, interviews, and photos. "Take a look at this picture. Does something seem off to you?"

While I studied the picture, Pops would hurry to the kitchen for "story sustenance" in the form of homemade popcorn with melted butter and foamy mugs of root beer. "This will help." He'd hand me a cold root beer and wait for my analysis. If I responded too quickly, he'd take a sip of his soda and encourage me to take another look. "A good journalist takes her time. Have another look. There's no need to rush."

I didn't realize it at the time, but he was teaching me how to craft a story and helping me ignite my creative spark. Mom and I had never quite found the same points of connection. With Pops gone, I wasn't sure it was even worth the effort to try to find them now.

She and I weren't exactly on speaking terms these days. I couldn't forgive her for leaving Pops. When everything fell apart before his accident, she walked out on him—no, on us. I never exactly understood their relationship. Where Pops was thoughtful and gentle, Mom was demanding and pushy. Gam said they balanced each other out. I wasn't sure. Maybe they did, but either way I was fine with our not-speaking-to-each-other arrangement; it was Mom who wasn't.

A swell of emotions washed over me as I swam beneath the moonlight. Would there ever be a time I wouldn't miss him? It felt impossible. I dove deeper, as if the water might somehow drown out my sorrows.

When I finally came up for air, the memories of better days with Pops lingered, but I was refreshed from the exercise and the crisp mountain air. I climbed out of the pool and carefully stepped into the hot tub. The water burned, causing my feet to turn a crimson shade of red. I slowly inched my way in deeper as my body adjusted to the heat.

The smell of chlorine and acid hit my senses just as something cold hit my nose. I brushed off a cold drop of water. *That's weird.* Another cold drop hit my head. I turned around to see if someone was playing a trick on me. The pool area was completely empty.

I shivered. An eerie feeling crept up my spine. Gam called this "a knowing." She said it was our higher self giving us a little tap, like, *Hey, pay attention.*

Was someone watching me?

I rubbed my eyes and scanned the pool. Nope.

Another icy drop pelted me. I looked up in the sky and shook my head.

Meg, you're an idiot. It's snowing.

FIVE

The snow continued overnight and into the next day. It snowed through our entire *Northwest Extreme* retreat. I watched from my creek-side vantage point as the snow began with a light dusting, as if someone were sifting powdered sugar onto the tops of the fir trees and coating the trails. Then the dusting turned into a dumping. Heavy, wet flakes fell with fury. Within a few hours, snow began to accumulate on the ground outside the lodge. The sky remained dark with bluish undertones.

Greg lit a fire as the temperature plummeted. So much for my flip-flops. I guessed I was going to have to break out those snow boots after all.

The scent of burning pine and the crackle of the logs made the lodge feel cozy as the storm picked up momentum outside. We mapped out the editorial calendar and new assignments and brainstormed how to better engage our readers online while the resort transformed into a winter wonderland. Greg cautioned that ad revenue continued to slump. Could that be why he'd been so upset on the phone? Seemed unlikely.

As the retreat was winding down, I stirred a packet of hot

chocolate into a boiling mug of water, and Greg came up behind me.

"You've got chains. Right, Meg?" He grabbed a tangerine from a bowl of fruit and began peeling it, studying me with concern.

"Yeah. Yeah. I think so. I'm pretty sure I do." I did, right? Pops had outfitted my car with an emergency kit before he died. There was just one problem—I had no idea how to install them.

"You better check before you head up to Timberline. That road's dicey on a calm day. I checked the snow report and chains and traction devices are required."

I concentrated on breaking up the clumps of chocolate on the top of the mug and gulped. What did he mean by "dicey"?

The last time I visited Timberline, I was probably seven or eight. Mom's relatives from Texas were in town and had never seen snow. Even though it was June, Pops assured them Timberline would still have powder. My cousins, who were both a couple years older than me, kept me entertained on the drive up to the summit. I didn't remember anything about a nasty road.

"Did you hear me, Meg? I want you to chain up before you go meet the Ridge Rangers. That's an order."

I tossed the stir stick into the sink and turned to Greg. "You got it. I'll chain up, I promise."

Damn. Chains. I should have watched some videos on how to install them.

No way was I going to ask Greg for help. I was finally starting to feel like I knew what I was doing; I couldn't let him see how much more I still had to learn.

Chains couldn't be that hard to put on, could they?

Apparently they could. Two hours later, with frozen finger-tips and a runny nose, I considered ditching the chains and walking to Timberline.

I heard a horn behind me. A dinged-up, rusty black Jeep

pulled over next to me. The top rack was piled with snowboards.

The tinted passenger window rolled down and a young guy I recognized, with shaggy red hair, stuck his head out. "Meg! I thought that was you. What's up?"

It was Henry Groves.

I met Henry last spring when an unfortunate turn of events led to me witnessing a man fall to his death on the summit of Angel's Rest in the Columbia River Gorge. Henry, the youngest member of the Crag Rats, helped me down the trail. We became friends over the summer.

Henry was twenty-four and lived with six roommates in an old, rundown house in Portland's Woodstock neighborhood. He worked at a skate shop in order to pay the rent, but spent every free minute on the slopes.

Two guys in the backseat rolled down their windows and elbowed Henry in the back of his head. "Hey, bro, who's the cutie?"

They were all outfitted in snowboarding gear: jackets in bright primary colors with psychedelic designs and funky stripes. Snowboarders had a distinctive look, from their tousled hair and knit caps to their skater style. It was one of the things that I admired about Henry. While our styles were different, we both gravitated to clothing and gear that was youthful and fun.

"Shut it." Henry opened the door and jumped out. "Need some help?"

My chains were twisted in a mangled pile in the snow. "Is it that obvious?"

Henry bent down to pick up the chains. "Where're you headed, Meg?"

"Timberline. Actually to see you—I'm doing a feature on the Ridge Rangers."

"Killer. No one told me." He began unknotting the mess I'd made of the chains. "They never tell me anything. But hey, in that case I'll just grab a ride with you." He turned to his friends and popped his board off the roof rack. "Go ahead. I'll catch up with you on Palmer."

One of the guys climbed over the backseat to occupy Henry's empty spot. Another threw a duffel bag and a hunting rifle out the window. The driver laid on the horn and the Jeep sped off, blowing snow in all directions.

"Thanks, Henry. You didn't have to ditch your friends for me. I would have figured these things out eventually."

"Like next week." Henry winked, and secured his board on my car.

I stepped back from his stuff. "What's with the gun? I didn't think you were a hunter."

Henry shoved the rifle and his bag in the backseat. "Nah, it's my grandfather's. They asked me to bring it. I guess one of the guys is going to do some demo of old-school gear and stuff."

My face must have betrayed the fact that I was terrified of guns. Henry jabbed me in the shoulder. "Don't worry. It's not loaded. The bullets are in my bag."

"Right." I nodded. I couldn't imagine laid-back Henry with a gun. Bullets or no bullets, I didn't want to be anywhere near it. Last spring I had a near miss with a crazed murderer and gun. Ever since, even the sight of a gun on TV made me a bit skittish.

Henry went to work, first unkinking the chains and then positioning them on my tires. Within a few minutes he had them tightly secured. "That should do it," he said, brushing snow off his hands. "Want to go?"

"Thanks, Henry. There's no way I could have done that," I said as I hopped into the driver's seat and cranked on the heat.

"No problem." Henry shook snow from his puffy jacket before getting in.

"You're officially a Ridge Ranger now?" I asked, keeping both hands on the steering wheel. The chains gripped the snow beneath my tires, causing the car to sputter. This was going to be a long drive.

"Dude, I don't know. It could be a bust." Henry's cheeks and nose were rosy from the cold. They matched his fiery red hair, which sprang out from under his knit cap. His face was spotted with freckles.

As an only child, I often wished growing up that I had a brother. Henry was exactly the kind of brother I wanted. We hit it off from our first meeting. His naturally laid-back attitude helped temper my fear. When we were out in the backcountry this past summer, he kept a pretty close watch on me. It was sweet.

"What do you mean?" I turned the heat down a couple notches. The car was like a sauna. I loved the heat, but noticed Henry removed his knit cap and unzipped his jacket.

"Dude, it's a mess. Everyone's kind of freaking out. They don't think Ben knows what he's doing. You remember Ben, right?"

Ben was Ben Tyler, the founder of the Ridge Rangers. Henry introduced me to him last summer. Ben was only twenty-six, but he made a gob of money in a tech start-up in Silicon Valley and was dumping a bunch of it into forming the new high-altitude guiding team. He was offering signing bonuses and consistent pay to entice the highly regarded volunteer Crag Rats to be part of his venture. Having even a handful of the Crag Rats on his team would lend instant credibility.

"Yeah, I did a quick phone interview with him to get some background for my story." In all honesty, I hadn't been that impressed. During our brief discussion, Ben made it clear that he thought there was big money to be made in helping novice climbers to summit the mountain. His pitch was slick: "It's about giving everyone access." I could tell that it was also about the money.

Henry twisted his knit hat into a long spiral. "He's got some swagger."

"I got the impression that he's pretty proud of his success, yeah."

"I'll say." Henry laughed. There was a hardness in his voice that I hadn't heard before. "The thing is the guy can tear it up out there, but I don't know much about him. A bunch of the other guys—especially the older ones—are talking about bailing. I think the whole thing is about to implode."

This news surprised me. And could mean disaster for my feature. Somehow I didn't think Greg would be interested in running a story about a new mountaineering team that was dismantling. Henry wound his hat so tightly, it looked like a long, thin piece of string. "Is it really that bad?" I asked.

"You don't know the half of it." He looked out the window. Snow piled on both sides of the winding highway to Timberline, burying the orange and white striped markers. They looked like the tips of swizzle sticks marking the road.

I kept my eyes focused ahead. The car was made for winter weather driving, but I wasn't. Nor was I experienced in driving in the snow. A line of cars had formed behind. I refused to go over the posted speed limit. A waterfall gushed on the cliff face to my left, cutting through the fresh powder. On Henry's side, I knew the land dropped off hundreds of feet. Shiver. *Stay focused, Meg,* I said to myself as I clicked my wipers on high to clear snow.

"This is between us, okay?" Henry asked, his gaze still focused on the dense cover of ashen white outside the window. "Off the record, okay?"

"Of course."

"Well, here's the thing. I've been getting some interest from Ten-Eighty.

Do you know the line?"

"Yeah." Everyone at *Northwest Extreme* wore Ten-Eighty

gear. It was one of the premier ski and snowboarding brands. It had been a staple with teens on the slopes for the last few years, but they went big when Olympic snowboarder Danny Powder wore their stuff at the Winter Games. Snowboarders were known for their unconventional style, both in terms of their tricks on the mountain and their fashion sense. The interesting thing I'd learned from Henry was that their jackets and baggy pants with patches on the knees and butt weren't just for show. They functioned as extra padding for kneeling and sitting while performing stunts.

"Isn't that what you're wearing now?"

Henry nodded. "They want to sign me to endorse the brand."

"That's fantastic news, Henry!" I almost swerved off the road in my excitement.

"It's not a done deal yet, but it could be pretty sweet if it comes through. I don't want Ben to know. He's all weird about doing outside stuff. Wants us to sign a non-compete."

"I won't say anything. Fingers crossed, though. That would be awesome."

Up ahead I could make out the parking lot of Timberline Lodge. Cars with ski and roof racks squeezed together in the expansive lot. It looked like the entire state of Oregon had descended on the mountain for opening weekend.

Henry jumped out of the car. "Catch you later, Meg. I'm off to find my bros. Don't say anything about the Ten-Eighty thing, okay?"

I promised and waved goodbye. As I watched him skate over the snow and shove the gun into the duffel bag slung over his arm, I felt unnerved. If what Henry said was true, and the Ridge Rangers were about to dismantle, I had *no* story. Great.

This was the worst-case scenario and something I needed to fix—fast. Greg had given me a huge break and a chance when no one else would. I couldn't let him down. I needed this job. I *wanted* this job. In a plot twist that was as surprising to me as it might be to anyone else, I loved writing for *Northwest Extreme*. I was—dare I say?—good at this job. Not the extreme sports part, but the being in nature and capturing Oregon's rugged beauty part.

Time to get creative. A new story had been waiting on the mountain somewhere.

SIX

I grabbed my gear from the back of the car and started through the thick snow-covered parking lot toward Timberline Lodge. The iconic building made famous in the horror flick *The Shining* looked anything but sinister. It could have been argued that Timberline was the finest lodge on national forest land, with its rock foundation, peaked roof line, and wood-paned windows.

The lodge was constructed in the 1930s as part of President Roosevelt's New Deal. With the economy struggling to rebound from the Great Depression, Roosevelt poured federal money into a new program called the WPA, or Works Progress Administration. The WPA funded the lodge's construction over a mere fifteen months.

Workers were trucked in several miles and paid ninety cents a day. Native materials, such as rocks from adjacent slopes and timber from the forest, were used by laborers who hand-crafted the massive masonry façade.

A throng of people tromped in front of me on their way into the lodge, their cheeks wind-burned and their bodies outfitted in boots, goggles, and helmets. I followed behind, feeling caught up in the excitement, especially as Timberline's towering architecture came into view.

Today I had to enter through a temporary winter structure, which felt like sneaking into a tunnel of ice. Each winter a tunnel to the main entrance was formed with parabolic arches. Snow piled up and banked on the sides, forming snowdrifts. The structure was illuminated, which resulted in a magical glowing igloo.

I sucked in a breath of cold air and skirted through the dazzling tunnel of ice and light. It was everything I could do not to stop and touch the structure.

As I climbed up old-growth timber steps to the lodge's interior, the smell of a hearty fire greeted me. Vaulted timber ceilings and archways carved from volcanic rock opened up in the common area. I scanned pine carved signs that pointed guests toward various Oregon-themed rooms—the Blue Ox, Barlow Room, and the Ram's Head. Nothing pointed to the Silcox Hut, though.

Around the corner, a Saint Bernard dog that probably weighed more than me sauntered over and rubbed his nose on my knee. I spotted a sign pointing to the reception desk and scooted that way.

An older woman in her sixties stood behind a wooden counter that reminded me of a ticket window in a train depot.

"Can I help you? Are you checking in?"

I dropped my suitcase on the hardwood floors. "I'm supposed to be meeting the Ridge Rangers? I think they're staying in the Silcox Hut?"

"Ooh, that's going to be a cold ride in this weather." She looked me over and furrowed her brow. "You're going to want to bundle up."

Bundle up? I was already sporting jeans, boots, and a ski jacket. "Sorry. What do you mean by 'ride'?"

"The snowcat. I'll call the driver. You sit tight by the fire and put on a hat and gloves."

To be honest, I'd never even seen a snowcat. The first thought that popped into my head when she said "snowcat" was an image of a white snow-covered kitten. Nope.

The front desk clerk sent me and my bags back outside to wait for my ride. I could hear the snowcat's rumble before it came into view. A huge red machine on monster revolving tracks chugged to a stop in front of me. It looked like a combination of a giant bulldozer and the cab of a London double-decker bus. The Timberline logo was painted in bright white on the side.

The driver hopped off, grabbed my bags, and waited expectantly for me to move. "You comin'? I've got a load of skiers in the back. You're gonna get toasty in the front with me."

I looked up at the cab. "We're going in *that*?" My stomach dropped.

He chuckled and led me around the side, giving me a boost up onto the giant tracks covering the wheels. From there I climbed into the cab. "You betcha. 1,000 thousand vertical feet. Should be a fun ride to the south side."

"How safe is this thing?" I shouted over the humming of the machine coming to life and the beeps warning skiers and snowboarders to make way for us. Black smoke chugged from a silver pipe.

"She's a one-ton wonder. She'll get us up there, no problem. You just sit back and enjoy the ride. I like to say it's an adventure just getting up the chute. Kind of like four-bying!"

The cat screeched to life and jolted forward.

You've done it again, Meg, I thought as I cinched my seat belt tight and clenched the side of the cat.

The snowcat plowed through the snow, sending icy waves in front of us. "Hold on!" the driver yelled above the sound of the rumbling engine.

My body flew back into the seat as the cat ascended the mountain. It was probably a good thing that my window was completely covered with steam.

"How can you even see where we're going?"

The driver flipped the wipers onto high and wiped the front window with a rag. "Better than a video game, isn't she? This is the real deal. I tell folks they leave the world behind when they step into my cat." He patted the dashboard and maneuvered the cat onto a path marked with poles and orange flags.

I peered out the front window. "How deep is it out there?"

"She's running over this no problem. Maybe six feet or so, no difficulty. You worried?"

"Have you ever gotten stuck?"

"Oh, yeah. Lots of times, but we'll be fine today. If it keeps dumping like this, tomorrow's another story. Hope you packed extra underwear." He chuckled and shifted into a higher gear.

"Up we go!" He turned to the skiers crammed in the back. "Who's ready to hit this?"

Cheers erupted from the back.

The driver grinned and said to me, "See, getting there's half the fun. Just ask the slope monkeys in the back. Relax!"

"Heights aren't really my thing." I kept a death grip on the handle, my knuckles turning white.

"Uh-oh, if you don't like this, you really aren't going to like the way back down." He steered to the left to give space to a group of climbers trekking on the side of the tracks.

I waved as we passed by them. *Who would climb in this weather?*

Ten long minutes later, we reached the Silcox Hut, elevation 7,000 feet. The hut was known as "Oregon's highest hotel room." I sucked in a deep breath, shaking slightly as I exited the cab. A break in the clouds revealed exactly how high we were. Oregon's highest hotel room was a fitting description. It looked like the timber-framed hut had been tucked into the mountainside, just below Palmer Glacier, like something out of Tolkien's *The Hobbit*. Stunning snow-capped vistas stretched on the horizon in every other direction. Ice crystals shimmered like shiny gems on the freshly fallen snow. The Cascade mountain range seemed to encompass the entire sky, stretching as far as I could see.

"Kind of Mother Nature to welcome you with this view. See why I'm never depressed?" The driver handed me my suit-case. He pointed to a bank of ugly black clouds moving as a mass in our direction. "Not going to last for long." The skiers jumped off and raced toward the lift.

I took my suitcase and thanked him for the ride.

He jumped back onto the snowcat. "Enjoy your stay. Maybe I'll see you tomorrow, but from the look of the weather I wouldn't count on it."

With that, the snowcat puffed out more black smoke and kicked up powder as it began its descent back to the lodge. I felt an uneasy longing to return with him. I hadn't considered that I might get stuck up here at 7,000 feet. Hopefully he was wrong about the weather, but I doubted it. Fat flakes of snow fell as I hurried inside.

SEVEN

I tugged my suitcase up stone steps, rounded a corner, and entered a dining hall where a stone fireplace at the far end of the room burned low. Its rock wall extended all the way to the ceiling with recessed cutouts for candles. The ceiling was nothing short of breathtaking. I dropped my suitcase on the unfinished volcanic rock floor and let my eyes soak in the sight of the arched exposed beams that crisscrossed the room. It felt like standing in the center of a snug cavern.

Stacks of split logs piled on both sides of the hearth were waiting to be burned. Iron screen doors etched with silhouettes of evergreen trees looked like they were aglow with the fire smoking behind them.

A large hand-carved timber dining table with matching wooden benches occupied the center of the room. Smaller two-person tables lined the windows along the walls. Overhead, two large wooden chandeliers cast a golden light. A galley kitchen and bar stood to my right.

Votive candles flickered on tabletops. I left my suitcase by the entry and wandered toward the fireplace. Indigenous Amer-

ican artwork and brightly colored blankets were tastefully hung
to add to the cheery and inviting vibe.

Now, this is more like it.

All I needed was a steaming cup of cocoa and the book I'd
brought along. I could pull a bench close to the fire and spend the
weekend inside, interviewing each Ridge Ranger individually.

"Can I help you?" The sound of a woman's voice startled
me from my daydream. "We're closed for a private event."

I turned around to see a young woman, not much older than
me, with a fitted knit cap and two long brown braids cascading
down. Her look was distinctly Oregon-lodge. She wore black
leggings, striped black and tan wool socks, and a pullover ski
sweater. The tan lines etched on her face were a dead giveaway
that she was a skier, and one who obviously wore ski goggles.

"Yeah, for the Ridge Rangers, right?" I approached her with
my hand extended. "I'm Meg."

She wiped her hands on her green Timberline apron and
appraised me. "You're with the Rangers?" She looked skeptical
as she shook my hand.

"No. No." I laughed. "I'm with *Northwest Extreme.* I'm
doing a feature about the Rangers for the magazine."

"Gotcha." She headed behind the counter and washed her
hands. "I'd go snag a bunk if I were you. It's going to get tight up
here."

"Where are the bunks?"

She pointed over her shoulder. "That way." Grabbing a dish
towel from an iron hook carved in the shape of a ski, she wiped
her hands. "I'm Lola, by the way. I'm the host for the weekend."

"Host?"

"Yep." She began chopping garlic and warmed olive oil on
the stove. "I cook, clean, take guests out on the slopes. You
name it."

"Cool job," I said, as I heaved my suitcase in my hand. "I'd love to hear more about it, but first I'll go find a space for this. Do you know when the Ridge Rangers are due to arrive?"

Lola scraped garlic into the pan. It sizzled and immediately filled the dining room with a pungent smell. "They're up on Palmer. Should be back soon."

I thanked her and made my way up the stone steps to the bunk rooms. The Silcox Hut was better described as a mini lodge. I was a research geek.

That was the best part of writing, in my opinion. Many of my colleagues wouldn't have agreed. They'd have said the best part of writing, well, at least for *Northwest Extreme* anyway, was the adventure. Nope. Not so for me. What I loved about my job was the time I got to spend researching. For this assignment, I stole away to the library for two days, flipping through periodicals and scouring the pages of glossy photo books of Timberline and its rich history.

It was nothing short of a marvel that eighty percent of the workers who built the lodge and hut were unskilled. They came to the rugged mountains of Oregon seeking employment and to learn a trade. The Silcox Hut originally served as the upper terminal for the Magic Mile, a revolutionary chairlift for its time. It was the second chairlift constructed in North America with a single-chair design.

That thought made me shiver as I pulled back the marine-blue curtains to one of the six bunk rooms and placed my suitcase on the bottom bunk. The beds were lined with hand-woven wool blankets in primary colors of red, yellow, and blue. A black raven was stitched in the center of mine.

Now that the lodge and hut were officially on the national historic register, all updates and upgrades had to be done in accordance with the style they were created in back in the 1930s. That meant when a blanket needed mending, Timberline turned to a trusted group of retirees who stitched each one by hand.

There was something magical about knowing that had I walked through the doors of this building eighty years ago it would have looked the same.

This focus on historic preservation would definitely have to be included in my piece, I thought as I peered out the picture window of the bunk room. Icicles hung from the rafters above. Dainty snowflakes fell on a picnic table outside. A group of snowboarders stomped past on their way up the glacier.

Palmer, where the Ridge Rangers were skiing, was actually a glacier and one of only two locations in the Northern Hemisphere where skiers could train year-round. Most of the U.S. Olympic Ski Team descended on Palmer to stay in top shape in the summer months.

Speaking of top shape, the sound of raucous banter and boots stomping off snow echoed near the front door. The Ridge Rangers must have arrived.

I left my suitcase on the bunk and checked my appearance in the mirror. My fair cheeks needed more color—I pinched them along my cheekbones, an old trick I'd watched Mom do every morning before she left the house. My lips felt dry and cracked. I glided an opaque pink gloss on my lips and ran my fingers through my shaggy blond hair. Adjusting the dangly typewriter earrings I'd found online at my favorite Etsy shop, I gave myself a nod of approval and scurried to the dining room with a notebook and pen under my arm.

Lola stood at the stove, stirring a giant cast-iron pot. A skier with black goggles on his head snuck up behind her and grabbed her butt.

I threw my hand over my mouth. Lola whipped around and backhanded him with a wooden spoon covered in red sauce. The sauce splattered on the wooden floor and the dude's face.

"Knock it off." She shot him a nasty look.

I was about to jump in, when he lunged toward her again. She flicked the remaining sauce on his face. He recoiled, wiping red sauce from his eyes. He muttered something under his breath that I couldn't make out and stormed past me.

"Let me guess, that's Ben." I rested my notebook on the wooden counter.

She rinsed the spoon in the sink and returned to her pot. "Yep. Ben Tyler. He's an ass." Shaking dried basil leaves in the sauce, she turned to me and gave me a serious look. "Do yourself a favor and steer clear of him."

I nodded, wishing that neither of us had to contend with him for the weekend. "I read up on him for my feature, so I have a sense of his personality."

"Lucky you. As head of the Ridge Rangers, he thinks he's the king of the mountain." She placed a heavy lid on the top of the pot.

"I've never met him in person, but that came through online."

She turned the burner down and came to the other side of the counter. Keeping her voice low, she cautioned, "I'm serious. Watch out for him. You're cute. Young. Just his type. I've been fighting him off for two days now. I'm over it. In fact, I'm going to say something to Clint tonight."

Clint, I knew. He was a retired professional skier and a famed broadcaster who covered every event in professional skiing from the X Games to the Olympics. I'd met Clint this past summer while immersed in the Crag Rats' outdoor survival training. Ben hired him to train the new team.

"Thanks for the heads-up," I said, noticing that Lola's hand shook slightly.

"Do you get to ski much?" I asked, intentionally changing the subject.

A smile spread across her face. "I do. That's the reason I took this job." She pointed to the window. "I get to ski out there every day. One of the most amazing places in the world."

"You're not from around here, are you?" I knew that look of

longing. Oregonians, like myself, had a tendency to take the awe-inspiring beauty of our surroundings for granted. We rarely commented on how green it was here in the summer or how much it rained every other time of the year. On the mountain they said we had two seasons—the Fourth of July and the rest of the year. Visitors, out-of-towners, and transplants from other states never really got over all this natural beauty. It was a good reminder for me to stop and smell the pine trees (so to speak).

"Vermont." Lola turned her gaze from the milky slopes outside the windows, which were beginning to steam. She twirled a shell necklace around her neck. "How'd you know?"

"Lucky guess." I grinned. "Hey, do you need a hand?" I motioned to a pot of boiling water about to spill over on the stove.

Lola swore under her breath and raced to the bubbling pot.

A swarm of Ridge Rangers clomped in, all wearing ski boots, neon-colored jackets with lift tickets dangling from the zippers, and puffy pants. Each of them carried a black backpack with the words RIDGE RANGERS and an outline of a compass embroidered in white. They nudged each other out of the way to get a space in front of the fire, warming their hands and shouting for Henry (aka "the kid") to grab them beers.

Henry waved to me as he made his way to the fridge and loaded his arm with bottles of microbrew beers. He held the bundle in his arms to me. I carefully freed a bottle of Ice Axe IPA from the pile and used the bottle opener on the counter to crack open the beer.

Clint Shumway, the oldest Crag Rat, threw a burly arm around my shoulder and squeezed it tight. "Meg, welcome. I was thrilled when Greg told me that you're doing a feature on our new guiding team." There was a gap between his front teeth. His leathered skin wrinkled in waves down his neck and was a giveaway that he'd spent years outside in the elements.

He emphasized "guiding," and I noticed Ben Tyler roll his

eyes and elbow the guy standing next to him. "That's right, Clint. We're going to be *guides*," he hollered. "That's all the old man cares about. No tricks. None of that fancy stuff. Just guide."

A few of the Rangers chuckled uncomfortably. Clint removed his arm from my shoulder and strode toward Ben. He poked Ben in the chest with his index finger. "You want to showboat? That's fine, but I'm not ruining my reputation. You pitched this as a mountain guiding group, yes?"

Ben threw his hands up. "True."

Clint clapped his hands together. "These things we do." He paused dramatically, waving his hands out in a gesture for everyone to join him.

"So others may live," the Ridge Rangers chimed in unison. This was the Crag Rats' mantra. Ben must have been successful poaching from the volunteer group.

"Right. Whatever. Let's eat." Ben took the seat at the head of the table and motioned for Lola to serve the food.

It seemed strange that this level of tension building right in front of me. From that brief exchange I could feel a bias starting against Ben, but as a reporter I knew I had to pull back—even if he was doing his best to be a jerk.

Everyone hurried to snag a seat at the table. I noticed Henry sat at one of the smaller tables near an oval window. "Is this seat taken?" I joked, joining him. The snow came halfway up the wood-framed picture window. "It's dumping out there."

He tried to grin but his face fell, a somber frown tugging at his lips. I could tell something was bothering him. Unfortunately, before I could ask, Clint launched into a speech about the pride and professionalism that have made the Crag Rats one of the premier mountain rescue teams in the country. "If you boys want to create that with the Ridge Rangers, we're going to maintain the same standards if I have anything to say about it." He threw a challenging look at Ben.

Ben shot his fingers like guns at Clint. "That's the plan, old man."

Clint ignored Ben and motioned for me to stand. "Troops, we're fortunate to have a young reporter with us this weekend, Meg Reed from *Northwest Extreme*. I know you're all familiar with the publication. Meg, can you explain what you'll be doing?"

I grabbed my notebook and pen and held them up like props. "It's very high-tech, as you can see. My strategy when working on a feature is twofold. I like to observe as much as I can to really get a feel for what you do. And I like to interview. I'll be asking you a bunch of questions and I promise I'll try my best not to annoy you with them."

The team laughed as I took my seat. Snow fell in heavy clumps outside the window. The fire crackled. Ceramic dishes of meatballs, pasta, salad, and warm bread were passed around the room. The mountaineers ate with gusto, listening intently to Clint as their forks clinked on plates and sauce was wiped clean with bread.

"Here it comes," Henry said, taking a swig of his beer.

"What?" I whispered.

"Listen."

"I think many of you may have guessed this." Clint's aging voice boomed in the toasty room. His plate sat untouched. "It's with a full and happy heart that I announce that I'm stepping down after nearly forty years with the Crag Rats and devoting my time to making the Ridge Rangers the best guiding team on the slope. Are you all ready to hit the trenches with me?" He sounded like a general rallying his troops.

"Hear! Hear!" someone shouted.

Another raised his pint. "A *prost* to the Rangers!"

Beer bottles and water glasses were held in the air as everyone stood and shouted, "*To the Rangers!*"

Clint waved everyone off. "Enough, enough. On to business. I'm determined that we elect a president to lead us forward before this weekend is up. Any suggestions?"

At that moment a cold gust of air blew in. A couple in color-coordinated ski gear burst into the room. Snow dusted their shoulders and floated to the floor. The man unzipped his coat and pulled the woman forward. "Sorry we're late. Had to get in one last run." He smiled, revealing veneered teeth the color of new-fallen snow. "Sounds like I'm just in time. I nominate the kid—Henry."

Henry dropped his beer bottle. It shattered in tiny pieces all over the floor.

EIGHT

"Henry, are you okay?" I jumped to my feet. Something was obviously wrong with my friend.

He stood frozen with his boyish eyes locked on the man, ignoring the shards of glass and splattered beer at his feet.

The man strolled over to Clint, seemingly oblivious that everyone else in the room sat in stunned silence. His slick black hair didn't move as he walked across the room. "Clint, old boy, I'm kidding." He threw his arm around Clint in a man hug.

Clint clapped him on the shoulder and let out an audible sigh. "Jackson, you made it."

Jackson released Clint and snagged a beer from the table. "What's up, men? Why the somber faces?" He popped off the bottle cap and chugged it.

Ben Tyler pushed the bench back. "Pretty Boy's here and he brought his lady friend." He blew an exaggerated kiss to the woman Jackson left standing by the entryway.

I couldn't decide if he was trying to be funny or if he was really that rude. It was clear that the Ridge Rangers were an old boys' club, and I wasn't a fan of so much toxic masculinity in one space. This was going to be a long weekend at this rate.

"Malory, come in, come in!" Clint greeted the woman with a hearty wave.

She sauntered to the table, clearly aware that her exacting posture was turning heads. This was a woman who knew how to make an entrance. Arriving at Clint's table, she kissed both his cheeks. He whispered something in her ear. She gave him a curt nod. Clint tapped his fork on his pint glass. "Sorry to ruin the stag party, men, but I've just confirmed that Malory and Jackson are engaged!"

I still couldn't tell what had happened with Henry. He remained frozen and stared off into the distance like he'd seen a ghost.

A round of cheers, whoops, and clinking beer bottles sounded in the room. Ben didn't raise his pint glass in a toast. He hardened his eyes at Malory. She ignored him and intentionally extended her hand so that everyone at the table could see the sparkling diamond on her finger.

"Congratulations, you two. Let me be the first to officially welcome you into the club, Malory." Clint gave a little bow. "Your boy here is going to be putting in a lot of long nights, you know." He spoke out of the side of his mouth. "We've got a lot of work to do to get in tip-top shape."

Malory didn't speak. She pursed her lips into a smile and sat on the rustic lodge bench as if she were seating herself on a throne. Her ski gear darted in at the waist, making me think it must have been tailored specifically for her. It probably cost more than an entire month's salary at *Northwest Extreme*. Lola weaved through the crowded room and delivered an empty plate to the table. Malory waved her off.

Lola mopped the beer on the floor by our table. When she finished, she scooted on the one-person bench next to Henry. She smiled broadly at me and then smirked, mimicking Malory. I tried to keep my face passive but had to admit that my first impression of Malory made me think we weren't likely to have much in common.

Clint stayed on his feet and addressed the group with a serious tone. "All right, men, back to business. As I was saying, all successful teams have a leader. My bum knee won't let me take on that role, so it's my pleasure to suggest that Jackson Hughes, one of the damn finest skiers I've ever seen—not to mention a doctor—is the *man* for the job." He grinned at Jackson.

What had I gotten myself into? The misogyny ran deep with Clint.

"Shall we put it to a vote? All those in favor, raise your glasses and give me a 'yay.'"

Ben jumped to his feet. He reminded me of an angry cat with hair spiking up its spine. "Uh, not so fast there, old man. I'm funding this sucker. I'll say who leads it."

Clint's jawline tightened. "Ben, we already discussed this."

The room went silent. Ben and Clint jockeyed for position while everyone else poked at their remaining pasta and avoided making eye contact.

Ben finally broke the tension by calling Lola. "Bring out another round, Lola. It's going to be a long night."

She rolled her eyes, gave Henry a squeeze on the shoulder, and darted to the kitchen. Clint's shoulders deflated. He gave Jackson a look that I couldn't decipher and sat down. Jackson smoothed his ebony hair and headed in our direction. He tapped Henry on the arm. "Did you bring it?"

"Huh?" Henry swiveled around. "Oh, yeah. Hang on." He threw his hat on the table, got to his feet, and almost slipped on the wet floor.

What was he doing?

Ben overtly flirted with Lola. She focused on squeezing between tables to deliver bottles of beer.

This was a disaster. I'd never witnessed such chaos in a

professional meeting. No way was I going to be able to write a feature about the Ridge Rangers if this was the way they operated.

Henry returned with the hunting rifle. He held it out to Jackson. "Not now, kid." Jackson furrowed his brow. He paused and motioned for Henry to take the gun away. "Our benefactor seems to have a different idea of how this training is going to go."

Ben cackled. He chugged the beer in his hand and walked over to Clint. Putting his arm around Clint's shoulder, Ben addressed the group. "Listen, bros, I think we're all here for the same reason. We like to live on the edge. We like to make money. Right? Who's with me?"

A few hands crept up.

"Right, so here's the deal. I say we forget about training for the night. Have a few drinks. Get to know each other—chill, you know." He spiked his hair with his fingers and slammed his beer. "The rest can be sorted out in the morning."

People nodded. Clint fumed.

Henry caught my eye and shrugged. He said something to Jackson and left with the rifle again. Hopefully he'd put that thing away for good. Even the thought of sleeping tonight with a gun in the hut made my stomach quiver. I wanted to follow after him. This wasn't what I'd signed up for. I wanted out of this drama fest—now.

NINE

The snow continued to pile up outside, falling in heavy clumps like the heavens were unleashing their anger on the mountain.

Lola stacked and cleared the dirty dishes and returned with carafes of hot coffee and chocolate brownies. I nibbled on a warm brownie at my window seat and felt oddly like a voyeur. I intentionally kept my notebook and pen on Henry's empty seat, finding solace in a fudgy brownie. The evening's events seemed perfect for the *National Enquirer* but not at all the vision I had for *Northwest Extreme*. Maybe I'd have to scrap the entire feature and take another route—but what?

My thoughts turned to Henry. Where had he disappeared to?

Ben knocked back beer after beer. His speech started to slur. "It's barfing snow out there. Awesome!"

Some of the other team members indulged, too. That just spurred him on to drink more.

Lola emerged from the kitchen with another round of coffee and a walkie-talkie in her hand. After refilling mugs, she gave Ben one look and shook her head. Passing by him, she whispered something in Clint's ear and showed him the walkie-talkie. There was an urgency in her face that made the tiny hairs on the back of my arm shoot up. Something was wrong.

"Hey, troops. Can I have your attention again?" Clint's commanding voice silenced the chatter. He caught my eye and winked as he looked out the window behind me. "I've just been informed that the weather has moved in faster than expected. Looks like we're going to be sardines tonight."

This news was met with an outcry.

"Sorry. I've been informed the snowcat's out of commission. We're stuck."

Another round of grumbles sounded.

"Easy, easy. Lola, our host, is going to scrounge up some extra blankets. Those of you who weren't planning to bunk up for the night can sleep in here. We'll push back tables and make space for you in front of the fire."

"Wimps!" a voice called out.

One guess who. Shocker. Ben Tyler was on his feet again—well, sort of. His neck struggled to hold up his head and his body swayed as he spoke. "I've ridden in worse, man. Let's do it. Who wants to ride?"

Snowboarders called boarding "riding." I'd learned that in my research. I made sure my notes reflected their tone. If this feature went anywhere, which was looking more doubtful by the minute, I wanted to get the lingo right.

"Absolutely not. It's a blizzard out there—you know that's the same as suicide. *No one* is leaving tonight. That's an order." Clint narrowed his eyes at Ben.

A handful of Rangers protested, but Clint refused to listen. He started stacking the benches and clearing space on the floor.

Ben made a "hang loose" sign with his hand. "Later, dudes."

Clint slammed a bench on the floor. "Ben, you're not leaving this building. Understood?"

Ignoring Clint's stern face, Ben threw his head back in a

laugh and snagged two more beers from the counter. "I'll do what I want." With that he sauntered toward the bunk room.

That was the thing about adrenaline junkies like Ben Tyler. They tended to see themselves as invincible. They'd never consider recommending a newbie ride in a blizzard, but they saw themselves as impervious to danger.

That was another thing I'd learned working with and around adventure lovers at *Northwest Extreme*. It came with the territory, and it was probably why they made good guides. You had to be willing to live on the edge if you were putting your life at risk to save someone else's. This mindset both fascinated and terrified me—that was the angle I needed for my feature. What was it that set the Ridge Rangers apart from the rest of us? Like firefighters who ran *into* a burning building while everyone else was running out, the Ridge Rangers intentionally sought danger.

Gam would have said they needed to find balance—build deeper roots. Mom would have said, "Mary Margaret Reed, you could learn a thing or two from this crew."

From the sound of it, I was going to be in tight quarters with thirty thrill-seekers for the next few days.

Great.

Just great.

On the flip side, maybe some of their fearless spirit would rub off on me.

The bad news was that the Silcox Hut only slept twenty-four. That meant six people would have to sleep on the floor. Good thing I'd snagged a bed.

Everyone who hadn't started playing rock, paper, scissors to figure out who was stuck with the floor.

I left the dining hall to find Henry. Maybe he could give me more background on Ben. Plus, I just wanted to hang with a familiar face. Being in the middle of drama wasn't my thing.

He wasn't in the bunk rooms. I checked the bathrooms and

the dining hall. No sign of him. I asked in the dining hall. No one had seen him since dinner. I searched all the rooms again. His skis and duffel bag stood propped against a bunk. He must have stepped outside—why?

One con of being highly curious and a reporter was that I had a hard time letting go. I should have been heading to my bunk for the night, but I was worried about my friend, so instead, I tugged on my purple-lined boots, zipped up my coat, and left the frenzy over bunks. It took all my strength to pull open the timber door. A blast of arctic air hit my face as I stepped out into the howling wind. It felt like someone threw a bucket of ice water directly in my face.

Why would he have come outside in this weather? And what was I doing out here? I told myself that I'd go as far as the picnic table and then turn back. I'd heard horror stories of climbers getting lost on the mountain, frozen bodies discovered after the spring melt, just a few hundred feet away from their tent or base camp. I wasn't about to let that happen to me.

My nose started to run immediately. I tugged the strings on my hood tighter and kept my head down. "Henry? Henry! Are you out here?" The sound of my voice evaporated in the ferocious gusts.

Snow pelted my back and the side of my face. It swirled all around me like mini tornadoes of white. I'd never experienced a whiteout before. I suddenly understood the meaning of a whiteout. With snow blowing in every direction, it was impossible to get my bearings. I could barely make out my hand in front of my face.

I took a few steps forward, my boots sinking into the deep snow. I called out again. "Henry! It's Meg. Are you out here?"

No response—just the rage of the wind.

I trudged on. The picnic table must be a few feet in front of me. I caught the scent of something minty.

Keeping my hands in front of my body to block the wind

and to ensure I didn't run into the table, I made my way blindly forward. The fingerless gloves left my fingers exposed. I shoved them back in my coat pockets.

"Henry!"

My toes felt tingly in my boots and my nose stung. How cold was it?

One more step and I banged into the bench of the picnic table with my knee. *Ouch!*

I cried out in pain. Then I felt my way around the table. I was sure I smelled smoke—and not the fire kind.

"Henry? Are you here?" Nothing.

I circled the table and shivered. *Time to get back to the Silcox Hut—and now, Meg.*

The problem was—which way? I couldn't see the hut through the blowing snow. *Meg, you're an idiot. What were you thinking?*

The negative voice in my head was replaced by Pops's kind and encouraging voice. *It's okay, Maggie. One step at a time. One step at a time.*

I felt my leg lift and bend in response to his voice in my head. What else was I going to do? Sit out in the snow? Um, no. One step at a time worked for me.

The wind assaulted me as I moved forward. That had to be a good sign, right? Hadn't it been at my back on the way to the picnic table? The table couldn't be more than twenty or thirty feet from the hut. I counted twenty steps. My hands were in front of me so I didn't hit the wooden timbers of the hut.

Thirty feet.

Nothing.

Maybe my steps were too small. I'd try forty. Nothing.

Now I was scared.

Which way should I turn? The snow fell with such fury, my footsteps disappeared in a blanket of white at my feet. I could turn around and try to count forty steps back to the picnic table.

What had I learned in my wilderness training this summer? Stay put. It was always better to stay where you were and let rescuers come to you. But that couldn't be true in this scenario, could it? I hadn't even told anyone I was going outside. No one was looking for me. In the mad scramble of bunks, no one would even miss me until tomorrow morning.

By then it would be too late.

TEN

That's when I heard Frank Sinatra's voice crooning again. *I must be losing it.* Why was I hearing big band music? Maybe I was closer to the hut than I realized?

I stopped and focused on the music, spinning in a circle to try to let my ears guide me back to safety. The relentless wind muffled everything.

Then I heard the shot—*bang!* I flinched in response and whipped my head in the direction of the sound. Standing frozen in knee-high snow, I waited. The howl of the wind was the only sound I could hear.

Get it together, Meg, I told myself as I sank deeper into the powder. After a few grueling steps, I heard the swell of the brass and woodwind instruments. That was *definitely* music. The bang must have been a snare drum. I had to be close.

Hurry, Meg.

Bang! Another loud crashing sound cut through the wind and startled me. A crash of cymbals?

That was no band. That was a gunshot.

Before I could take another step, I ran smack into someone. I let out a scream and fell backward into the snow.

"Meg? What are you doing here?" Henry's arm reached down and pulled me onto my feet.

"Henry!" I threw my arms around him. "I've been looking all over for you!"

"For me? Why?"

"I couldn't find you after—well—you know, the whole weirdness with Ben." I released him from my grasp. "I thought maybe you came outside, but then I got kind of turned around in the blizzard."

Henry wrapped his arm around my shoulder and rubbed it with force, like he was trying to ignite my jacket. "Meg, you're shivering. Come on, I gotta get you inside."

Fine by me.

"Which way is the hut?"

Henry tromped through the thick snow with ease, cutting a path for me to follow. "It's right here. You shouldn't have come out on your own, Meg. Rookie move. Don't you remember anything from wilderness survival school?"

Wind lashed my face. "Yeah, but—I—"

Henry cut me off. "But nothing, Meg. Dude, this is how people die. You *never* wander blindly in a blizzard. You could have frostnip."

I could feel my internal body temp rising a degree with anger. "Whatever. I came out looking for *you*."

"Well, you shouldn't have." He yanked me forward through the snow.

"Henry, stop." I tugged on his jacket sleeve and tried to stop my boots from sliding on the slippery snow.

"Meg, you need to get inside."

I didn't budge. "What's going on with you? Why were you out here, anyway?"

Henry looked over his shoulder. "I'd had enough of Ben. I had to get out of there."

"Yeah. I get that. Believe me, I don't think you're the only one."

Henry shrugged. "I think I'm quitting."

"Really?" There went my story, but I didn't blame him. "It does seem fairly old-school in mentality and not in a good way."

"You don't know the half of it." He sighed.

"I'm here to listen."

"Meg, not now. Come on." Henry grabbed my arm and started moving forward through the snow. "You need to get inside." Why did he keep saying that?

I let him steer me through the blizzard. My depth perception had disappeared. He was right. We were only a few feet from the front door of the Silcox Hut. How had I gotten so turned around?

We stomped snow from our boots. "Hey, did you hear a gunshot earlier?" I asked, kicking my foot free from my wet boot.

"What?"

"A gunshot. I thought I heard a shot. A couple, actually. Right before I bumped into you."

Henry shook his head and held my arm to steady me as I tugged off my other boot. "No. I didn't hear anything. Must have been a branch snapping in the wind."

I nodded and stepped into the warmth of the Silcox Hut. My double layer of wool socks was soaked. The heat stung my face and fingertips. I could smell popcorn and cider. The sound of trombones and saxophones reverberated from the dining hall. Someone was blaring Harry Connick Jr.—my kind of music.

So my imagination had gotten the best of me. The gunshots were just in my mind. I was safe.

I would soon learn I was still lacking Gam's heightened level of intuition. Let's just say I was wrong about my imagination—and about being safe. Really wrong.

ELEVEN

Sleeping bags and woolen blankets lay in rows in the middle of the dining room. The tables had been pushed to one side and were piled with backpacks, ski helmets, and gloves.

Whatever animosity had occurred earlier had been reduced by the bottle of whiskey being handed around the room, along with heaping bowls of popcorn and the upbeat sound of music playing on the speakers. This was more like it.

I weaved my way to the fireplace and took a seat on the stone hearth. The rocks were almost hot to the touch and warmed my buns immediately. One of the Ridge Rangers grabbed a wooden spoon from the kitchen and jumped onto a table. He began serenading the crowd.

Lola caught my eye and pointed to cider on the stove. I nodded vigorously. She ladled some into a ceramic mug and brought it over to me.

"You look like you need this." She surveyed the room. "Or better yet, maybe a shot of that whiskey going around. Were you outside? It's freezing out there, isn't it?"

I took the cup and wrapped my hands around it. The heat burned, turning my fingers red. I didn't care. At least feeling was starting to return. "That's an understatement. Wait. Were you out there, too? I got a little turned around. Fortunately, Henry found me."

Lola shook her head. "No way. I won't go outside in that."

"What happened in here? It's like a party."

"Ben must have gone to bed." She moved a pair of wet socks from the hearth and sat next to me. "I don't understand why they're thinking of joining forces with him."

I blew on the cider, taking in a whiff of cinnamon and nutmeg. "He's got deep pockets, right?"

Lola shrugged. "So they say."

An impromptu karaoke had begun, with everyone taking turns hopping onto the table and singing a line and then passing the mic (aka wooden spoon) on. Lola and I laughed as each guy tried to outdo the next. One of them slid on his knees across the floor, landing at Lola's feet and caressing her hand.

She grabbed the bottle of whiskey, took a swig, and joined the Ranger in a dramatic waltz around the room. Someone scooped me up into the action. Before I knew it we were both being twirled and dipped, spinning in wild circles from partner to partner. When the music finally stopped, we collapsed in giggles on the floor.

"See what I mean?" Lola pulled me back to the hearth. "This is why I love my job. If it weren't for the Ben Tylers of the world, it would be perfection." Her jaw tightened at the mention of Ben.

"I know I'm supposed to stay unbiased, but I have to admit I agree," I confessed. "I'm worried that I might have to scrap my story. I don't want to write about in-fighting and drama and unchecked masculinity. I want to write about Oregon's adventurers who are putting their mad mountaineering skills to work so that people like me can summit. That's what our readers want."

"Good luck with that. Ben brings out the worst in this crew.

Unless you leave Ben Tyler completely out of your feature. Come to think of it, do it. That will really make his blood boil." She squeezed my knee. "I better go turn down that cider."

She danced her way to the stove. I wished I had her confidence. It was probably a job requirement for a position like this, but still I felt envious at her self-assuredness. Gam said we became more comfortable in our skin with each passing year. It was like the layers of memories and knowledge filled up the space between our cells. If only I could have hurried up the process. At twenty-three I felt like my skin had some serious toughening up to do.

"This seat taken?" a seasoned voice asked. Clint towered above me.

Little flecks of snow dusted his scruffy cheeks. I scooted to the side to make room for him.

He kept his right leg extended as he sat. His face flinched in pain for a moment. "Damn thing, getting old. Enjoy your youth. Let me tell you, it's a pain in my ass getting old."

"Sorry."

"Don't be. It's life, kiddo."

"You should see my grandmother. She's a Reiki master and healer. She might be able to help."

He brushed snow from his cheeks. "I'm not into any of that mumbo-jumbo New-Age stuff." He patted the pockets of his ski parka. "That's what these are for." He removed a bottle of pills, twisted off the cap, and popped one into his mouth. "The drugs get better with age. That's for sure."

That could be true. I wouldn't know. I'd been graced with good health. I attributed it to Gam. She always encouraged me to "go within" and activate the part of my body that knew how to heal itself. I should clarify. That didn't mean Gam didn't believe in Western medicine. It was more like she took a dual approach. If you had strep throat, she'd advise you to take an antibiotic, would make you her homemade chicken noodle soup, and would place her healing hands on your throat chakra to speed up the healing process. It worked for me, like a charm, every time.

Clint stuffed the prescription bottle back into his pocket.

"Were you outside?" I asked, noting the snow dripping from his parka and melting on the hearth.

"Huh?" He massaged his knee.

"You look like you were out in the blizzard."

"Reporter at heart—I see you don't miss a detail. We could use more kids like you on this motley crew."

I may have blushed. I wasn't sure. It could have been the heat from the fire crackling behind us. "I just noticed the snow, that's all."

"Good eye. Good eye. Yep. I took the doc, Jackson, outside for a quick look with me. One of the worst I've seen. Must be blowing eighty. Maybe more with gusts. I stand by what I said earlier."

"You mean about no one leaving?"

Clint shifted his weight to his left leg and held on to the iron fire grate. He pulled himself to his feet. "That's right. It's not safe out there even for us pros. You stay put too, young lady. Understand?"

I held up the remains of my cooling cider. "I'd be fine sitting here all weekend with a cup of this. Don't worry."

He limped off. Watching him in obvious pain made me think about his perspective on aging. Gam said, "We manifest what we believe."

I chuckled to myself as I finished the rest of my cider. What would Gam have said about me convincing myself I was lost out in a blizzard? Apparently I'd been lost in a crowd. I hadn't been alone out there at all. In the last half hour I'd learned that Clint, Jackson, and Henry had all been outside. It just went to show that perception was everything.

TWELVE

I didn't sleep well all night. I tried texting Matt and Jill, but couldn't get service on my phone. It would have been nice to chat with a friend. The wind rattled the windows, and the sound of snoring in the bunk above me kept me awake. It smelled like a gym locker room that hadn't been cleaned in weeks. Too many people in a small space. Even with such tight quarters, the room stayed cold. The woolen blanket might have been a work of art, but I woke up early with frozen fingertips and an ice cube for a nose.

Leaving my bunkmates in a symphony of throaty snores, I pulled on a pair of leggings, hiking socks, and a pink fleece hoodie. I tiptoed into the dining room, stepping over two sleeping bodies in the dark hallway.

The dining hall sat in a quiet, glowing white dimness. Overnight, the snow had accumulated so quickly that it blocked the windows, only letting in an inch of light. We were literally buried in the snow. Have I mentioned that I was a tad claustrophobic? I would do just about anything to avoid being cramped in tight spaces, elevators, closets, that sort of thing.

I found myself breathing shallowly. *Stop, Meg. You're fine. It's just snow.*

Lola was in the kitchen scooping coffee grounds into a carafe. The scent of the dark-roasted beans helped my breath to slow.

"You're up early." She motioned to the empty pot on the counter. "Can you hand me that?" It looked like she'd slept in her braids last night.

I passed her the coffeepot and inched closer. "Is everyone else still asleep?"

She poured water into the pot. "Not once they smell this."

A couple of the Rangers stretched in front of the fire. Lola chopped pineapple. I found an extra apron and helped her dice peaches. Maybe I could swap my focus to a story on the lodge. Lola's job seemed interesting.

"So you like working here?" I asked.

Lola scooped pineapple into a bowl. "Best job on the planet." She turned toward the snow-covered windows. "Except when we're stuck in here."

"It's pretty bad out there, isn't it?" I asked, scooping peach slices into a salad bowl.

"Yeah. We lost contact with the main lodge last night. I've been trying to get in touch, but there's no signal."

"What do you mean?" I gulped back a sense of panic.

No signal? That couldn't be good.

She rinsed raspberries in the sink. "The satellite phone isn't working."

"Is that bad?"

"No, why?"

I wiped peach juice on a hand towel. "That means we're cut off, right?" The fire crackled behind us. I jumped.

"Relax. It's okay. Happens all the time in weather like this. I have enough food and wood to keep us going for days. Plus, you're with the best mountain rescuers in the country." The coffeepot beeped. She poured me a cup. "Here, go chill out by the fire."

She was right. I thanked her for the drink and took it with me. Everyone began to stir as the aroma of coffee filled the room. The team rolled up their sleeping bags, stuffing them in nooks and crannies. We moved the tables back into position, gathered our mugs, and sat down.

Clint hobbled in. He looked like a cautionary tale for this rugged lifestyle. Poor guy. He really should go see Gam.

After multiple cups of coffee and a farm breakfast complete with a fresh fruit salad, eggs, sausage, and homemade biscuits drizzled with Oregon honey, Clint called everyone to attention.

"All right, troops. Here's the deal. Doesn't look like we're getting out for training this morning. I suggested to Ben that we go over a brief history. I know this will be review for some of you, but some of you are new. Then Jackson, our resident doctor, can talk through med-evac procedures. If we're taking novices up the slope, we have to be prepared for every scenario." He squinted and put his hand above his eyes. "Jackson, you here?"

Jackson waved from the back of the room. Malory clutched his forearm.

"Excellent. Excellent." Clint saluted Jackson. "You want to come up front?"

Malory released him from her grasp, and he sauntered to the head of the table. Unlike last night when his ebony hair had been plastered with gel, this morning it curled and twisted in unruly waves. I was sure Malory wouldn't have approved.

Clint clapped him on the back and leaned in to say something I couldn't hear.

"Ben, where are you?" Clint squinted again.

Silence.

"Where's Ben?" Clint couldn't hide the irritation in his tone as he scanned the room.

"Probably sleeping it off," someone hollered.

Hungover or not, I couldn't believe Ben wasn't leaping over tables to get to the front of the room.

"Go find him. We have work to do, troops."

The guy scrambled out the entryway. He returned a few minutes later with a look of concern on his face. "Sir, he's not here."

"What do you mean 'he's not here'?" Clint boomed.

"He's not here. I checked everywhere. The bunk rooms are empty. So are the bathrooms. He's not here."

"Did anyone see Ben this morning?" Clint barked. More silence.

I picked up on an uncomfortable energy. I took a deep intake of breath, trying to get a read on why Clint's face was suddenly fixed with a look of concentration like he was seriously stressed. Something was wrong. My heart rate ticked up in response to Clint's reaction.

Clint scrunched his face so hard it made my jaw hurt. "Jackson—you're a doctor. Grab your gear." He shouted orders to other members of the team, who sprang into action.

Clint stormed out with Jackson on his tail.

What happened to Ben? Had he actually tried to ride last night? After being momentarily lost in the blizzard last night, I hoped he was hungover and hiding out somewhere.

I followed Clint and Jackson. I might finally be on to a story—a real search and rescue in process.

Henry raced up to Clint. "Hey, I'll go. It's freaking terrible out there."

Clint appraised him and after a second threw him a pile of rope. "You want to go, kid?"

Henry threw the rope over his shoulder. "I want to go. I need the training."

Jackson put on snowshoes and pushed open the door. Icy air pushed back.

"You know what to do, right?" Clint asked Henry as he tied one end of the rope to the door handle.

"I've got this." Jackson carefully looped the rope around his thick ski gloves. "You coming?"

Henry nodded. "I'm good. Gotta grab my gear."

"What's the rope for?" I asked Clint.

"They'll follow the rope in one direction until they come to the end. Then they'll follow it back. They'll repeat it in a grid around the cabin. Search the perimeter. See if there's any sign of Ben."

It reminded me of a story from *Little House on the Prairie* that Pops read to me as a kid. To find their way from the house to the barn, Laura and Mary Ingalls had to follow a rope in the cold Wisconsin winters. It was hard to believe that with today's technology, the rescue team was using a hundred-year-old survival technique.

Henry returned wearing his Ten-Eighty ski jacket. "I think I should go with you," I announced.

Jackson, Henry, and Clint all looked at me like I was speaking a foreign language.

"What?" Henry punched me in the arm. "Dude, didn't you learn anything being out there last night?"

"That's exactly why I think I should go. What if what I heard..." I trailed off. Henry shook his head frantically, all the color draining from it.

"What did you hear?" Clint asked.

I looked at Henry. He shook his head. "Nothing. The wind."

Henry gave me a look of appreciation. I continued on.

"Can I go?" I almost begged. "It'll be really good research for my story. It's best if I can be part of the action, when I'm working on a story. You know what I mean?" I didn't tell them that the real reason I wanted to go was because I had a bad feeling something had happened to Ben.

"No," they replied in unison.

"You know how some actors go all 'method' when they're preparing for a role? It's like that. If I can actually experience what you do, it'll make the article on you so much easier."

What was I thinking? What was wrong with me? Why did I want to go out in a blizzard again? It didn't have anything to do with research. I could write a paragraph in my sleep about holding on to the rope for dear life. Perhaps I'd title it "The Life Rope." No, wanting to join them had nothing to do with research and everything to do with the nagging feeling that my ears hadn't deceived me last night. Plus, I needed to prove to myself that I could handle situations like this. Otherwise my summer training was wasted.

Jackson shrugged. Henry looked incredulous as Clint patted me on the back and said, "Knock yourself out, kid. Stick with these two and don't let go of that rope."

"Yeah, no problem. I won't let go. Don't worry."

I climbed into my snow boots, zipped up my parka, and took the ski mask Henry offered me.

Clint ushered us out the door and we scrunched out into the snow. Over the sound of the wind he called out a warning to stick together and check back before taking the next pass.

Jackson led the way. The snow was to my waist. Of course that wasn't saying much since I was a shorty. It was slow going. Jackson acted as a personal snowplow with his snowshoes, cutting through the whiteness as far as the eye could see.

The wind felt sinister, not only its high-pitched cry, but the way it blew around us, like we were caught in its vortex, with no escape.

I clutched the rope. Each step took triple the normal effort. My heart rate spiked. I wheezed from the effort of lifting my body through the snow and the lack of oxygen at 7,000 feet.

"You doing okay?" Henry turned to check on me, his eyes hidden behind goggles.

Gasping for breath, I gave him a quick nod and focused on my feet. I didn't want him to know that I felt like I was about to pass out.

"End of the line!" Jackson shouted over the roar. "Time to turn around." That meant I became the front of the line.

"Just follow it straight ahead, Meg!" Henry yelled. "Stay in our tracks."

"I got it!" I wished I had snowshoes.

The way back felt longer. Thoughts whizzed in my head. What if the rope came undone? Had Clint tied it tight enough? The brightness of the white sky hurt my eyes. Now I understood why boarders and skiers wore goggles.

The ski mask Henry lent me helped to shield the wind, but it became wet with my sweat and the barrage of snow pelting my face.

Finally I felt tension on the other end of the rope. I gave it a tug and fell backward into Henry. "Made it!"

Jackson took a compass from his pocket and held it into the air. "You want to stick with us, or head in?"

I gave him a thumbs-up. "I'm good. Let's go."

He returned the compass to his pocket and started off in a new direction, clearing a path.

We hadn't gone far when I spotted something out of the corner of my eye. Any flash of color stood out in the unending whiteout.

I stopped and tapped Henry on the arm. "What's that?" I pointed to my right.

Henry came to a halt and grabbed Jackson. "Hang on, dude. Meg sees something."

Did I? Or were my eyes playing tricks on me? "Over there. See that?"

They both trudged forward in a hurry. I couldn't keep up. I felt like the rope was dragging me down.

"It's just the picnic table," Henry announced, brushing mounds of snow from the top.

I caught up as Henry dug all around the table. Was he looking for something?

"Nothing here," Jackson announced. "We better head back to the hut and start over. My grid's messed up now."

"Uh, dude. I think you better come take a look at this." Henry sat on his knees next to the picnic bench.

Jackson and I moved closer.

Henry held up a mound of snow covered in brownish red specks. "Is this blood?"

"Nah. Why are you digging through the snow anyway?" Jackson pushed his goggles on the top of his hood to get a better look.

"I thought I saw something." Henry scooped snow near the base of the picnic table.

"Come on, man. Let's head back." Jackson secured the goggles on his face.

Henry didn't budge. He kept digging like a golden retriever on the scent of a buried bone. What was he doing?

Jackson wrapped the rope around his wrist and started the slow process of yanking us back to the Silcox Hut.

"Stop!" Henry yelled. "Dude! Stop!" I felt my stomach drop.

Jackson froze in midstride. "What now?"

"Come here!"

We looped back to the picnic table. My stomach lurched when my eyes caught sight of the red snow surrounding Henry's knees. "This isn't dirt, bro."

Jackson's hands shook as he dropped to his knees and examined the stained snow with Henry.

"That's blood, isn't it?" My voice sounded squeaky. Neither of them responded. I wasn't sure if it was because they couldn't hear me over the storm or because they didn't want to confirm it was true. Something serious had occurred. That was a lot of blood.

I put my hand to my stomach. *Center, Meg, center.* I could hear Gam's voice in my head.

So many questions swirled in my mind. Whose blood was it? Ben's? An animal's? If it were the latter, I wouldn't want to meet up with whatever attacked it out here.

"This way!" Jackson yelled, plunging forward through the snow and allowing the rope to drop to the ground.

Henry raced after him. They reminded me of kids digging at the beach.

Only I was pretty sure they weren't going to find any treasure.

Jackson made a grunting sound. Henry threw his hands up in the air, like a goal post.

"Meg—don't look." He whipped his head around. His boyish freckles seemed to disappear into a solemn and sober stance.

"Okay," I agreed. "Is it an animal?" I asked with a false sense of hope.

"No." Henry shook his head. "It's Ben."

THIRTEEN

Jackson hollered for Henry to give him a hand and ordered me to follow the rope back to the hut. "Get Clint. Now."

I stood in stunned disbelief.

"Can you do this?" Jackson stood and gave me a hard look.

"Yes, sorry." I grabbed the rope at my feet.

"Go!" Jackson yelled.

I hurried to the hut, the rope flying between my gloves, creating rough, warm friction. My mind hadn't been playing tricks on me last night. I *had* heard a gunshot. Ben Tyler was dead.

How had this happened again? I had just begun to erase the memory of seeing a body fly off the top of a cliff last spring. Now the vision of blood-coated snow flashed in front of my eyes.

An even scarier thought emerged as the rope became taut. I couldn't have been that far away when Ben was shot last night. His body was only twenty—maybe thirty—yards from the picnic table. My knees gave a bit at the thought. I could have been killed. A stray bullet could have sailed right at me.

I reached the hut in record time. I banged on the front door. "Clint! Clint!"

Clint burst open the door. "Meg, come in, come in. Where's Jackson? Henry?"

"B—B—Ben." My lips chattered together.

"Ben?" Clint stepped to the side and pulled me through the heavy door. He shut it behind him with a thud. "Did you find him?"

"He's dead." My words slurred from the cold. My body felt strange, like it was moving in slow motion.

Clint put his arms on my shoulders and gave me a little shake. "Meg. You're not making sense. Are you okay?"

I peeled off my gloves and rubbed my cheeks. "I'm fine. Ben's dead. They found him out there buried in the snow."

Clint's fingers dug into my shoulders. It hurt and would probably leave a mark. He noticed me cringe and dropped his hands to his hips. "Sorry. Sorry. Ben's dead?"

Nodding, I massaged my jaw and wiped my nose with the back of my hand. "He's dead. Someone shot him."

"What? Shot? How do you know? Lots of things could have happened out there. Let's not jump to conclusions."

"We found a ton of blood out in the snow." My nose dripped. Hot tears stung my eyes. My voice didn't sound like my own. It sounded like it originated somewhere outside my body. Gam would have said I wasn't grounded. True. I wasn't.

I tried breathing in and out of my nose slowly. She always said, "The mouth is for eating. The nose is for breathing."

"You need to sit down. Have a shot of whiskey. Come with me." Clint steered me up the stairs and into the dining hall. "Make some room!" Clint barked. The Rangers jumped to their feet. Someone pulled out a bench for me.

"Sit." Clint forced me down. He motioned to Lola. "Whiskey and water—stat."

Another Ranger knelt at my feet and took my arm in his

hand. He placed two fingers on my wrist. "Just checking your pulse. Keep up that nice, slow breathing. You're doing great."

Clint thrust a shot glass in my hand. "Knock that back." The glass trembled as I lifted it to my lips.

"Do it quick." Clint watched me.

I opened my mouth. The smell was intense. I'd have to drink it fast, otherwise it wouldn't go down. I plugged my nose and threw it down.

The alcohol burned the back of my throat and made me cough.

Clint appeared to have anticipated this. He ripped the shot glass from my hand and replaced it with water. "Now drink this —slowly. Sip."

He caught the eye of the Ranger assessing me. "How's she doing?"

The Ranger scooted next to me and rested his hand on my knee. "She's going to be just fine. A little touch of shock, but she's not in any danger."

Danger? Did he say "danger"? And why were they talking about me like I wasn't there? I could feel my cheeks begin to burn. My heart rate quickened.

"Easy, easy. Keep up that slow and steady breathing. You're just fine." The Ranger patted my knee.

"My bad." He hit his chest twice. "I shouldn't have said 'danger.' We just wanted to make sure you didn't decide to pass out on us. You're good. Don't worry."

I took a sip of water. Unlike the whiskey, it felt cool and refreshing.

Clint waited and watched me, along with the rest of the team, for what felt like an agonizingly long time. When he was satisfied that I wasn't going to faint, he addressed everyone. His tone was solemn and his hand shook slightly as he spoke. "I'm sorry to have to say this, but we have a serious situation. Ben Tyler has been found out in the elements."

A hush rippled through the room. The only sound was the crackling fire and wind assaulting the hut.

"I need a team to suit up. Any volunteers?"

Hands shot in the air.

Clint picked three Rangers. "You—you—and you. Bring rope, gear, and someone grab a blanket. Are you going to be okay here?"

"I'm better." I swallowed the tight lump stuck in my throat and nodded. "Thanks."

"Good, good. You sit tight."

"Wait, Clint," I called as he started to hobble toward the entryway. "Shouldn't we call the police?"

"Police?" He paused and supported his knee with his hand.

"Yeah, shouldn't someone call the police? If Ben's been murdered?"

He cut me off. "No one said 'murdered.' I'll take a look at the body."

"But..."

"Can't call them anyway, can we, Lola?"

Lola held up the satellite phone. "No service. I'll keep trying."

"Good plan. Good plan. We'll get out there and see what's what."

After Clint and his team set off, Lola came over to me with a cup of coffee. "Here, I warmed this up. Might be a little bitter, but if you're like me, coffee always helps."

"Thanks." I tried to smile and took the mug from her. "Everyone's being so nice. I'm fine. Really. I am. It just kind of hit me suddenly when I got back here that someone's dead. Dead, you know?"

Lola scowled. "Couldn't have happened to a nicer guy, if you ask me."

I must not have disguised the look of distaste on my face.

"Sorry." She sat with one knee crossed beneath her,

revealing a hole in her brown tights. "I didn't mean to sound callous. I know it must have been terrible to see Ben dead."

"It's okay." I took a sip of the piping hot coffee, not caring that it burned my tongue.

"No, it isn't. Really, I'm sorry. I've never seen a dead body. I shouldn't have been sarcastic like that. He just was a total pain in my ass." She stood and looped her fingers together. "I should go try to call the main lodge again."

I watched her as she walked into the kitchen. Regardless of her apology, she certainly seemed almost pleased with the news that Ben was dead. Could she have killed him? I didn't think so. If it wasn't Lola, then who killed Ben? Maybe I should slow down. Like Clint said, "No one said 'murdered.'"

As I sipped my coffee, I retraced my steps from last night, trying to piece together what I could remember. Well, that's not exactly true. My steps were erratic. Impossible to retrace. Instead, I tried to think about the timing and what I'd seen.

Henry had left after dinner—with the gun. I'd looked everywhere for him, so he must have already been outside. Then there were Clint and Jackson. They both were outside. Clint claimed they were checking on conditions. Could he have lied? What if one of them, or both, had followed Ben outside to kill him?

I thought about the picnic table, the sound of gunshots, bumping into Henry.

Henry. It couldn't be him—could it? Why had he brought a gun? He claimed it was part of a historical presentation. That hadn't happened yet. It could be because the Ridge Rangers were in such disarray—or it could be that Henry had another reason for bringing it.

As much as I didn't want to believe my friend had anything to do with Ben's death, it sure didn't look good for him. He had led us straight to Ben's body this morning. How had he known to dig in the snow? Because that's where he killed Ben? That didn't make sense. If he killed Ben, why would he lead us to the scene of the crime?

One thing was for sure. I had to talk to Henry. And I had to do it before Lola got in touch with the police. I'd learned a few things last spring when I discovered a body. The first of which was that if all the evidence pointed to one person—it wasn't good.

Breathe, Meg. I pressed my fingertips together. *Remember, this might not even be a murder.*

FOURTEEN

The next few hours flashed by. Clint directed the team to rope off the area around Ben's body. I wasn't sure how they were going to keep the rope from blowing away in the storm. Ben's gear and snowboard were stored in a bunk room.

"No one touches a thing—understood?" Clint held the mantel for support. "Any luck with the phone yet?"

Lola shook her head from the kitchen as she chopped vegetables for soup. It took me by surprise how normal activities could resume in the midst of a crisis. I mean, I guessed we needed to eat, but who could think of lunch after seeing a teammate slain in the snow?

The vibe in the dining hall was muted as Lola served steaming bowls of vegetable beef soup and homemade rolls.

I pushed around carrots in my soup. It smelled hearty and exactly what I'd imagine you'd feed a group of hungry skiers and snowboarders, but I couldn't shake the image of Ben's blood splattered in the snow. Ben hadn't made a great first impression last night, but I didn't wish him dead.

It was decided that as soon as there was any break in the weather, Jackson would ski down to the main lodge for help.

Apparently it would take a while for the snowcat to get moving and plow a trail back up to the Silcox Hut. Skiing wasn't without risk. All the fresh snow meant that avalanche danger was running high.

Henry, who slurped down his bowl of soup across the table from me, explained that it could take a couple days, sometimes even weeks, for avalanche danger to subside after a major snowstorm.

He picked up the salt shaker and shook some into the palm of his hand. "Feel this? That's what the top layer is like out there right now. Same texture as salt or sugar."

He shook some into my hand. I rubbed the granules together. "Feels pretty good to me. I don't get it. Doesn't everyone covet powder?"

Henry brushed the salt on his hands onto the floor. "Yeah, the powder's pretty sweet, but it's the layer underneath that you have to worry about. The weak layers are just below the new snow. There are layers under there that formed maybe a few weeks ago." He shook more salt into my hand. "Think about it— that's pretty weak. It's not going to hold."

"Should Jackson risk it?"

"He'll be fine. My grandpa used to do avalanche patrol. He told me in the old days they used to strap rifles to their pack and use them to shoot off the cornices."

"That's bonkers."

He shrugged. "Plus, Jackson can take an avalanche bag."

Avalanche bags I knew about. I'd done a product review on them for *Northwest Extreme*. They were like airbags in a car. Backcountry skiers and boarders carried them in their packs. In the event of an avalanche they yanked on a cord, like a parachute, and the bag inflated with air. It served as a buoyancy device to keep the skier from being buried under the snow. The odds of surviving an avalanche without one were bleak.

The afternoon lingered on as the restless vibe increased

inside the Silcox Hut. The Rangers passed the time by playing poker, watching movies on the projection screen, and snacking nonstop. I hoped Lola was right about having enough food. With the way the team noshed as the afternoon wore on, I wondered if there would be anything left for dinner.

A tap on my shoulder startled me. "You're Meg, right?" Malory, Jackson's fiancée, stood with her glittering diamond hand extended.

I smiled. "Yep, and you're Malory."

She bent her hand in a dainty shake. "Do you have a minute?" She eyed Henry. "I was hoping I could speak to Meg —in private."

Henry offered her a seat. "I was about to snag a beer anyway." He gave me a look like, *Good luck with that*, and left.

"Congratulations." I pointed at the ginormous ring on her hand. It literally made me want to shield my eyes from its glare. It wasn't my taste—a princess-cut stone set in a thick gold band. If I ever got engaged, it would be antique platinum for me.

"Thanks." She positioned her left hand over her right in order to showcase the ring while we talked.

"When are you and Jackson planning to get married?"

"Soon. Definitely soon."

"Maybe you could do it up here? It would be so romantic. Think candlelight, the fireplace."

"You mean here?" She pursed her lips and angled her carved cheekbones. Her face looked taut and dewy. Probably the result of expensive moisturizer. Her dark eyes were lined with bronze liner and dusted with copper eye shadow.

I pinched my cheeks in hopes of giving them a shot of color. "Yeah, wouldn't it be so cozy and romantic?"

"Uh. No. Jackson's a prominent physician. The entire reason I came to this *little gathering* is to check out a wedding down at Timberline." With her non-bling hand she flicked her hair and arched her neck.

"Oh, funny. One of my friends from college is getting married at the lodge later. It must be the same one. Don't you just love weddings?"

She flared her nostrils. "Jackson's so enamored with the mountain that I promised him I'd take a look, but our guest list is going to top five hundred. I'll go take a peek at Timberline, but it's not going to be able to accommodate our needs."

"Wow. That's a big wedding."

She shrugged. "People expect it. He's on track to be the youngest chief of staff ever at the hospital."

I should introduce her to Mom. They'd hit it off instantly. Or they'd come to blows fighting over who was the better name-dropper.

Was I being childish? Yes. I swear, I was trying to work on it. Gam had been helping me. She would say, "Margaret, you're always *at choice.* You can choose to dive into a situation that's less than optimal, but how is that working for you? The only behavior we can change is our own."

"Did you want to ask me something?" I dropped the wedding convo.

Malory surveyed the room. Her eyes lingered straight ahead. I turned to see what she was staring at. It was Lola. She had her back to us, scrubbing the soup pot in the kitchen.

"I noticed you and Lola have buddied up pretty quickly." Malory returned her attention to me.

The way she looked at Lola made me put up my guard. "I guess." I didn't offer more.

Malory tapped her jeweled finger on the table and leaned in. "Listen, I think that we have some mutual friends. I just want you to watch who you associate with. You seem sweet, but a bit naïve."

Naïve, really? That was a leap. Even if it were true, it still stung. "Who are our mutual friends?" I asked, trying to remain breezy.

"Will Barrington and I went to school together." She removed a silver tube from her pocket and twisted off the cap. It smelled of burning mint.

Oh, Gawd.

Will Barrington. He was the last person on the planet whose opinion mattered to me.

"Will. Yep. He's dating my best friend." I tried to play it cool with Malory. "What's that?" I asked, pointing to the minty tube she ran across her hands.

"It's just lotion. My hands get a bit tight in the cold." She twisted the tube closed and reached across the table to pat my hand. Her fingers felt cold. They matched her charcoal tunic and dark eyes. "What a lucky girl your friend must be. Rumor has it, he's going to make partner before he's thirty."

Big whoop. Social climbing was right up there with having a root canal for me. Not that I'd ever had a root canal, but I'd heard they weren't much fun.

"What does that have to do with Lola?"

Removing her hand from my arm, she made sure to reposition her hands so that the rock on her finger caught the light. She lowered her voice.

Let me just say, I was highly suspicious of anyone who wanted to confide a secret within minutes of meeting me. That was weird, right?

"Lola's not the kind of person you want attached to your name."

"Why?"

Malory looked annoyed. "Portland's a small town. Word travels fast. I'm trying to help you out."

Help? Yeah, right. Although she was right about Portland being a small town. I'd learned that the hard way after Pops's death. He'd been a revered journalist at *The O*. Before his death, he became immersed in a meth investigation that led to him being fired, Mom walking out, and maybe even murder.

Being known as Charlie Reed's daughter suddenly meant that people whispered in hushed tones when they met me or they gave me a look of pity. I didn't love it, but nothing compared with losing him and trying to live without him. I'd have taken the gossip about him any day in exchange for even five minutes with him.

I took a deep breath, willing those ugly memories to the back of my mind. "Believe me, I know it's a small town. I'm just trying to understand how Lola plays in? She's a host up here in the middle of nowhere."

Malory's voice turned as icy as the wind outside. "There's no such thing as the middle of nowhere in Oregon."

She had to be kidding. I considered debating this fact. The state of Oregon boasted more wild space than cities. Sure, maybe along the western valley, but had she ever traveled east? Should we talk about the desert named Hells Canyon or the acres upon acres of forest where someone could literally disappear? I'd read somewhere that nearly half of Oregon's land was held by the U.S. Forest Service. I begged to differ. There was most certainly such a thing as the middle of nowhere.

"Lola's name has been circulating in some less than savory circles, if you know what I mean."

What *did* that mean?

"No, I'm not sure I do." I looked at her for clarification, but she shrugged and rolled her eyes with a flash of annoyance as if to say that if I didn't get it, she wasn't going to spell it out for me.

"Well, thanks for the heads-up." I picked up an empty cup and got to my feet. "I'm going to grab some coffee. You want anything?"

Malory declined my offer and glared at Lola, who was chatting with a group of Rangers while passing around beers in the kitchen.

As much as I didn't like Malory's snobbish vibe, our conversation left me feeling unsettled. Was she simply a social climber who didn't want to associate with Lola because in Malory's world you don't interact with "the help"? Or could it be that Malory really knew something serious about Lola? I thought back to first meeting her yesterday. Ben had been trying to make a move on her. Was it possible that she could have something to do with his death? Could she have gotten fed up? I tried to remember exactly what she'd said—something about staying away from him. I liked Lola. She didn't strike me as the revengeful type, but I decided to keep my intuition tuned up.

FIFTEEN

As the afternoon wore on, the storm front passed. Lola paced back and forth in the galley kitchen with the satellite phone in her hand, attempting to contact the lodge. The Silcox Hut smelled of musty bodies cramped inside for too long. "No luck." She held the phone out.

We were going to be here for a while. I decided I might as well use the time to interview some of the team. I was in a prime position to cover the story, and had to come up with something to show Greg. Clearly there was ample material for me to mine. I wasn't sure yet how it would all fit together, but not only could I gather intel for my feature, but I could also use it as opportunity to learn more about everyone's relationship with Ben.

Jackson, who was momentarily free from Malory's clutches, stood chatting with Lola in the kitchen. As I approached them, they looked like they were posed for a Silcox Hut brochure. Jackson wore expensive jeans, a wool arctic sweater, and moccasin slippers. Lola's Timberline apron and sun-kissed cheeks seemed picture-perfect for a tagline that would read: HOSPITALITY WITH A VIEW.

"Hey, can I steal you for a couple minutes?" I asked Jackson." Lola jumped backward. "Sorry, I didn't mean to startle you."

She brushed off her apron and scooted toward the stove. Jackson set the walkie-talkie on the counter. "What's up?"

"I wondered if I could ask you a few questions for my story."

"Sure." He leaned on the counter. "Shoot."

"Tell me about yourself—what's your background? You're a doctor and a skier?"

He pulled a piece of fuzz from his sweater. "Guilty of both. Yep. I've skied all over the globe."

"What are some of your favorite spots?"

"Here." He extended his hands. "Obviously. I love the east too, especially Vermont."

"Oh!" I motioned to Lola. "Did you know Lola's from Vermont?"

Jackson gave me a wry smile. "We were just talking about that."

Strange coincidence, I thought, but he didn't offer more, so I continued with my questions. "What are your thoughts on the Ridge Rangers?"

"I doubt that it's going to take off."

Lola turned from the stove. I lowered my voice. "I don't get it. If Ben was funding the team, who's going to run it now?"

Jackson shrugged. "Who knows? Ben had all kinds of crazy plans. He wanted to partner with advertisers for exclusive endorsement contracts. Upsell clients with branded gear and packs." He motioned to a table where Clint was playing poker. "Clint pulled me into this, but the Crag Rats are more my speed. This weekend is a bust."

Henry ambled past us with his snowboard under his arm. He pulled Lola out of the kitchen and flipped his board for her to see. Jackson's eyes followed them. "Your friend there knows what I'm talking about."

"Henry? About the Rangers being a bust?"

Jackson didn't respond.

Had word gotten out about Henry's deal with Ten-Eighty? I wasn't sure how to ask him without revealing Henry's secret.

Jackson saved me. "Listen." He tore his gaze away from Henry and Lola to the window. "I can't hang out here any longer. I'm going to ski down to Timberline. Someone has to alert the authorities."

I agreed, but as he geared up I wondered what he knew about Henry.

Everyone traipsed outside after him, trying to shake the stir-crazy feeling of being shuttered inside for the past twenty-four hours. I couldn't believe my eyes as I stepped outside. The mountain was completely transformed. Dark clouds hung on the ridgeline to the south, another storm looming. The sun, low on the horizon, and clearing skies directly above gave me a sense of freedom.

"Remember," Clint hollered as Jackson stepped into his skis. "Small mistakes equal death."

An icy chill went down my spine, sending a fresh wave of fear from the top of my head to the tips of my toes as I thought of Ben. *Noted.*

The team dug snow from the entrance to make a pathway and assessed the snow for stability. They measured it systematically. Henry explained that not only were they measuring how much snow had fallen overnight, but they were trying to get a sense of avalanche risk.

"Four feet, troops." Clint held a yardstick in his hand. "Four feet in eighteen hours. That storm packed a mighty punch."

The lift wasn't running, but I could see Timberline Lodge buried in snow far below. Somehow even the distant sight of the hotel made me feel better.

Sooner or later they'd have to send up the snowcat to check on us and test the upper runs for safety.

There was discussion amongst the group about whether or not they should trek up to Palmer and trigger an avalanche intentionally. Clint shot this down immediately. "No way! No one's going up there in this unstable snow. The base is ready to crumble. My guess is ski patrol will be sending up the avalanche team soon."

After a winter storms dumped fresh powder in record amounts like this one had, ski patrol and the Forest Service would work in conjunction to keep skiers safe by aiming ammunition at the chute and creating an avalanche. It was also common practice in backcountry skiing for individual skiers to intentionally trigger an avalanche.

The concept was that if a backcountry skier triggered an avalanche from the top of the slope, they'd mitigate their risk of being consumed by one as they skied down. There was a big debate in the ski community about the safety of this method. While it could reduce the risk for the individual skier, it put anyone farther down the slope in harm's way.

Many critics claimed the practice was selfish and irresponsible, while uphill skiers maintained that was the risk everyone experienced playing in the wild.

I didn't have to solve the moral dilemma today since Clint put the kibosh on anyone trekking up the slope. Instead, a spontaneous snowball fight of sorts broke out. In fairness, there weren't many balls involved in the battle. Probably a better description would have been snow flinging.

They were wrestling on the opposite side of the hut from the picnic table and makeshift temporary morgue for Ben Tyler's body, but I didn't want to take any chances. I took myself out of the game and returned to the kitchen. I figured I could help Lola with dinner prep and see if she'd divulge anything about her relationship with Malory.

After kicking off my wet boots, I made my way to the

kitchen, where Lola stood near the stove waving a bread knife in her hand at Malory.

"You heard what I said. I won't say it again, but you keep your distance from me." Malory poked Lola on the shoulder and whipped around. She almost knocked me over on her way out and didn't even bother to apologize.

"What was that all about?" I asked, hanging back a little.

Lola brushed a stray strand of hair from her eyes and tucked it back into her braid. "You can come closer," she said, resting the knife on the counter. "I'm not going to use this thing on you."

"What's her problem?" I stepped into the galley kitchen.

"Who knows? She thinks I'm after every guy here." She peered toward the snowed-in window. "Did Jackson leave?"

Lola sounded casual, but I noticed her hand shook slightly as she tried to twist open a jar of peanut butter. Malory had shaken her—literally.

"Yeah." I motioned to the jar. "You want me to get that?"

"Thanks." She handed it to me.

I twisted off the cap in one move. "Why would she think that?"

"No idea. She's self-obsessed."

"Do you two know each other?"

Lola nearly dropped the peanut butter as I handed it off to her. "No. I mean we met up here, but I don't know her. Why?"

"I just wondered what her deal is."

Lola didn't respond. She pulled butter from the fridge. "You want some help?"

"Sure, thanks. I'm making peanut butter cookies. Figured a little hit of sugar might help lift everyone's spirits. How is it out there, by the way?"

"It's beautiful. Gorgeous. I can't believe it. It's like the storm came through and blew in new energy or something." I sounded like Gam. Mom would not have approved.

"It does." Lola scooped peanut butter into a mixing bowl. "There's nothing better than taking the first run after a storm. In fact, I was thinking if I get these in the oven in time I might have enough daylight to get out there for a few."

I unwrapped the paper lining from the butter. "You can't. Clint says no."

"Clint's not my boss."

What was it with adventure types? If someone told me not to ski, I'd gladly curl up on the couch with my latte. In fairness, I would do that anyway, even when the conditions weren't dangerous.

Lola and I worked in silence, creaming butter and sugar. The oven hummed to life, and the smell of sweaty bodies that lingered in the room began to shift to the scent of baking cookies. What would happen to the Rangers now that Ben was dead? Would Clint take the helm? He seemed like the natural choice, but what about financing? It had to be a huge undertaking to invest in outfitting and training high-altitude guides.

A rumbling sound and a sharp beep of a horn startled both of us. The snowcat had arrived. I hurried to the front door and pulled on my boots. Sure enough, the cherry-red snowcat had tracked its way up. Members of the ski patrol emerged wearing their red jackets with white crosses on the back and carting all kinds of gear and equipment.

I recognized the last person off the cat. He and I got to know each other last spring when he investigated the murder of an adventure racer. Plus, he'd been seeing Gam on and off for a few months. Sheriff Daniels hopped off the cat and locked his wise eyes straight on me.

SIXTEEN

"Sheriff Daniels! What are you doing here?" I had to resist the urge to throw my arms around him. Seeing his familiar, weathered face sent a wave of relief through my body.

"Ms. Reed?" He furrowed his silver eyebrows. "I could ask you the same question."

Before we could continue our mini-reunion, Clint interrupted. "Sheriff?" He offered his free hand; the other rested on a wooden cane. His leg must have been hurting.

Sheriff Daniels returned Clint's handshake and unbuttoned his suede coat. He wasn't dressed for the elements. He wore a pair of tight, broken-in Levi's, cowboy boots, a cowboy hat, and a bolo tie. No wonder Gam's eye sparkled whenever the sheriff was near. He looked like he'd stepped out of a Western movie.

He pulled a silver badge from his suit pocket. "I'm Sheriff Daniels. As you can probably tell, I wasn't prepared for professional duties. I'm up here on personal business, but when word came through that there'd been an incident up here, I offered to come take a look. It's going to be a while before the road from Government Camp is passable."

I felt sorry for Sheriff Daniels. Being an officer of the law must be like being a doctor. When there was an emergency, you were forced to drop your personal plans.

"I'm going to need to see the body, and then I'll take everyone's statement inside. I know you're all professionals, so I'm sure this goes without saying. No one is to leave the Silcox Hut until I've secured the perimeter and had a chance to speak with each of you."

Everyone nodded. Clint ordered the team inside to await questioning while he led Sheriff Daniels to Ben's body.

Once Sheriff Daniels returned, we all huddled to the far side of the dining hall and in the bunk rooms while the sheriff held court at a table pushed to the back wall near the fireplace. Total privacy was nearly impossible. I tried to eavesdrop without looking obvious. Sheriff Daniels caught my eye twice and gave me a stern look.

After a few of the team members had given their statements, Malory stood and demanded that she go next. "Look, I have to get down to Timberline. I'm supposed to be meeting the coordinator so I can get a sense of the venue. It's the only reason I'm here."

Sheriff Daniels gave her a strange smile and motioned her over.

Malory stormed over to Lola once she was done with the sheriff. "Can you tell the snowcat we need to go now?"

Lola shook her head. "Sorry. It's not leaving until the sheriff's finished."

"What? I need to get down to the lodge—now!"

She seemed pretty spun up. Jackson might have a bridezilla on his hands.

Clint ambled over and tapped her on the shoulder. "If it's okay with the sheriff, I'll ski down with you. Does that sound okay?"

"Ski down? Go to a wedding in this?" Malory motioned to her black jeggings and tunic.

"Probably fine," Clint responded.

"Fine. I've got to get out of here." Malory turned to leave.

Sheriff Daniels stopped her. "Wait." He stood and addressed the group. "You're free to ski, but no one is leaving the mountain yet. I've secured the perimeter. Do not disturb that area. The coroner is on his way."

Malory huffed out of the room. Clint followed her, dragging his leg. Wait. How was he going to ski on an injured leg?

Sheriff Daniels finished interviewing the other Rangers. When he finally motioned that it was my turn, I could tell from the scowl on his face he wasn't happy with me.

"Ms. Reed, do you want to explain how you've managed to land yourself in the middle of another suspicious death?" He clicked his pen shut and removed his cowboy hat. His silver hair gave away his age, as did the rough wrinkles on the edges of his kind eyes.

"I—I—didn't." I stumbled over my words.

"You're here, and there's a body right outside this window, correct?" He tapped on the windowpane, buried in snow.

He and Gam shared an ability to cut to the truth in a matter of seconds. It unnerved me. It wasn't like I planned this.

"You said 'suspicious.' Was Ben murdered? Or do you think it was an accident?" I asked, not able to contain the questions rattling around in my brain.

Sheriff Daniels frowned. "Ms. Reed, I'll ask the questions. Where were you last night?"

I told him about the Ridge Rangers, my feature story and everything I could remember from last night.

"Slow down, Ms. Reed." He jotted notes on a Timberline Lodge notepad. "What can you tell me about Henry Groves? I hear he brought a gun?"

"I know it looks bad for Henry, but I know—well, at least I'm pretty sure—there's no way he could have done it."

Sheriff Daniels rubbed his temples. "Here we go again."

"No, really. Ben was awful to everyone. He groped Lola. He was trashed."

"Trashed? Is that a technical term?" Sheriff Daniels tried to conceal a small smile.

"You know what I mean."

"I don't. I'm afraid I don't speak twenty."

"I mean drunk. He was totally gone."

Sheriff Daniels clicked his pen shut and tucked it in the pocket of his suede jacket. "Thank you for your insight, as always. Now, young lady, I want to remind you once again that you're here to write a story, not involve yourself in my investigation."

I thrust my notebook toward him. "Do you want to see my notes? I've written down everything I can remember."

"That won't be necessary. Unless there's anything you haven't told me?" He raised his brow and waited.

I shook my head.

"In that case, I have a few things to wrap up outside, but when I'm done, what do you say—you want to take a ride to the lodge with me? There's someone there who would love to see you."

"Who?"

He held his finger in the air. "Get your stuff. Meet me outside in five minutes."

I hurried to my bunk to layer up. Who could Sheriff Daniels be referring to? Who did we both know, other than Gam? She would have told me if she were coming up to the mountain at the same time as me.

Whew—I was going to be free of the Silcox Hut at last. Plus, I might actually get to go to the wedding and see Jill. I unpacked my party dress and dug through my clothes to find my swimsuit. I'd bring both along. Timberline Lodge had an outdoor pool that was heated year-round. As guests of the Silcox Hut, we had full access to all of Timberline's amenities. A swim would refresh my spirit and maybe help put Ben's death out of my mind.

The question was, where was it? I searched through every item in my suitcase. I would have sworn that I put it in the zippered pocket on the top of my suitcase when I left Government Camp. I checked around and under the bunk. No swimsuit.

Could someone have taken it by mistake? *No, Meg. Duh. Who would steal a swimsuit?*

I scurried into the bathroom. Maybe I'd accidentally stuck it into my toiletry bag. After a quick search of the bathroom, my swimsuit was nowhere to be found.

Now I really wanted to swim. I decided to check the other rooms just in case. Mom said I was too trusting. Maybe it fell out of my bag and someone accidentally moved it? I know. It's a stretch, isn't it?

I did a quick survey of the bunk rooms. If anyone found me, they would think I was snooping. My search yielded a plethora of soggy wool socks, ski jackets, and a few unmentionables—aka men's boxer shorts. But no sign of my suit.

Just as I was about to say "forget it," I saw Ben Tyler's gear piled in the corner. Worth a shot, right? I unzipped his bag and removed wadded-up long johns, T-shirts, and underwear. My hand felt into the bottom of the bag. I pulled out a piece of paper.

My internal voice said, *Put it back, Meg.* But my hands moved like they were possessed. I opened the folded sheet of paper. A handwritten note in pink pen and a woman's scrawl read:

Ben, you're still the one. Meet me after dinner. Let's talk.

I dropped the note as if it were diseased. Who would send Ben a love note? *You're still the one*. Double gag.

I stuffed the note back into the bottom of the bag, returned the clothes, and zipped it shut. As I went to place the bag back in its original spot, something caught my eye. My swimsuit! What was it doing here?

SEVENTEEN

Sheriff Daniels waited for me by the snowcat. He offered me a hand up and I immediately launched into what I'd just discovered.

"Who would have sent Ben a love note?" I asked Sheriff Daniels. My swimsuit caught the wind. I clenched it under my arm. "And why would someone move my suit?"

The sheriff signaled the snowcat driver to go. "Ms. Reed, I have a more important question."

I waited, grabbing on to the handle as the snowcat jerked to a start.

"What are you doing contaminating my evidence?"

"I, uh, um, was just looking for my swimsuit," I protested, feeling my cheeks start to flame. Why did he have to be so good at his job?

"In the duffel bag of the deceased after I made it clear no one was to touch any of his belongings?"

"When you put it like that it sounds bad, but I didn't mean to disturb any evidence." I chomped the inside of my cheek. Damn, he'd caught me red-handed.

Sheriff Daniels focused his gaze out the windows and shook his head. "Your grandmother isn't going to be happy with me."

"What does that mean?"

"It means that I want you to stay out of my investigation." We hit a bump in the snow that tossed us both in the air.

"Sorry about that," the driver yelled above the sound of the cat's engine. "Needs grooming. We'll be down in a flash."

We were down in a flash, but not the kind of flash that I enjoyed. Snow shot underneath us as we barreled down the slope. I made the mistake of looking out the front window. *Bad idea, Meg.* It literally looked like we were going to fall off the mountain. I kept my eyes focused on my feet for the remainder of the descent. My knuckles were white by the time the sloped, shingled roof of the historic lodge came into view.

I let out a sigh of relief as Sheriff Daniels helped me climb off the cat. We had to plod through knee-deep snow to get to the entrance. He steadied my arm as my boots sank into the snow. A sparkling layer of crystals had formed on the top. It felt like crunching through a snow cone.

Once inside, I grinned at the sight of exposed timber beams running across the towering ceiling. "It's so beautiful, isn't it?"

Sheriff Daniels nodded in agreement.

A wall with mosaic tiles designed with native animals and plants greeted us. In the Barlow Room, a kid banged on the piano playing "You Are My Sunshine," and guests played table tennis with wooden paddles.

There was a palpable excitement in the air—ski season was officially on.

Skiers gathered in front of the massive stone fireplace in the lobby, warming their hands and drying their socks. I turned around to take it all in. Sitting dead center with her hands on the lodge's resident Saint Bernard was Gam. She wore a turquoise party dress, pantyhose (as she liked to call them), and black flats with tiny sequins adorning the top.

"Margaret!" She clapped her hands together and raced over to me. The Saint Bernard trailed behind her.

She wrapped me in a huge hug. "Surprise! Can you believe it?"

We rocked back and forth, oblivious to the mob of skiers and guests pushing past us. It was impossible not to feel captivated by Gam's joyous and brilliant energy.

Finally releasing myself from her hug, I stepped back, holding her hands. "Gam, what are you doing here?"

Her eyes darted to Sheriff Daniels with a wink. Her face was aging to perfection. Tonight it radiated. Her eyes were dusted with blue shadow and lined with a dark pencil, and sparkled with excitement. Her cheeks were alive with color.

"Bill surprised me with an invite to his nephew's wedding. We're going to boogie! Can you believe it?" She twirled me toward her and planted a kiss on my cheek.

Gam had a unique ability to take pleasure in just about anything in life, from meditating quietly in the forest to watching "shoot 'em up" movies, as she liked to call them. Dancing was like trekking to Mecca for her. Line dancing, swing, the foxtrot. It didn't matter. She loved it all.

"I can't believe it. Why didn't you tell me you were going to be here?"

"I didn't know. Bill surprised me. You know how I like surprises." She squeezed Sheriff Daniels's arm. He tipped his cowboy hat. "We came up yesterday. I planned to ride in that snowcat up to see you. I can't wait to get in that thing. It looks like so much fun. But then the storm hit."

"Did you tell her about Ben?" I asked Sheriff Daniels.

Gam's expression changed. "He did. I don't like it one bit that you're involved in another investigation, Margaret."

"I'm not involved, Gam. I just happened to be there when it happened."

She ran her hands from the top of my head to my feet.

"Let's clear that energy out, shall we?" I closed my eyes as she drew air over my body in gentle waves. It felt like she'd enclosed me in a warm, glowing bubble. Her hands radiated heat. My heart rate slowed and I unconsciously shifted my breathing.

When she finished, she brushed her hands together and looked from me to Sheriff Daniels. "What do you say? You want to come boogie with us?"

I smiled. "You two go enjoy yourselves. I want to go for a swim. How about I come join you in a little while?"

"Yes! We can have dinner with—" She stopped and threw her hand to her mouth. "Oops. I'm not supposed to say anything. Go swim. Come find us upstairs when you're done. You brought your party dress?"

I held up my tote bag. "Yep. I'm all set."

Sheriff Daniels wrapped his hand over Gam's and escorted her upstairs. She came to his shoulder as she leaned into his sturdy frame. I felt strangely protective. If anyone deserved happiness, it was Gam. She'd been alone since my grandfather died years ago. She brought joy and light to everyone she met. I wasn't convinced that Sheriff Daniels was a match for her energy. Was Gam ignoring her own inner guidance? Was she jumping in too quickly? I wasn't used to seeing Gam with her head in the clouds.

I'd have to tread carefully. Gam was usually my personal advisor. How would she respond if our roles were flipped?

For now, I had enough on my mind with Ben's death and the fact that I had nothing solid for my feature yet. I stopped at the front desk for directions to the pool. The receptionist pointed me down the hall. I walked past the gift shop, which was jammed with tourists purchasing Oregon marionberry jam and Pendleton blankets.

The long passageway gave me the creeps. It made me feel like I was in *The Shining*. I tried to avoid watching horror flicks. I was too impressionable. Pops called it the creative curse.

"Don't worry, Maggie, it comes with the territory. The creative force allows our brains to open up and filter the world differently. It also means that sometimes we have to be more protective about what we let in."

I shivered as I scurried down the hall. I never should have let *The Shining* in. It was Jill's fault. We watched it at her birthday party. I couldn't remember, but I thought we were fifteen. Her birthday fell right before Halloween, so she usually threw a spooky-themed party. She was a mystery junkie. I was pretty sure she had seen every episode of *Midsomer Murders*. I could handle those, but for her fifteenth birthday she opted for a horror theme. I hid in my sleeping bag while she and our other friends chomped on Swedish fish, screaming in delight as *The Shining*, *Scream*, and *Night of the Living Dead* played on her movie projector. I crawled deeper into my sleeping bag. I didn't sleep at all that night.

Pushing the image of a crazed Jack Nicholson and the words "Red Rum" out of my mind, I rushed into the women's changing room. A mother with twin girls was trying to wrangle them out of their wet suits.

"Are you going to swim?" she asked, as she twisted a suit above the drain on the floor. "It's amazing. We were the only ones out there. I can't believe it. It's so warm."

We chatted while I unpacked my tote and pulled on my swimsuit.

"Great suit. You look like one of the travel postcards from the gift shop."

I thanked her, left my tote on the bench, and grabbed a towel from the stack by the door to the pool.

"Be careful. It's slick out there!" she called after me.

Wrapping myself in the towel, I thanked her and made my way outside. The alpine air blasted my exposed skin. Thin clouds stretched like taffy between the treetops. Steam hovered above the pool's surface.

The pool was enclosed with a wooden fence. The far section shouldering the ski slope had four-foot windows cut out. As I was swimming, I'd be able to watch skiers and boarders coming down to the lodge.

Snow piled around the pool. I tiptoed on the icy deck and found a chair to hang my towel. My feet burned with cold. As soon as I was close enough, I plunged right into the warm water.

The smell of chlorine and heavy steam rose around me. I dove under the water and swam to the far end. There was nothing like the sensation of losing myself in the water. I could feel my worries fall away as I swam back and forth.

I stopped to catch my breath and treaded water.

This is more like it, Meg, I thought as I practiced my breast-stroke, losing track of the time. After my muscles felt loose and rejuvenated, I took a break and braved the cold to hop into the hot tub.

Within a few minutes I looked like a lobster. Blame it on my Irish skin.

Time to cool off again.

I jogged across the deck and nearly slipped. My arms flew in the air like windmills. Once I'd regained my balance, I chose my steps carefully and dove back into the pool.

The water felt like it had dropped by ten degrees after being in the hot tub. I swam to the middle and started doing laps. It was a surprisingly harder workout than usual—maybe due to the elevation. After I'd gotten my heart rate up and my cheeks nicely pink from exertion, I took a break and floated on my back. The lodge with its sloping roof and glass-paned windows reminded me of a gingerbread house.

In one of the windows above I caught sight of two familiar faces—Malory and Jackson. That must have been the room the wedding reception was in.

I blinked chlorine from my eyes, trying to focus on the window three stories above me. Malory and Jackson didn't appear to be enjoying the wedding. They stood in front of the window, clearly fighting. Malory waved her arms and looked like she was hurling insults at Jackson. He didn't back down from whatever she was saying. He pointed his finger at her and launched into some kind of tirade himself.

What was going on with those two? Maybe Malory wasn't impressed with Timberline as the site for their exclusive wedding. Yep. I'd pegged her correctly—a bridezilla.

If only I could hear what they were saying. Was Jackson standing up for his vision of their wedding, or were they fighting about something else?

At that moment they both looked down at the pool and caught me staring at them. Uh-oh.

I treaded water and threw a hand up in a cheerful wave.

Hopefully they'd think I'd just spotted them.

Neither returned my greeting. They both hardened their eyes. Jackson pushed past Malory and out of my line of sight.

Malory continued to glare at me. I waved again and dove under the water. It would look too obvious if I got out of the pool now, so I swam a few more laps. My fingers were wrinkled, and despite the water's warmth and my exertion, I was starting to shiver. Time to get out.

As I grabbed the towel that I'd left on one of the deck chairs, a loud bang sounded from the heavy wooden doors to the locker room shutting. Funny timing. Someone else must have been coming out for a swim.

Only no one appeared. The doors banged again.

"Hey, is anyone there?" I shouted, wrapping the towel around my waist. Silence.

I skated across the cold, wet deck. The twilight above revealed the first stars of the night. No storm tonight.

The sound of footsteps crunching in the snow made me pause. I whipped around. "Hello?"

My stomach felt hard as a rock as the hairs on the nape of

my neck tingled. My senses were on high alert. "Hello? Is someone here?" I squinted, trying to see in the dim light.

I hesitate to describe what happened next because I know it's going to sound kind of "out there." As I made my way closer to the locker room, I had what Gam described as a "knowing" that I wasn't alone.

Had Malory or Jackson come down to tell me to stop spying on them?

I was only a few feet from the door when that knowing turned into a reality. I heard the sound of the snow crunching under someone's feet again and caught a whiff of a familiar scent I couldn't place. Mint? No. Something more earthy?

The next thing I knew, something whacked me on the back of the head, and I fell onto the deck.

EIGHTEEN

When I came to, I sat up slowly and felt the back of my head.

Ouch.

I winced. A huge bump was growing from my skull like a volcano's bulging lava dome. My legs and butt felt numb. I began to shiver uncontrollably. I wasn't sure if it was because I was sitting on the pool deck in a swimsuit, soaking wet in the snow, or because of what had just happened. Either way, I needed to get inside.

My damp towel provided no protection from the cold. I wrapped it around me anyway and crawled onto my knees to push myself up to standing. Dizziness flooded my body. I grabbed the back of a chair to steady myself. My towel fell to the ground.

Forget it, Meg. Get inside.

Every part of me shook as I edged toward the door. My jaw clenched and emitted weird sounds that seemed to come from somewhere within.

I reached the door and yanked the wooden handle. It didn't budge. I tried again, this time using all my weight. It didn't move —at all. Someone had locked it.

Now what?

Maybe if I walked to the other side of the pool I could flag someone upstairs? I could get back in the pool or hot tub to warm up, but the lump on my head left my body feeling foggy. I kept blinking my eyes to try to clear the blurriness. It didn't help.

First I should try to find someone inside to come help me. If that didn't work, then I'd think about getting in the hot tub. I shuffled around the pool deck, stepping over my soaked towel.

I peered up at the windows. My head throbbed. Lifting it made me woozy. I sucked in a breath and wrapped my arms around my chest. All the windows looked empty. I scanned each of them, trying to ignore the fact that each time I moved my eyes, it felt like my center of gravity shifted.

No luck, Meg. Plan B.

The hot tub didn't seem like a smart idea with a woozy head, but if I didn't raise my core body temperature soon, vertigo would be the least of my worries. I padded toward the hot tub. I felt like someone was watching me. I took one more glance to the windows above.

Malory reappeared. She stood with one hand on her hip and the other near her eye, like she was looking for someone. Me?

Could she have hit me? Would she have had time to run down, knock me out, and get back to the window? Probably. She was an expert skier. Navigating a couple flights of stairs wouldn't be an obstacle. That scent—the minty smell—I remembered why it was familiar. Malory's hand lotion. It had to have been her.

I debated whether I should hide behind one of the snow-covered lounge chairs or try to get her attention. Not that it mattered, because Malory caught sight of me and fixed her gaze in my direction. She looked surprised.

I motioned for her to come down. She didn't acknowledge that she'd seen me and raced away from the window.

Crap.

You have to get out of here, Meg—now.

I listened to my inner voice and inched back to the door. Maybe if I pounded on it loud enough, someone inside would hear.

"Help!" I threw my body weight into my arm. "*Help!*"

It didn't budge.

I lifted my fist again just as the door burst open.

"Megs!" Someone scooped me into their arms as my knees buckled.

NINETEEN

"Matt?" I steadied myself in his arms. "You're here, too?"

My knees buckled again, but this time not from the lump on my head.

Matt Parker, my friend and current crush, grinned down at me.

"I came with Jill. I wanted to surprise you." Matt pointed behind him.

Jill Pettygrove appeared in the doorway. "Surprise!" She stopped in midstride staring at me with concern. "Meg, are you okay?"

My body broke into another wave of shivering. "Uh, I'm kind of a little out of it." My hand instinctively went to my head. Everything was already fuzzy, and now Matt was here to complicate things even more? I blinked hard, trying to clear my vision and concentrate.

"We better get her inside." Matt held the door open with his foot and practically pushed me into Jill's arms.

Jill yanked me into the women's locker room and wrapped me in a towel while she turned on a hot shower. My teeth chattered as I spoke. "Matt's here?"

"Hop in the shower." Jill held open the curtain. "You need to warm up."

"Yeah, but I didn't know Matt was coming." I dropped the towel on the floor and stepped into the steamy shower.

Jill tugged the curtain shut.

Water sizzled on my skin. I wrapped my arms around my chest and plunged my head under the burning stream. "Why didn't you tell me Matt was coming?" I shouted to Jill.

She lifted one side of the curtain and poked her head inside. "Warm up. You look like a Popsicle."

"I feel like one." My body continued to quake despite the heat from the shower. I turned the dial to make it hotter. "But why didn't you tell me Matt was coming?" I knew I was disorientated from the bump on my head, but everything felt like it was moving too fast, and I was struggling to keep up. I couldn't believe Matt was here.

Jill waved steam from her face. She wore black ski pants and a gray puffy ski coat with a navy-blue woolen scarf tied in a slipknot around her long neck. "He was planning to come up the whole time, but I wanted to surprise you. Will's meeting us at the wedding soon. We'll make a perfect foursome."

That was right. Of course Will would be here. Gag. Maybe he and Malory could hang out and swap social-climbing techniques.

Will and I didn't have much in common. He wore three-piece suits (no one our age in Portland even owned a suit) and preferred martinis to microbrews. I had to suck it up for Jill. I kept hoping she'd step into herself more, as Gam would have said. The Jill I knew was adventurous and insanely creative. I was waiting for the day when she decided that it was time to reveal her true self, but for the moment, she seemed content—or maybe more like resolved—to keep that part of her locked away. Was it a glaring red flag? Yes. Jill rarely brought up her art or traveling these days, but was it my issue to fix? Sadly, no.

Gam liked to remind me that Jill (and everyone else) was on her own path. "Margaret, one of the biggest lessons in this life is learning to understand that we—and we alone—manifest our dreams. You can't force someone else's dream."

I knew she was right, but I wished I could. Will was wrong on every level for Jill.

"Did I miss the actual wedding? I hope Mike won't be mad that I'm just coming to the reception." I pumped shampoo into my hands from the dispenser on the wall. It smelled like coconuts. I gently massaged the shampoo into my throbbing scalp.

Jill closed the shower curtain and raised her voice in order to be heard over the water. I couldn't see her face, but I could hear the smile in her tone. "No, no, not at all. The wedding was just a few people. I think just their family. Mike wanted that part to be low-key. Tonight should be fun, a chance to dance with Matt, yeah?"

Maybe Jill wanted to help me manifest a dream, too. Matt Parker and I had been friends since my junior year of college. We met when Pops came to present a lecture on "Meth Madness," a feature story he'd been working on for two years at *The O.* His investigative work led to national coverage on Oregon's growing meth addiction, congressional legislation, and eventually his downfall.

Pops became obsessed with the story and was convinced that he'd just scratched the surface—that the real story was about how entangled high-ranking officials in the state were in drug trafficking all along the West Coast. His sources informed him of tunnels and underground railways that snaked from Mexico to Oregon. As *The O*'s leading investigative reporter, his editor poured money and resources into the exposé until the *New York Times* released a report that Pops had inflated his statistics and used unreliable sources. His name was discredited, he was put on leave from the paper, and Mom walked out.

That didn't stop him. In fact, if anything, it fueled him to dig deeper. He went "off grid" and tracked sources down in Mexico and out in Hicksville towns in eastern Oregon. Having his name become synonymous with crazy conspiracy theorists was hard to come to terms with. I was away at school, though, and didn't have time with the close of the term and finishing off my last few credits before graduation to focus on Pops's problems.

I wished I had. I wished I'd dropped everything and paid closer attention. He died in a biking accident before I had a chance to really understand what he was working on.

Matt and Pops hit it off when they met during that first lecture. From that day on, Matt saved me a seat in the lecture hall with a stick of peppermint gum. Pops was partial to Matt and helped him land a job writing the technology beat for *The O* after he graduated.

No one else seemed to believe that Pops was working on a legitimate story, but Matt did. And what was even more disturbing was that Matt thought Pops's "accident" may not have been an accident after all. He thought Pops was killed because of what he'd learned.

My brain told me he might be right, but my heart wasn't ready to face that yet. I'd been on shaky ground since Pops died. He was my rock, and nothing felt solid without him. I was just starting to find my footing. What if looking into his death brought all those memories back up to the surface?

Shampoo dripped into my eyes, startling me back to the present. I rinsed my hair and turned off the shower.

Jill handed me a dry towel. "Feel better?"

"Yeah. I can't believe you're all here. Gam, too. Did you know that?" I dried myself off, still feeling like everything was slightly off-center.

She unzipped her parka and twisted off her scarf. Even in the steamy locker room, Jill looked perfectly put together.

"I did." Jill winked.

"I love it. You have no idea how relieved I am to have you all here." I ran a towel through my chunky blond hair. "You didn't happen to bring a blow-dryer, by chance?"

"There's one in my room. We can head that way after you're dressed. I have makeup and extra clothes if you want to, you know, look cute for anyone special."

I threw my wet towel at her. "Matt and I are friends. That's all."

"Right." Jill nodded.

"Just friends." I tugged my ski pants back on.

"Got it. So all this talk lately about 'Should I, shouldn't I go for it with him' is just talk?"

"Shh. He's right outside." I wrung my swimsuit over the sink. "Let's go."

Jill gave me a knowing smile. "You got it." Her voice turned serious. "Meg, listen, I know that Matt really cares about you. Don't take too long deciding, okay? He may not wait around forever."

I rolled my eyes and folded my suit in a towel. "I have enough on my mind for the moment."

She followed me out of the locker room. "What's that supposed to mean?"

I didn't have a chance to respond.

Matt stood leaning on the door to the men's locker room. "Took you long enough." He winked and tapped an imaginary watch on his wrist. "What's what supposed to mean?"

"Meg apparently has a lot on her mind."

"Megs?" Matt put his arm around my shoulder. He stood a good foot taller than me, so I had to look up to meet his eyes. They were the coolest shade of blue. Watching him gaze down at me made my stomach flop. "What's on your mind?"

Before I had a chance to answer, Malory burst into the hallway, followed by Clint limping behind her.

"There you are." Malory's eyes darted from Matt to Jill.

"Hold up!" Clint bellowed.

Malory snapped her head around. "Well, hurry."

Clint shuffled down the hall.

Malory stood with her hands on her hips, directing a glare at me. "What's going on?"

"What do you mean?" I snapped back.

Clint caught up and squeezed into the tight passageway.

She pointed to the pool. "What were you doing out there? I thought you were in trouble. Why did you signal me?"

Matt tightened his grasp on my shoulder.

There was that smell again—something minty. Had Malory hit me? I put my hand to the bump on my head again. I wasn't sure how to answer. I didn't want to let her know she'd spooked me. "Yeah, I got locked out." I pointed to Jill and Matt. "My friends let me in. I'm cool now. Thanks."

Clint cleared his throat. "Good thing. I ran into Malory running down the stairs like there was a fire raging. Said she had to come help you. I tried to hurry as fast as I could on this bum leg." He tapped his leg with his cane.

Malory shifted on her feet. "Yeah. Glad you're okay." She didn't sound sincere.

Clint saluted all of us. "I'm heading back to the Silcox Hut. You want me to hold a seat on the snowcat?"

I shook my head. "No, thanks. I'm going to hang with my friends for a while."

He turned and hobbled down the hall. Malory watched him intently and then returned her attention to me. "I need to get back to the wedding." She pivoted away.

"What was that all about?" Matt asked, releasing me.

"I'm not sure. That's what I was going to tell you both, before they interrupted. You're not going to believe this, but one of the Ridge Rangers was murdered—well, at least I think it was murder—last night."

"Murdered?" Jill grabbed my arm. "Why didn't you tell me?"

"I haven't had a chance."

"Start talking."

I explained about Ben's death and the storm. Jill and Matt listened intently. "After I ran into Gam, I decided to take a quick swim. Clear my head, you know?"

They nodded.

"I don't know how the door locked. I didn't even think it had a lock."

Matt interrupted. "It doesn't."

"What do you mean?"

"I mean, it doesn't." He paused. "We ran into Gam. She said you were swimming. When we got here, there was a stick wedged in the door, to keep it shut. At first I thought maybe the hotel had done it as a temporary fix, but then I heard you yelling."

I took a quick breath. "That means that I'm not imagining what just happened."

"What happened?" Jill and Matt shouted in unison.

"I think Malory tried to knock me out. I saw her in the window fighting with Jackson, her fiancé. The next thing I knew, someone came out onto the pool deck and hit me on the back of my head."

"What?" Matt pulled me toward him. "Where?" He started separating strands of wet hair.

"Here." I guided his hand to the back of my head.

"Jeez, Megs. That's a wicked bump." He turned to Jill. "We should get some ice on this."

"I'll go check with the front desk." She sprinted down the hall.

"You're shivering again." Matt ushered me in Jill's direction. "Let's get you in front of the fire."

I let him guide me to the roaring fireplace in the lobby. Matt whispered something to a group of skiers warming their hands. They bunched together, making room for me right in front.

The warmth and earthy smell of the fire helped calm my nerves. Having Matt by my side helped, too. My body trembled even as my temperature warmed. I knew it was an emotional response to being attacked. Why would someone hit me?

While we waited for Jill to return with ice, I spotted Jackson weaving his way between boarders and skiers to the Blue Ox Bar. There was no sign of Malory.

Shouldn't he be upstairs at the wedding? What was going on with the two of them? The feeling of calm evaporated from my body. Could Malory have really tried to hurt me? Why?

TWENTY

Jill returned with ice and gently put it to the back of my head, where it stuck to my damp hair. After she and Matt were both satisfied that the swelling had gone down a little, we agreed to meet upstairs in the Cascade Dining Room in an hour.

Matt ambled to his room, but not until he gave Jill firm directions to keep an eye on me. "If she starts feeling dizzy or nauseous, call the front desk right away. She could have a concussion."

"I'll keep her safe," Jill promised, patting Matt's arm.

Back in her room, Jill lugged an overstuffed suitcase onto the bed. She dug through neatly folded piles of scarves, turtle-necks, jeans, and ski gear until she found her hair dryer.

"Dry your hair." She handed it to me. "It'll help you warm up."

I plugged in the dryer and clicked it on high. Usually I blew my hair upside down. It gave it body and just a little hint of tousle. When I bent my head forward, the room started to spin. I grabbed the bedside table and dropped the blow-dryer on the floor.

"You okay?" Jill hurried over and turned off the dryer.

"I'm fine."

She didn't look convinced. "Maybe we should see if there's a doctor on site."

"No, really. I'm fine. I promise. I just won't bend over." I took the dryer from her hands and clicked it back on.

Jill appraised me from the bed. Once my hair was dry and I looked less like a drowned rat, she tossed her makeup bag to me.

"Thanks. Do I look that bad?" I teased, dusting my cheeks with powder. I fluffed the taffeta skirt on my ivory and green mid-century dress.

"Not at all." Jill pointed to a silver tub of expensive lip gloss. "You should use some of that shimmer gloss."

Jill and I shared a love of makeup. My obsession came from Gam. Even in her seventies, she never left the house without her "eyes done."

I applied a touch of the shimmer to my lips, brushed on a thin layer of gold eye shadow—which brought out the green flecks in my hazel eyes—and pinched my cheeks.

"You look great." Jill threw me a creamy ivory cashmere scarf. "Wear this. It'll keep you warmer and will look perfect with your rosy complexion."

I wrapped the scarf over my shoulders. "Thanks." I ran my hand over my cheeks. "It's more like windburn."

She shook her head.

"You want to get a beer before dinner?"

She searched through her clothes. "I'm going to jump in the shower myself, if it's okay? I want to get out of my ski clothes. I told Will that we'd meet him upstairs."

"Speaking of Will, where is he?"

"He wanted to get in one more run."

"Cool." I tucked her makeup bag and hair dryer back in her suitcase. "You take a shower. I think I'll go grab a pint at the bar."

Jill arched her brow. "What are you up to, Meg? I know that tone."

"Me? Nothing. Never." I winked and pretended to massage my head. "A pint should help numb the pain, right?"

"Right." Jill narrowed her eyes. "Meet you upstairs in thirty?"

"Yep." I breezed out of the door before she could say anything else. I wanted to see if I could catch Jackson at the bar. Maybe I'd be able to find out what was going on with him and Malory.

I hurried through the crowded corridor, past the crackling fireplace in the main lobby to the hidden iron cave-like entrance to the Blue Ox Bar. The centerpiece of the cheery bar was an opaque glass mural that covered the far wall. Crafted by hand by the Works Progress Administration artisans, the mosaic featured Paul Bunyan and his blue ox designed in bright orange, yellow, and blue tiles.

The smell of wood-fired pizza and hops greeted me at the door. *Man, I would give anything for a slice of pie right now.* I hadn't realized how hungry I was.

Wooden benches and tables ran the length of the narrow space and were jammed with snow lovers munching on pizza and knocking back pints. Exposed beams crisscrossed the ceiling, and one giant beam stacked the bar. I spotted Jackson, sitting on a bar stool and nursing a beer.

I pushed my way through the throng of rowdy drinkers.

"Hey, Jackson." I squeezed between a group of skiers gathered round the bar.

He almost spilled his beer at the sight of me. "Meg? What are you doing here?"

The bartender caught my eye.

"Can I get an IPA?" I shouted over the crowd.

"You're an IPA fan, huh?" Jackson set his pint glass on the wooden bar.

"Yep. The more hops the better."

"What are you doing down here? I thought you were up at the Silcox Hut." He sat up on his stool and glanced behind me.

"I came down with the sheriff. I'm meeting some friends for dinner." The bartender handed me a frothy pint of beer. I took a long sip, letting the scent of hops linger in my nose.

"What about you? I thought you and Malory were checking out a wedding?" I tried to keep my tone light.

"Huh?" Jackson's gaze was focused on the beer in front of him. His eyes shifted from his beer to my dress. "Are you sure you write for *Northwest Extreme*?"

"Yeah." I laughed, then tried another tactic. "Are you taking a break from all the wedding planning?"

He picked his beer up, but didn't take a drink. "Sorry, what did you say? It's loud in here."

True. The combination of sweaty bodies and flowing drinks had raised the decibel level in the compact space, but Jackson definitely had heard me. He looked distracted.

Pops used to say the best way into a source was to join them where they were. That was his trick. It was no surprise that he and Gam got along so well. He parlayed her spiritual slant into his reporting—*Be in the moment. This moment,* now.

I leaned closer to Jackson. I could smell a faint whisper of stale, sweet beer on his breath. "I'm feeling kind of rattled about Ben's death," I confessed.

His beer sloshed in his hand. He snapped his eyes up to meet mine. "Why?"

It worked. He was fully present. I could feel his energy shift and noticed his back become stiff.

"Well, I mean, what if he was murdered? Right outside last night. Doesn't it creep you out?"

Jackson's hand shook slightly, unsettling his beer. He placed it back on the counter. "No. There's no need to be worried. The police are up there investigating now. I bet he accidentally shot himself. He was so drunk. I've seen way too many self-inflicted firearm injuries in the ER."

"But if it wasn't an accident, that means that someone at the Silcox Hut must have done it."

"Not necessarily." Jackson scanned the room. His foot tapped on the checkered floor, as if he were keeping the beat to imaginary music.

"Who else could have done it? We were the only ones snowed in last night."

"That's up to the police now. It's not my problem. I've got my own stuff to worry about." He grabbed his beer and slugged a big gulp.

"You mean about taking over as the leader of the Rangers?"

Jackson took another swig. "Nah, that worked itself out." He finished his beer and stared at something behind me. I swiveled my body to see what he was looking at. Malory stood in the doorway, with her hands on her hips. They said looks could kill. If that were true, Jackson was a dead man.

"I better go." He jumped from the stool.

"Hey, not to pry, but I noticed you and Malory fighting upstairs when I was out in the pool earlier. Is everything okay?"

Jackson held his index finger in the air at Malory. "Just go enjoy your party and leave it alone." He nearly knocked me over as he elbowed his way to the door.

Granted, I knew I was too pushy, but his reaction seemed strange. Plus it was my job as a reporter to ask the tough questions. Why had he blown off Ben's death? With Ben out of the way, did that give Jackson a chance to take control of the Rangers? But was that a position he'd kill for? As a prominent doctor, it wasn't like he needed the money. And what was going on between him and Malory? They were obviously fighting.

Was it just a case of pre-wedding jitters? Was he having second thoughts about marrying a bridezilla, or could it have something to do with Ben's death?

My mind ran wild.

I sipped my Total Domination IPA, not feeling like I was dominating anything at the moment. It was probably time to meet Jill, Matt, and Will for dinner. I polished off my drink, paid the bartender, and made my way toward the door.

Between the beer and the boisterous crowd in the small space, my entire body finally felt warm. I caught a glimpse of my reflection in the mirror behind the bar. My cheeks were pink with color and Jill was right. The cream scarf around my neck pulled out the honey color from my hair and softened my face. The emerald tone of the dress made my eyes appear greener. I didn't look half bad, especially given the events of the past few hours.

Something else caught my eye in the mirror. I threw my hand to my mouth, not caring if I smeared the shimmer on my lips.

Tucked in a corner booth near the back of the Blue Ox sat Will Barrington. His tanned arm was wrapped around a leggy brunette woman as they nestled together in the booth, with her head resting on his shoulder. I thought Jill said he was taking one last run? Apparently not.

What should I do?

I scooted out of the bar. Once back in the well-lit hallway, I tried to steady my breath. Had I just witnessed my best friend's boyfriend with another woman?

TWENTY-ONE

"Megs!" Matt waved from the far end of the hallway. He maneuvered through a crowd of tourists who'd stopped to examine the artwork displayed. Reaching me, he grabbed my hand. His touch made my stomach quiver.

Knock it off, Meg.

He looked like he'd showered, too. In place of his ski gear he wore a relaxed pair of khakis, a white dress shirt, and a blue tie. His light, shaggy hair looked like he'd tamed it with gel. Jill thought he looked like a younger Justin Timberlake.

"I've been looking everywhere for you." He squeezed my hand. My heart skipped.

His transparent blue eyes lingered on mine. "You look amazing," he whispered.

Jill's scarf slipped off my shoulder, exposing my skin. Matt repositioned it. "Listen, I know you have a lot on your mind this weekend, but I really need to talk to you. Maybe we can find a little time after dinner?" He paused. "Megs, are you okay? Is it your head?"

I'd forgotten all about my head.

"No, I need a minute. I have to think about something." I dropped his hand.

Matt took a step back and shrugged. "Okay. Guess I'll head upstairs, then."

I watched him turn, his shoulders sagging as he walked away. I didn't mean to brush him off. I really did need a minute. Could this weekend be more messed up? A death, an attack, catching my best friend's boyfriend in the arms of another woman—and now sending the wrong signal to Matt?

I sighed. For the moment I'd leave it. I needed to eat. I needed space to think. I needed to talk this all through with someone older and wiser. Someone like Gam—she'd know what to do.

Taking a deep breath, I pulled the scarf tighter and hurried up the stairs to the Cascade Dining Room. Helmets and boots hanging from pegs lined the hallway. Since the natural wood floors had to be repaired by hand due to Timberline's status as a National Historic Landmark, staff tried to keep ski boots off the stairs—not an easy task with hundreds of boot-clad guests rotating through the lodge every day.

Stepping into the expansive dining room felt like stepping back in time into a scene from a Bing Crosby movie. Ten-foot-tall wood-framed windows piled with snow showcased the mountain's slopes. Timber-exposed beams framed the room. Skiers gathered in cozy, plush red chairs in front of a giant basalt fireplace burning in the center of the room.

The Ram's Head, the bar above, swept around the open room. People congregated at tables and on comfy chairs. An older man caught my eye as I surveyed the balcony and he leaned over the wooden fence to blow me a kiss. Yuck.

Our friend Mike posed with his new bride in front of the fireplace. With the official ceremony complete, the reception was in full swing. Couples queued at a buffet set up on the far side of the fireplace. A sunken dining room nearby was lit by tapered candles and adorned with garlands of fall flowers. I spotted Gam and Sheriff Daniels at a table for two in the romantic room.

Jill and Matt sat at a table with legs carved like rams, near the windows. A four-piece jazz band played quietly. On the circular balcony above us, couples danced and swayed to the music.

"This is *gorge*," I teased, as I squished into the booth.

"Gorge?" Matt socked me in the arm. "And you call yourself a journalist."

"Ouch." I feigned pain. "Isn't that what the kids are saying these days?" Matt shook his head and laughed.

I gave him a flirty smile. "Whatevs."

Jill rolled her eyes. "Should we order drinks?" She surveyed the room. "I'm surprised Will's not here yet."

I bit my bottom lip. Mom claimed I had the worst poker face. She was probably right. "Yeah. Drinks. Should we get a pitcher?"

Will strolled up to the table as we were deciding which beer to order. He planted a kiss on Jill's cheek.

"Hey, I was just wondering where you were." Jill scooted to make room for him. Her sheer black dress caught on the chair. "Good run?" she asked, carefully extracting her dress from the chair.

He removed his suit jacket and hung it on the back of the chair. Sliding in next to Jill, he wrapped his arm around her shoulder. If anyone other than Will did this, I'd think, *Oh, sweet.* But the way he pulled her close to him made me bite into my lip more. He held her like she was a possession.

"The powder was so good. I had to get another run in." Will let this lie roll easily from his tongue. He clearly was a better poker player than me.

Matt leaned closer. "Are you okay?" he whispered.

I pursed my lips. I could taste a hint of blood from where I'd bitten my lip. "Tell you later," I said so that Jill wouldn't hear.

Will proceeded to snatch the menu from Jill's hand and ordered her a cocktail when the waitress came by. Matt shrugged and ordered a pitcher anyway.

Good thing I wasn't responsible for driving the snowcat back up the mountain.

Jill kicked me under the table. "Tell Will about the murder."

Will didn't bother to make eye contact with the waitress when she returned with our drinks. "Murder?"

Jill practically bounced in her chair. "Yeah. Meg discovered a body."

Will popped the olive from the side of his martini glass and squished it in his mouth. "Really?"

Jill strummed her long fingers on the tabletop, ignoring the pink Cosmo in front of her and helping herself to a pint of the amber beer Matt had ordered. "Yeah, one of the Ridge Rangers was shot last night. Meg found the body."

"Well"—I hesitated—"I wouldn't go that far. I was with them when they found the body. But I didn't find it. And the sheriff hasn't said for sure that Ben was murdered. It could have been an accident."

Jill blew me off. "What about what just happened at the pool? Someone hit you. That's too much of a coincidence, if you ask me."

Something about her almost-manic excitement over Ben's death made me wonder if Jill suspected that Will wasn't telling the truth. She was completely obsessed with British mysteries and after she helped me solve a murder last spring, she'd been on a new kick. I remembered one summer when she read the entire Nancy Drew series, then moved on to Sherlock Holmes and Miss Marple. Lately she had been breezing through culinary mysteries, even though she couldn't cook.

Matt sighed. "She might be right. You need to be careful."

He handed me his menu. "Are you hungry? You should probably eat something."

"Starving." I scanned the mouth-watering options. Mike and his new wife had spared no expense on the reception. Between rent and my student loans, my meager salary at *Northwest Extreme* barely covered my expenses. I refused to complain. I had a job—a real-life writing job. That was more than half my graduating class could say. Most of them were blogging or trying to bill themselves as social media consultants. The landscape of journalism was changing so fast, even our professors couldn't keep up.

I opted for the baked chicken and a hazelnut and cranberry salad. While we waited for our food, Will made it clear he didn't approve of Jill's excitement or my involvement in a potential murder investigation.

"You two need to stop acting like you're crime solvers and leave it to the professionals." He sat back, crossed one leg over the other and stared at Matt. "Am I right?"

Matt moved his head from side to side and lifted his hands as if to say, *Who knows?*

Our food arrived before Will could push it further. We ate in silence. I listened to the sultry sounds of the jazz band and watched as Sheriff Daniels whisked Gam around the dance floor.

"Your grandmother has some smooth moves." Matt finished his steak and gave me a little bow. "Want to go give it a whirl?"

I caught Jill's eye. Her body was rigid, and not from her Pilates practice.

She forced a smile and told me to go.

Matt led me to the floor, clutching my hand in his. It felt good. Too good. The band played Etta James's "At Last." He pulled me close, wrapping his arms around the emerald-green satin on my waist.

I wasn't sure if it was the melodic sounds of the band, the

glow of a wedding, the candlelight, the cedar scent of Matt's aftershave on my cheek, but I forgot about Jill, my head, and Ben's death as Matt held me and we swayed in rhythm to the music.

Time faded away in his arms. Everything felt normal, steady, and blissfully off-center at the same time. Matt gently stroked my hair as we circled the dance floor. I rested my head on his warm chest. When the music stopped, he didn't release me. Instead he placed his hands on both my cheeks and bent his face toward mine.

He tilted my chin. His eyes looked at me with a longing that I'd never seen before. I sucked in air. This was it. He was finally going to kiss me.

My heart pounded. I wondered if he could feel it beating on his chest.

Just as he inched his face closer to mine, a loud crash echoed throughout the room. He dropped his hands from my face as we both swung toward the sound.

Malory stood a few feet away. She was covered in red sauce. A large silver tray had splattered by her feet. Waitstaff scurried with rags and a bucket of water to clean up the mess. Malory glared at Jackson, who had escaped the mess. He grabbed napkins from a nearby table and began dabbing Malory.

She pushed him off and stormed out, leaving a trail of red streaks on the floor behind her. Jackson bent over to help clean up her mess.

Matt broke the silence. "What do you think that was all about?" His face had returned to normal. Our moment had been lost.

"Bridezilla."

Matt chuckled. "The lifestyle editor is doing a feature on bridezillas. I should hook her up."

"Malory's textbook from what I've seen so far. You should."

The band began to play again. Couples crowded the dance floor around us.

Matt cracked his knuckles. "I could use another drink. You?"

I felt a twinge of regret that he didn't ask me for another dance. "Sure." I followed him from the floor. He didn't take my hand this time.

As we wound our way back to the table, we passed by the sheriff and Gam. She intentionally bumped her hip into mine.

"Margaret! Isn't this the best?" The lines around her eyes crinkled deeper as she beamed at me.

"I'm glad you're having fun, Gam." I squeezed her hand.

She squeezed mine back. I started to pull away, but she stopped me. "Margaret, what's wrong?"

How did she know?

She asked Sheriff Daniels for a "refresher" and tugged me to their secluded table in the dining room.

"Sit." She motioned to the empty chair. A votive candle flickered, wax spilling down its sides and pooling in the glass below.

I plopped into the chair. Gam was best described as serenely directive. As an energy healer, she exuded calm and an inner-knowingness that I could only hope to achieve someday. She was no pushover, though. Quite the opposite. She held the space around her, firmly occupying it with her commandingly calm presence.

She wrapped my hands in hers. I could feel heat radiate immediately, sending warm waves up my arms. "Okay, Margaret. Out with it."

"Gam, I'm fine."

She scrunched her aging face. "Honey, it's me." Her hands pressed firmly into mine. "I can feel it. You're all spun up."

Everything came spilling out. I told her about Ben's death,

the attack, Jill, and finally my confusion over my relationship with Matt.

One of the things I appreciated most about Gam was that she didn't jump in. She sat comfortably, watching the candle flicker, absorbing everything I said. I tended to rush in, trying to fill silence, acting before I thought, even though I strived to become more Gam-like.

She released her grasp, brushed her hands off, and ran them over her body from her head to her feet. It was how she cleared someone else's energy. "Which one of these challenges is yours?"

"What do you mean?"

Her brown eyes narrowed. "I mean, which one of them is *yours*?"

"All of them?"

She laughed and shook her head. "You think so?"

"No?" I wrinkled my nose.

"Margaret, I've said it a thousand times. We're always at choice. In every minute we're at choice. This moment—this very moment—holds the most power." She animated this point with her hands. "What choice do you want to make at this moment?"

"You mean Matt, don't you? He's the only challenge that's mine."

"I didn't say that." She raised her eyebrows.

"What if I'm not ready to move forward?"

She placed her hands together in front of her in a prayer position and closed her eyes. A serene smile crossed her face. I watched her face transform. After a couple of minutes she opened her eyes and nodded. "This is important for you to understand." She held up a finger. "Doing nothing is also a choice."

I took a moment to let her words sink in. "Right." I sighed. "I guess after Pops's death I feel like every decision I make is so much more important."

"Mm-hmm." She ran her fingers along a blue onyx crystal pendant around her neck.

"I guess I also feel guilty."

"Guilty, how?"

"If I move on, move forward, it's like I'm leaving Pops behind. I'm starting to forget things about him, Gam." I swallowed back tears.

"I understand." She clasped her hands over mine and held them there. "Have you heard of the poet Kahlil Gibran?" she asked.

I shook my head.

"He said that sorrow carves the heart to contain more joy. Your heart is open and waiting for more joy. That's the gift of grief. It makes space for more love, light, and joy. That doesn't mean that sadness won't linger, but when our hearts break, they also break open if we let them."

"So you think I should give Matt a chance?"

She considered this for a moment. The flickering candlelight reflected on the sequins on her turquoise dress. "I didn't say that. I think you should ask for guidance. Spend some time being quiet—asking your higher self what brings it joy. Then set your intention for that."

A waitress passed by with a tray of desserts.

She gave me a soft smile and changed the subject. "Oh, I see chocolate cake. Shall we indulge?" She took two plates of chocolate Bundt cake from the tray.

"About this death." She stabbed her fork into the cake, and molten chocolate oozed from the center.

"I already know what you're going to say." I carved a chunk of the dense cake and popped it in my mouth. Divine. Gooey chocolate melted on my tongue.

Gam rested her fork on her plate and waited until I met her eyes. "Margaret, this is a job for the professionals. You already have enough to think about, right?"

Licking chocolate from my lips, I agreed. "The problem is I just have to know. It's like once I've started on this path, I can't stop."

"You can't force it either." Gam gave me "the look."

I hung my head. "I know."

"Margaret, forcing something never helps. The Universe reveals everything in its own time. It would be like you planting a new flower. Imagine trying to force it to grow by pulling it up by its roots every day, saying, 'Grow, grow.' Then putting it back in the ground again and again and wondering why it doesn't grow. This is the same thing. If you try to force finding answers, I'm concerned that you'll end up on a path you don't want to travel."

"I get it."

"Good on you! Okay, shall we go boogie again?" She munched another bite of cake and scooted to the dance floor. I watched her body sway to the music—letting it envelop her as she danced her way to Sheriff Daniels. She practiced what she preached. Throughout the restaurant people took notice of her, smiling and nodding with appreciation of her joyful abandon.

I poked my cake with my fork. Gam was right, but I couldn't drop it that easily. I blamed Pops. He taught me from an early age that tenacity won.

"Maggie." He would stroke my head when he tucked me into bed at night. "You know if you really want to be a reporter when you grow up—and that may change, my sweet—the one thing, the only thing you need to do is to follow the story all the way through to the end."

He'd kiss my cheek. "The biggest pitfall I see in this line of work is that people give up too easily. Don't give up. Keep on your story—whatever it may be."

I knew, even then, that Pops was talking about more than just reporting. I'd modeled my career, my life, after him. Had it been a mistake? Staying on a story could have been what had gotten him killed. I didn't want to repeat his pattern, but I also couldn't let Ben's death go. I wasn't done with the story yet.

TWENTY-TWO

The wedding had begun to wind down. Guests toasted with champagne as the bride and groom made their exit down the historic staircase.

Matt spotted me. He patted the empty seat next to him and held up a pint of beer. I weaved through the crowd.

"Is this for me?" I asked, taking the empty seat. "Where's Jill?"

"Yeah. Where'd you run off to?" Matt handed me a full pint glass. "Your beer is getting flat. Totally unacceptable."

"Thanks." I grabbed the beer and took a sip. "Sorry, I had to talk to Gam."

"Megs, please. That beer has been sitting on the table for at least"—he paused and checked his watch—"fifteen minutes. Drinking flat beer is like drinking cold coffee. If you don't understand this basic principle, I'm going to have to take it away from you. You must follow my motto."

"Your motto?" I nearly spit beer on him. "Since when do you have a *motto*?"

Matt looked injured. "Since I took my first-ever home brew

class last week. I took an oath to revere the beer." He caressed the side of his pint glass for effect.

I rolled my eyes. "P—l—ease! Revere the beer? Are you a poet now, too?"

"Do not make fun." Matt pointed his index finger at me. "Or else you are not going to get a taste of my first batch."

Matt was a beer snob in the best way. It didn't surprise me that he'd decided to take the plunge into home brewing. If anything, I wondered why he hadn't done it before now. Homebrew shops were prolific in Portland. Hop vines had replaced wisteria on front porches of bungalows. You'd find them snaking up the side of brick buildings and home brewers clamoring to get the latest seasonal varieties. Homemade keg stands rolled out of garages and took over backyards year-round.

Hipsters flocked to dive bars to order old-school watereddown beers produced in mass which, shockingly, were trendy again. Don't ask. I refused to touch a drop of the cheap swill. Neither would Matt. Like Portland's true beer aficionados, Matt spent his time and paychecks at one of the city's hundreds of microbreweries where corporate beer was never on the menu.

A bridesmaid waltzed by our table, clutching a bouquet of peach and red roses with white lilies. The bouquet had a touch of greenery and wooden branches and was tied with natural raffia ribbon.

I caught a whiff of their fragrant scent as she passed by us. "Those are beautiful."

Matt watched the bridesmaid float away. "Duly noted."

"What?"

"Nothing." He blushed slightly and hesitated. "I'll just remember you like flowers like that. That's all."

"Stop." I laughed.

Matt's cobalt eyes held mine. "I wasn't kidding."

I swallowed another taste of the beer. He was right; it was flat. Not that I'd admit it. My hands felt sweaty. I pinched my fingers together under the table to try to center myself. Usually the trick worked. Not tonight.

"Megs?" Matt ignored the sounds of the band nearby. You'd think we were the only people in the room by the way he searched my eyes, his gaze unwavering.

I cleared my throat. I didn't trust my voice. "Yeah?"

He reached his hand across the table and folded it over mine. His fingers felt like they were radiating heat. "We have to talk."

Was this it? Matt and I had had a steady flirtation for the past few months as our friendship had shifted. I knew that sooner or later we were going to have to make a leap. One of us would propel our friendship forward to something deeper. I just didn't think it was going to happen now. While I knew I cared about Matt, I wasn't ready now.

"Matt, wait." I pulled my hand free.

An injured look flashed on his face. He recovered quickly and sat upright in his chair.

"I don't think I can do this tonight." I waved to the candlelit room. "I know it's gorgeous and romantic and hard not to get swept up in the moment, but I just have too much on my mind right now. It's not you. It's—it's—"

Matt threw his head back. Then he sat up and pounded his palms lightly on the table as if he were keeping time for the band. "Megs, I'm not an idiot."

"Well, I just..."

"Stop." He shook his head. "Really, come on. Give me a little more credit. I'm not going to make a move."

"I thought—"

He rested his hands on his palms and leaned closer to me. "Megs, I promise you one thing." His firm gaze made my heart flip again. "If I ever make a move, you'll know. You won't have to think."

I gulped. This time I could feel my cheeks flame with heat. *You're such an idiot.*

His voice softened. "Listen, Megs, there's something I have to talk to you about. It's about your dad."

"Pops?" I leaned back in my chair.

Matt looked around the room and scooted closer to me. "Yeah, remember how I told you I found one of his sources?"

I nodded. My stomach clenched. This was worse than Matt trying to take our friendship to the next level. I wasn't sure I could handle whatever he wanted to tell me about Pops.

Everyone had assumed that when he was killed in a biking accident a year and a half ago, it was a straightforward tragedy. He was on the wrong stretch of road at the wrong time.

Pops was an avid cyclist. It was one of the many hobbies that he and Matt shared. Believe me, I know what you're thinking—I was attracted to Matt because he reminded me of Pops. It's true. I was. Maybe that was one of the reasons why I was hesitant to move forward.

In any event, Pops used to ride his bike from our farmhouse on the outskirts of Portland to the coffeehouse and shops nearby. Some days he'd bike all the way into the city. It was an hour's ride, but Pops didn't mind. He used to say that biking was like meditation.

"There's something magical about the stretch of open road out in front of you, the wind on your face, the rhythmic sound of your tires rotating. I do some of my very best writing when I'm not writing, Maggie. When you find a way to clear your head, it opens you up to so much more."

Unfortunately, the stretch of road connecting our farmhouse to the city was also dangerous. The two-lane road didn't have a bike lane, let alone much of a shoulder. The police theorized that whoever hit and killed Pops didn't even see him.

The case was still open. Despite a year-long investigation,

the police weren't any closer to discovering who'd killed him. They'd run stories on the local news stations with a description of the hit-and-run scene and opened a phone line where callers could leave anonymous tips. Someone out there had to know something. The car that killed him would have had damage to the hood.

So far, the few leads that had trickled in had been a bust. Mom kept track of all of them. I didn't know why. She walked out on Pops before he died.

Maybe it was her way of dealing with guilt. But I ignored every one of her chipper messages on my phone, saying things like, "Mary Margaret, good news. The police got another tip. This one sounds promising. Call me back, dear."

No way. I wasn't going to get sucked into her halfhearted attempts to mend things between us. She made her choice.

"Megs, you still with me?" Matt tapped my hand.

"Huh?" I blinked. "Sorry. What were you saying?"

"You have that faraway look in your eyes again. You okay?" Matt looked concerned.

"Yeah, yeah. I'm fine." I cracked my knuckles and yawned. "I'm just tired, that's all."

"Right." Matt rolled his eyes.

"What?"

"Megs, look, I know you don't want to talk about this, but there's something major you have to know, and it impacts your job." He rubbed his temples and puffed up his cheeks with air.

"My job?"

Blowing out the air in his cheeks, he scanned the room again. "Yeah. I've been going back and forth for the last few days about whether I should tell you or not, but you have to know."

Sweat beaded on his forehead. Something was really wrong. I'd never seen Matt react like this.

"Matt, I don't understand. What does Pops's death have to do with *my job*?"

He sighed and dabbed his forehead with a napkin. "Let me start from the beginning, okay?"

TWENTY-THREE

My foot bounced under the table with anticipation as Matt moved his chair so close to mine that our knees touched. He snuck a final glance behind him and launched into his confession.

"Remember last spring when you found that name on the calendar at your dad's house?" He loosened his tie.

I nodded. I did remember. In fact, I couldn't forget. When I went to Pops's house to pick up some things, I found a strange entry on his calendar. On the day that he died, he'd scheduled a meeting with someone with the initials P.D.J. The note below the meeting read: Bring MM file.

MM was Pops's code for "Meth Madness," the story he'd been working on.

I shuddered, remembering the day Mom called me with the news that Pops was dead. When I found the meeting on his calendar I thought it was strange, but I probably would have forgotten about it, if it weren't for Matt.

Matt, without my knowledge, had been combing through all of Pops's files at *The O* in his spare time. Even after everyone else believed that Pops had lost it, Matt stuck on the story. He dug through every file he could find at *The O* and talked to his fellow reporters about their take on the story. Before Pops had been discredited, an entire team had been working on the exposé.

Last spring, Matt found what he believed to be proof that Pops's death wasn't an accident. Pops's source, P.D.J., had called *The O* on the morning that Pops died to warn him that he was in danger. Of course Pops never got the message. He'd been fired months earlier and the receptionist who'd taken the call logged it as another "junk lead."

Matt discovered the message in a file of calls, many of which were from unreliable sources. He was convinced this one wasn't, and when I told him about the meeting on Pops's calendar, he started looking for P.D.J.

He hadn't had much luck. Tracking a source who didn't want to be found, especially in a city where it was easy to disappear on the streets, proved challenging. Matt had a few good leads since the spring, which all led to dead ends.

The sound of the band announcing this was the last song startled me. I'd forgotten we were surrounded by a hundred people.

"You okay?" Matt placed his hand on my knee.

"Yeah, go on. Sorry."

Matt scanned the room before continuing. "I found him."

"You found who?"

"P.D.J.," Matt whispered.

"*What?*" I threw my hands on the table.

"Shh." Matt hushed me. "Keep it down. I don't want anyone to hear this."

"Sorry." I sat on my hands. "You found P.D.J. How?"

"It wasn't easy. I've been scouring your dad's files for months, trying to crack his code. He was really good at making sure his sources stayed secret. It's pretty impressive, actually."

That was the thing about Pops. He never went after

sensational headlines. Ethical journalism was his passion. He spent a night in jail once instead of revealing a source. As new media embedded with AI began evolving, he expressed deep concern about the lack of integrity as "journalists" (he used that term loosely) rushed to scoop each other on social media.

"Maggie, being first doesn't always mean being right. Every story requires due diligence."

"I know, Pops, but social media isn't going away. In fact, it's completely changing the landscape of journalism."

He'd sighed, removed his glasses, and rubbed his temples. "Then we're going to have to work even harder to vet our source material and maintain our values as journalists, aren't we?"

Had I been doing that? If Pops had still been alive, I would have wanted him to be proud of me. What would he have thought about me writing for *Northwest Extreme?*

"Anyway, I finally cracked it last week." Matt continued. "He used a mnemonic trick. Turns out each initial rhymes with a real letter of P.D.J.'s name."

He took a drink of his beer. "This is getting flat, too." He stuck out his tongue.

"Keep going. You're driving me crazy." My knee bounced with anticipation. "Did you actually find P.D.J.—or whatever his real name is?"

Matt grinned. "I did." Then his face turned serious. He grabbed my knee. "Listen, Megs, this is important. You cannot tell anyone—I mean anyone, not even Jill, about this. Deal?"

I nodded. "Okay."

"No." He squeezed my knee. "I need you to understand how serious this is, okay? It's a big deal."

"I got it." I rubbed my knee.

"Here's the deal. I met with P.D.J. last week."

"Who is he?"

"I'm not telling you P.D.J.'s real name. It's too dangerous."

"Matt, come on. What's going on? You're acting like this is some kind of huge conspiracy or something."

He ran his finger around the rim of his beer glass. "Megs, I'm still not sure what all your dad was entangled in with this story, but he wasn't delusional. And I can tell you without a doubt, he didn't go off the deep end or make up facts. This is big. It's so big that I don't know who to trust. I've been sitting on this information. I haven't even gone to the editor in chief yet."

"Matt, you're scaring me."

"Good. You should be a little scared. We're in over our heads on this one, Megs. Your dad had been in the business for thirty years. He knew his way around the streets. I have no idea what I'm doing."

"Tell me. Let me help."

Matt scanned the room again. He was making me feel jumpy. What could he possibly know that would make him so skittish?

"P.D.J. had been living in a camp for the unhoused under the Burnside Bridge. You know me, it's not like I'm not familiar with Portland's housing crisis, but I write technology. People send me cool gadgets, and I cover geeky conventions. I don't usually spend my days trying to find sources out in the field."

"Matt, you didn't have to. I didn't ask you to do this."

"I know. I know. I'm not saying you did. I had to. I still do. Now that I've come this far, I'm not stopping. It's just I want you to understand I'm out of my comfort zone here."

"So you found P.D.J. under the Burnside?"

"Eventually. I had to put the word out. I guess that's how it works on the streets."

"I always saw Pops at his desk, typing away at *The O.* I never imagined him out looking for sources under bridges."

"He was the real deal. The only reason that anyone down there would talk to me was because I used his name. They really respected him. He treated them well."

Tears flooded my eyes. That was Pops. It didn't matter if you were a top advertiser or an addict, he treated everyone with the same level of respect.

"Hey, Megs, sorry. This is too much, isn't it?" Matt offered me a napkin.

I dabbed my eyes. "No. I want to hear this. I have to hear this. Please, keep going."

Matt hesitated. "If you're sure?"

"I'm sure." I wiped my nose with the napkin and held it in my lap.

"P.D.J. was a heroin addict."

"Ugh." I shuddered. I couldn't stand the thought of needles. Getting shots was like torture for me.

"I know." Matt scowled. "It's a whole other world out there. And honestly, I had no idea the scope of how many people—I mean people our age—are living on the streets. It's like its own separate city."

"It puts things into perspective, doesn't it?"

"Yeah. Some of the things I saw are burned into my head." Matt gave his head a little nod as if trying to shake the images free. "Anyway, even with the drugs, P.D.J. was a credible source."

I twisted the napkin tighter. This was my fault. I'd gotten Matt mixed up in Portland's drug culture.

"Apparently P.D.J. had been feeding your dad information for years. Like we thought, it's huge. Tons of drugs are being funneled through eastern Oregon."

"Really?"

"That's just the beginning."

"Why would he want to help Pops uncover that? Wouldn't that cut off P.D.J.'s source?"

"Funneling drugs is just the tip of the iceberg, Megs. P.D.J. confirmed there are some major players involved in this and big, big money."

"Okay, so we go to the police. We can talk to Sheriff Daniels —tonight."

Matt held up his finger and shook his head. "No. It's not that simple, Megs. I'm serious. You can't talk to *anyone* about this yet."

"The police can help."

"The police may be involved." Matt propped his arms on his hips.

"Not Sheriff Daniels."

"No, but people higher up than him. Megs, this is huge. I can't even begin to tell you. We're talking government officials, business leaders, politicians—so many people are involved in this."

"Isn't that why we should tell Sheriff Daniels? If we're in over our heads, we need help."

"Not yet. It's too dangerous. I need to do some more legwork first. The day that your dad was killed, he and P.D.J. were scheduled to meet with the mayor. Your dad convinced him, promised him immunity, safety. He had it all worked out to send him directly to rehab and then a safe house."

Matt started to take a drink of his beer and set it back on the table.

"P.D.J. tried to warn your dad. The night before he died, a bunch of guys came by and roughed up a few of P.D.J.'s friends, looking for him. Someone found out they were going public. That someone killed your dad. Once P.D.J. heard, he went into hiding. I was the first person he'd spoken to about this since." Matt hung his head.

He stared at the table.

"Matt, what is it?"

I thought he wasn't going to answer. It took him a while to respond.

When he finally lifted his head, I saw tears form in his eyes. "Megs, P.D.J. is dead."

TWENTY-FOUR

"What?"

He blinked back a tear. "I don't know what to do. I can't believe it."

"Matt." I reached for his arm. He pulled away.

"If I'd left it alone, this never would have happened."

"I don't understand. Didn't you just meet with him? How did he die?"

Matt stared into his pint glass. "They found him two days later. Drug overdose."

"Maybe that's true? You said he was a heroin user, right?"

"Megs, come on. You're not that naïve. What are the odds? More like a convenient way to knock him off, if you ask me."

I sat back for a moment, trying to take in everything Matt had just said. Part of me felt relieved to know that Pops hadn't been crazy. This validated everything I'd known about him. If he and his source had been killed over the story, that meant that Matt could be in big danger.

"Matt, we have to tell Sheriff Daniels, your editor, someone. This is too much."

"Not yet. I have to finish reading through your dad's files. I don't want anyone else to get hurt."

At that moment the sound of Jill's voice interrupted our conversation. "Hey, you two." She stopped short. "Sorry, am I interrupting something?"

Matt pushed to his feet. "No." He grabbed his pint glass. "Not at all. I was just going to grab a fresh pint."

As he made his way toward the bar, he furrowed his brow and gave me a look like, *Don't you dare say a word.*

"Everything okay?" Jill watched Matt stroll away.

"It's cool." I stood. "I guess I should probably head back up the mountain before it gets too late."

Jill wrinkled her nose. "What's up with you and Matt? Did you have a fight?"

"No." I crumpled the napkin next to my empty beer glass. "Not at all."

I changed the subject. "What's your plan for tomorrow? I'm going to be up at the Silcox Hut covering the training. You should come by if you have a chance."

She glanced at the fireplace where Will stood with a group of skiers. "Yeah, I'll check with Will. I think he might ski anyway."

"Just come on by. I'm sure we'll be easy to find. Just look for me and a bunch of mountain men." I hurried toward the stairs before she could stop me.

I had too much to think about as I bundled up for the ride back to the Silcox Hut. No wonder Matt had been acting so distracted for the past few weeks. I wasn't sure I could keep this secret. Especially not from Jill and Gam. They'd see through me right away.

They said things came in threes. First Ben's death, then Will's cheating, now all this with Pops. At this point I couldn't take much more.

I zipped my parka and stepped outside in the night air.

There was one major question I still needed to ask Matt. He said that Pops's death had something to do with my job. I couldn't imagine what. Jill had interrupted us before we'd finished our conversation.

Oh, well, I sighed. I had enough to think about for one night.

The snowcat hummed as I climbed on board. Jackson and Malory were cuddled together in the seat behind me. They barely acknowledged me as I buckled my seat belt and the driver revved the engine. I guessed they must have made up from their fight. Malory nibbled Jackson's ear. I kept my eyes to the front. I wasn't a fan of PDA. Gross.

The snowcat plowed its way up the trail in the dark. Last night's storm had given way to clear skies. Stars multiplied above us. It looked like someone had tossed a handful of glitter into the sky. Something about seeing the flickering tiny lights above me made me feel calmer.

Skiers and boarders had long since abandoned the upper runs, leaving empty slopes, just stillness, starlight, and the loud churning of the snowcat. I used the opportunity to focus inward as Gam had suggested.

I steadied my breath and focused my attention on a star dancing above the summit.

What brings you joy, Meg?

My inner voice didn't answer. *Thanks a lot.*

By the time we made it to the Silcox Hut, Malory and Jackson were arguing again. That didn't bring me joy. They didn't seem to bring each other much joy either. Jackson stormed off the cat, pushing past me and ignoring Malory's pleas to wait. I noticed crime scene tape stretched around the picnic table, but thankfully Ben's body had been removed.

The vibe inside the hut was much more subdued than last night. The bunk rooms were dark and sounded with snores and grunts from Rangers who'd gone to bed early. A group of

Rangers played cards in front of the fire in the main room. Lola scrubbed the countertop in the kitchen.

I pulled up a bar stool next to the counter. "Quiet night, huh?"

Lola grunted. "Hardly. You missed all the action. The coroner and police just left. They've been through everything inside and out." She ran a sponge over the countertop. "This fingerprinting dust is hard to get off."

I ran my hand over the surface. "Why were they dusting the kitchen for prints?"

She shrugged and glanced at the clock on the wall. "It's late. How was the wedding?"

"Beautiful. Really simple, but gorgeous."

She stacked a set of ceramic plates on the counter. "That's the best kind. I love understated events."

I checked to make sure Malory and Jackson weren't around. "Me too. I hope I don't get invited to Malory and Jackson's. She's so intense. They got in a huge fight."

The plate in Lola's hand slipped and fell into the dishwasher. A crash sounded, startling everyone in the room. "It's okay." Lola held up the chipped plate. "Just a plate." She tossed the plate in the garbage. "What were they fighting about?"

"No idea. I saw them from down in the pool and then again on the snowcat ride. One minute they were all over each other; the next minute he stormed off. I can't figure them out."

Lola finished wiping the counter and untied her apron. She moved a stool next to me.

"Wait till you hear this." She lowered her voice. "I saw Malory with Ben last night." Her freckles blended into her skin as color rose in her cheeks. She studied my face, as if waiting for a reaction. "Okay, you don't get it, do you?"

"Uh—no?"

"I mean I saw Malory and Ben together—you know—as in

together." She tapped her fingers on the counter and held out her hands in an exasperated gesture.

My eyes must have bugged out, because Lola nodded her head vigorously and leaned even closer. She smelled like dish soap.

"They were going at it." She stuck out her tongue. "Ugh. Ben. Can you imagine?"

"Malory and *Ben*?"

Lola pulled the knit cap from her head and tossed it on the counter. Her hair frizzed and curled in natural waves around her face. She reminded me of a model for an outdoor clothing line with her sun-kissed face and athletic curves. I'd have a serious case of hat-hair if I'd been wearing a hat all day, but not Lola.

"Ben!"

I rested my chin in my hands. Malory was cheating on polished, professional Jackson—with Ben Tyler? I couldn't picture it.

"Are you sure?" I rubbed the base of my neck. My head was starting to throb.

Lola put her finger to her lips as Clint walked into the room. He gave us a salute and headed over to the fireplace to join the card game.

"I went to find extra blankets and stuff in the storage closet in the alcove and they were in the bunk room, totally making out."

"You're sure it was Ben?"

"Positive." She ripped a thread from her hat. "I couldn't stand him. Not that Malory's much better, but I don't get how she could go after Ben."

I adjusted my position on my stool. "Right. Especially because she's so possessive of Jackson. I mean, they're constantly all over each other."

"Exactly!" Lola snapped her fingers together. "PDA is

always a sign that a relationship is on the rocks."

"Why?"

"Because it's a sign you're trying too hard. It's like you have something to prove. Trust me, the couples who put on the biggest show are always the ones about to implode."

She might have been on to something. I thought about Jill and Will. He constantly pawed her. I couldn't remember a time when we went to a pub that he didn't spend the entire meal caressing her leg or with his arm wrapped possessively around her shoulder. This usually led to Matt and me kicking each other under the table in disgust.

It made sense. If Malory was cheating on Jackson with Ben, could she have killed him in a lover's rage? Or had Jackson found out? Maybe that's what they'd been fighting about at Timberline Lodge. My mind spun.

Lola tapped me on the shoulder. "Meg, you still with me?"

I massaged my temples. "Yeah, sorry. I have a headache. Is there any coffee left that I can nuke in the microwave?"

"Of course. I'll get it." Lola pushed back her stool and hurried around the counter. She grabbed a coffee cup and poured stale coffee into the cup. She held it up. "You sure you want this? I can make a fresh pot."

"Will you drink any? Don't make a new pot for me."

"I'd love some. Give me one sec."

While she ground beans, I considered what I'd just learned. The note I'd found in Ben's bag could have been from Malory. Was she planning to break it off with him and things took an ugly turn? Maybe he decided to break it off and she flipped. Either way, I was more convinced than ever that Malory must have killed him and come after me, too.

Lola handed me a steaming mug of coffee a few minutes later. "I can't believe we're drinking coffee this late. I'm never going to sleep." She motioned to the dust on the countertop.

"It's probably good. I have a bunch of cleanup to do with this mess."

I took a sip and wrapped my hands around the cup. "Not me. I can drink it anytime—day or night. It doesn't affect me."

She gave me a knowing smile. "That won't last for long. How old are you—twenty-one, twenty-two?"

I puffed up my shoulders. "I'm a very mature twenty-three, thank you very much."

"Right. Sorry. You're sooo mature. Trust me, give it another year or two and you'll notice a shift."

"What's that supposed to mean? It's hardly like you're old."

"Believe me, there's a shift that starts to happen in your late twenties."

The coffee warmed my hands. I took another drink. "Not with this. I live on coffee. If I ever have to cut back, I don't know what I'll do."

"You can always switch to decaf."

"That's what I call 'why bother?'"

"Funny." Lola finished her coffee and took her cup to the sink. She rinsed it and let the water run. I could tell she was distracted.

Jumping down from my stool, I joined her. "Is everything okay?" I shut the water off.

Lola wiped her hand on a dish towel. "Sorry, it's just that Ben reminds me of my stepdad." She shivered.

"Wasn't Ben kind of young to be like your stepdad?"

"I don't mean in age. I mean in attitude. My stepdad is an ass." She twisted the towel.

"Do you want to talk about it?"

She busied herself cleaning the coffeepot. "There's not much to say. My mom married him when I was fifteen. He treated her like dirt. Flirted with every woman within arm's reach. It made my mom miserable, but she keeps going back to him. I can't even begin to count how many times she kicked him out when I was in high school. My sister and I would help her toss all his stuff on the front lawn and she'd change the locks. Then, a week later, he'd show up on our doorstep with a bunch of cheap roses or chocolate and she'd let him back in."

"That must have been rough."

She didn't make eye contact as she scrubbed the inside of the coffeepot with such force, I thought it might shatter. "It was. Not just for me, but for my little sister. I tried to be a role model for her. What sort of example was my mom setting?"

I knew a thing or two about mother/daughter relationships, but didn't bother to interject my thoughts.

"He's the main reason I left. Now I'm working to get my sister out here, too. I can't stand that she's stuck back in Vermont with them."

"How old is your sister?" Hadn't Jackson said something about being in Vermont?

"She's about your age. She'll be twenty-one soon. She's almost done with school, so I've been saving everything I can scrape together to afford a plane ticket and a bigger apartment for her."

I knew a thing or two about scraping together cash, too, but I let her keep talking.

"She's a skier, too. Better than me actually. I'm hoping I can get her a job with ski patrol, or maybe she can get an endorsement gig or something. Anything to get her out here."

I admired Lola's dedication to her sister. It was sweet to hear how concerned she was. I'd always wanted a big brother or sister, especially one like Lola, who seemed so invested in making a better life for her family. However, the way she talked about Ben Tyler left me feeling unsettled. I really liked her, but I couldn't help but wonder if there was a chance that Lola could have something to do with Ben's death.

Add it to the list, Meg, I told myself as I bid everyone good night and crawled into my sleeping bag. Despite my assurance to Lola that late-night caffeine wouldn't keep me awake, it did. Between the coffee pulsing through my veins and the rotating list of worries rapid-firing in my brain, sleep eluded me. The last twenty-four hours had been a blur.

I spent half the night tossing and turning in my sleeping bag, replaying the night of Ben's death, practicing how I might tell Jill that I'd seen Will with another woman, wondering about Pops's mysterious source, and dreaming of Matt leaning in to kiss me. At some point I finally fell asleep, only to awaken an hour later with my heart racing—I'd completely forgotten to start writing my feature story.

TWENTY-FIVE

When I awoke the next morning, it was threatening to snow again. Gray clouds hovered, blocking the sun and casting a dreary haze on the rugged ridgeline. It matched my mood. Between lack of sleep and my inability to silence the growing list of worries in my head, I felt depleted.

Gam would have advised me to sit in stillness and center before rising, but she wasn't there, so I unzipped my sleeping bag and popped out of bed.

I'd forgotten about my head. Black dots and bright white stars flooded my vision. I grabbed the side of the bunk. I might hit the floor. The room swayed, rocking back and forth like I was on a cruise ship, not 7,000 feet above sea level.

I steadied my body and braced my way to the bathroom, using the wall as my guide. I splashed water on my face and tried to position myself to see the bump in the mirror. To get a better view, I climbed onto the toilet lid. Parting my hair, I could see an area of my scalp was deep purple, but fortunately it was hidden. I pinched my cheeks, ran my fingers through my hair upside down, and found a bottle of Tylenol in the first-aid bag. I swallowed three. That should do the trick.

The smell of cinnamon rolls baking in the oven made me hurry to the dining room. I didn't want to miss out on Lola's homemade creation. The Rangers didn't let a crumb go to waste. The dining room was bright and cheery. A new fire roared and crackled, sending wispy ribbons of smoke up the chimney. The long shared table was set with coffee, teas, fresh fruit, berries, and a mouth-watering assortment of pastries. Everyone was gathered round, enjoying Lola's elaborate spread. I slid into an empty chair and poured myself a coffee.

"Morning, troops." Clint tapped his cane on the hardwood floor. "I have some news. The police have informed us that Ben's death was a murder. They'll be up here again this morning and have asked that all of us cooperate with their investigation. No one is to leave. I'm sure that won't be a problem."

The team responded with solemn murmurs and nods.

It wasn't like I hadn't expected this news, but somehow the confirmation that Ben's death was officially a murder made me feel heavy-hearted. It was easy to get caught up in the game of playing detective, especially with Jill and Matt, but the reality of murder felt much bleaker.

Clint continued. "Ben had a vision and I intend to see it through. Guiding expeditions up here is serious business. I say eat your breakfast. If we're stuck up here anyway, we might as well continue training."

I wondered how the Rangers would continue without Ben's financial support.

The mood seemed subdued as Lola sent around trays with cinnamon rolls bigger than my hand, vanilla frosting drizzled over the top of the sweet, warm bread. My mouth watered.

"Hey, Henry"—I plopped on the bench next to Henry, helped myself to a cup of coffee, and let out a long breath— "how's it going? Terrible news, huh?"

Henry scooped two cinnamon rolls onto his plate and passed me the tray. "Yeah." He didn't look like he'd slept any better than me. His shaggy reddish hair needed a wash. Dark circles hung beneath his normally bright eyes.

"You don't look so great," I said, taking the tray. "Rough night, too?"

"Dude, you don't even know." He cut his cinnamon roll with his fork.

"What's wrong?" I handed the tray with one lonely roll to the table next to us.

Henry rubbed his temples, making his hair look even more unkempt. I took a bite of the roll and frowned. It tasted flavorless. I was sure it wasn't. "Really, are you okay?" I asked Henry through a mouthful of roll.

He checked around us to make sure no one was listening. "Nah, not really." He didn't touch the cinnamon rolls in front of him. "Dude, the sheriff thinks I had something to do with Ben's death."

"What? Why?" I licked frosting from my lips.

Henry ruffled his hair again. "My gun. Everyone's talking about it."

"Anyone could have taken it. I'm sure Sheriff Daniels knows that."

Actually I wasn't, but I planned to meet Matt and Jill at the lodge later anyway, so I could talk to the sheriff then.

"I guess." He shrugged. "I've never been a suspect in a murder before. Not sure what this is going to do to my chances of signing with Ten-Eighty."

"Come on, Henry. Don't sound so dejected. I know you didn't kill Ben. Sheriff Daniels is a reasonable guy. I'm sure he'll figure out who did."

"Yeah? I hope so. 'Cause he told me not to leave."

"That doesn't mean anything." I swallowed a bite of cinnamon roll and reached over to pat his arm. "He told everyone not to leave."

Henry frowned. "Maybe." He stood, leaving a plate of

unfinished cinnamon rolls in front of him. "I gotta go grab my gear. See you out there."

I brought our plates into the kitchen for Lola. Clint hovered near the sink, swallowing pills by the fistful.

Lola took the dishes from my hands and scraped Henry's uneaten rolls into the garbage. "Thanks, but you know, you're a guest, too, Meg. You don't have to clean up. It's my job."

"I know. It's just I like to be part of everything when I'm working on a story." I motioned to the pile of dishes in the sink.

"Really? Doing dishes?" She took an empty water glass from Clint.

"Well, maybe I'm looking for a distraction. I really should start writing," I said, giving them both a sheepish grin. "I haven't written a single word yet."

Lola's eyes widened. She clutched the shell necklace around her neck. "You haven't? But you've been writing in that notebook all weekend."

I grimaced. "Yeah, but that's mainly background info, plus I may have taken a few notes about Ben's murder that I passed on to the sheriff."

Clint coughed on his medication. Lola clapped him on the back. His gruff voice brushed her off. "I'm fine," he said, limping out of the room.

"Notes on the murder?" She gave me a strange look.

"Not like that." I rolled my eyes. "But I do need to work on my *actual* story." I left her and the dirty dishes and headed to my bunk. It was clear that while everyone was trying to act normal, we were all on edge.

Today was day three of the four-day training weekend. Since the blizzard and Ben's death had put a halt to yesterday's activities, today was going to be action-packed. It felt strange that we were moving forward, but I guessed Clint had a point. Sitting around doing nothing felt worse.

I tugged a pair of pink and brown striped tights on, followed by pink long johns (I know what you're thinking—and yes, they made pink long johns), my ski pants, a chocolate-colored turtleneck, and my parka. I was definitely ready to face any inclement weather; however, moving with all these layers on might prove challenging.

I unpacked a camera that I'd borrowed from *Northwest Extreme* and looped it around my neck, careful to avoid the lump on my head. Greg liked us to take as many candid shots as possible when we were out in the field. The magazine employed several freelance photographers for cover shots, but I posted candid shots on our social media. It also helped me to document as much as I could in the moment to use when writing my final draft. My phone was fine for visual references and social media but I needed a legit camera to catch everyone getting big air.

With the camera secured around my neck and my notebook under my arm, I shoved my feet into my ski boots and put on my gloves. I had never written in gloves. It could be interesting.

I tromped outside, where Clint barked orders to the Rangers. My eyes scanned the area where Ben's body had been discovered. The glaring two-toned gray and white sky hurt my eyes. I pulled my sunglasses from my coat pocket and positioned them on my face. Crime-scene tape stretched from the picnic table, which had been cleared of snow, to a set of stakes strategically placed around a ten-foot perimeter.

"All right, troops. Off to the summit, then?" Clint pointed to the snow-capped peak behind him.

One of the Rangers shouted, "Why don't we get in some runs before it's a mob up here? We'll do it for Ben!"

Everyone cheered in agreement.

"It's gonna be lit," someone else echoed. He flipped the lift ticket pinned to his jacket. "Opening weekend!"

Clint snarled at the Rangers. "We're here to train."

"Why? Powder. Fresh powder, man!"

Someone else shouted, "This whole gig is a bust with Ben gone."

I couldn't have agreed more. It didn't make any sense to me that they were pushing ahead when there was no clear future for the team.

Clint was losing ground and was outnumbered. These snow junkies needed their fix.

He threw his hands in the air. "Fine. Two runs each. Then it's straight to training. Understood? Ben paid for this weekend to get you all up to speed on high-altitude rescue, and come hell or high water, I'm going to finish the task."

The team whooped in delight and clambered for the slope before Clint could change his mind.

"Are you going to get a run in?" He turned to me.

It should have been obvious from the fact that I wasn't toting skis. "Nope. I need to work on my story. What about you?" The second the words were out of my mouth I regretted them. As a word girl, I tended to do better with paper and a pen or my keyboard than live. Mom said I spoke before I thought. It was a great trait in writing. When I was in the zone, the words flew from my fingers, but not so much when I said the wrong thing without thinking.

A look of regret flashed across Clint's face. He quickly clenched his jaw and massaged his leg. "Afraid I can't do much on this old boy these days."

"Right. Sorry." I fumbled over my apology.

He brushed me off. "Nothing to be sorry about. Comes with age. Enjoy that fresh face and your youth while you can, young lady."

I gave him a salute. "Yes, sir. Hey, would you have a minute to answer a few questions while we're waiting for everyone to come back from their runs?" I flipped open my spiral notebook. Even with my sunglasses, the bright light was killing my eyes.

Probably from your killer headache, Meg, I thought, rubbing the base of my skull.

"Hurt your head?" Clint asked.

"I'm fine. Just a little headache this morning. It's so bright."

He put his hand up to shield his eyes and scanned the slope. "Yep. Fire away."

I squinted as we both watched the Rangers expertly fly down the mountain.

"Wow! That's impressive," I said, as one of them caught huge air over a jump.

"The best on the mountain."

"What's going to happen now? Will the Ridge Rangers keep going? Wasn't Ben funding this venture?" Writing with my gloves on made my usually neat handwriting look like a preschooler's scrawl in my notebook. Hopefully I'd be able to decipher the scribbles later.

"I can't say anything on the record." Clint motioned to my notebook and looked around to make sure we were alone. He leaned closer. "Let's just say I'm exploring new avenues of financing. We already have clients lined up and waiting. Money's going to start coming in. I might have to trim the team a bit, but otherwise I see us getting this off the ground in the next few weeks."

"Really?"

"I can't say more." He moved back and turned toward the ski run. On the slope another boarder showcased his jumping techniques, launching twenty feet in the air. Snow sprayed in his wake as cheers erupted.

"Show-off," Clint muttered.

I wondered if it irritated him to see the younger members of the team performing stunts he could no longer execute. It might make for an interesting angle in my feature. I'd have to tread carefully, though. Writing a story from the vantage point of a struggling personal narrative could go south fast. I wouldn't want to paint Clint as an aging skier without something to balance it.

The upside was I was thinking about crafting an article for the first time in two days. "What do you have in store for training today?" I asked.

Clint checked his watch and shielded his eyes from the gray sky. "Looks like the troops are heading in. Good timing."

He acted like he didn't hear me.

"Yeah, what's the plan?" I pestered him.

"What's that?" He scratched his head and tapped his watch. "Does it look like they're taking another run to you?"

I followed Clint's line of sight to the trail. "I can't tell."

Clint pointed to the ski lift. "Looks like they got the lift up and running. That means this place is will be packed soon. The troops better head this way." Magic Mile chugged to life, rotating empty chairlifts that swung from side to side in the gusty morning air.

"Sorry to keep bugging you, but what's the plan for today? It would really help to have an overview of what you're all going to be working on for my story."

"No, no, happy to help." He bolstered his shoulders. "Sorry about that.

Just got to keep the troops in line. What do you need to know?" His demeanor returned to drill sergeant. I felt like I should stand at attention and prepare myself for an inspection.

"Can you walk me through your training regimen?"

"Yep." Clint gave one last glance at the chairlift and slope. Assured his "troops" were on their way back to the Silcox Hut, he launched into an explanation of the training program he helped to design thirty years ago.

My hand flew over the page. I mastered shorthand in college with my own twenty-first century spin. Most of my fellow journalism students blew off the "archaic" form of hand-writing notes, claiming shorthand was dead. Not me. There's something about handwriting when I was interviewing that allowed me to make a deeper connection. I could make eye contact with my subject while scribbling on my notepad. Don't get me wrong. When it came to actually writing a piece, I loved my laptop, but there was an art to interviewing, and call me old school, but I didn't think it could be done well with a glowing screen in front of your face.

"You've heard by now that we're pioneering guided trips to the summit?"

That seemed like a stretch. I didn't say anything to Clint but I knew guided climbs were big business. People paid thousands of dollars to summit peaks like Everest and Kilimanjaro.

Clint continued. "We'll be taking a range of climbers from novices to experts to the summit with the best safety team on the mountain—emphasis on safety."

"That's important to you, isn't it?" I shook my hand to loosen my fingers while I waited for him to continue.

"It's the only thing that matters. I'll be using an MRA protocol to train the Rangers."

"What does MRA stand for?"

"Mountain Rescue Association. Today there are over one hundred teams and two thousand professional volunteer rescuers that are accredited through MRA."

Good background info for my story.

"MRA's primary goal is keeping rescue teams educated and safe." Clint pursed his lips. "Emphasis on 'safe.' It's a dangerous, dangerous job. Prior to launching this venture, none of us ever made a dime. We volunteered anytime we got a call. We put our lives on the line. Making money doesn't change anything."

He motioned for me to write that down and kept going. "MRA helps track the four major things that can go wrong: aircraft, operator error, equipment failure, and, of course, the big one—Mother Nature."

My hand started to cramp. I flexed my fingers. The tips of

my fingers, sticking out from my fingerless gloves, were turning bright pink.

"Aircraft?" I asked after getting the last note about Mother Nature on paper.

"Yep. A chopper is only as good as its pilot."

"I didn't know you used a chopper," I interrupted.

"That's all part of the next phase of rollout. We'll drop backcountry skiers off in areas they can't access otherwise. Of course that's where Mother Nature comes into play. Fog rolls in on the summit. Suddenly your visibility is down to nothing, and the ceiling drops. Total nightmare."

"Really?"

Clint shot me a look of disbelief. "Mountain guiding is not to be taken lightly. We've lost good climbers to ice falls, had a group of rescuers swallowed by a crevasse while taking a lunch break. It's serious stuff. If we want to make money and be taken seriously, we have to know our stuff."

I let out a breath. "Scary."

"No one's died on my watch and I'm not about to let that change." Clint twisted his spine toward the mountain. "She's a beauty." He paused and turned back to me. "And a beast."

I gave him a sheepish smile. "That's an awesome description. Maybe I'll have to use it as the title for my piece."

He didn't laugh. His eyes darkened. "Did you hear a word I said?"

I gulped. "Yeah." I held up my notebook. "I wrote it all down. I'm impressed. I mean, I already was, but I didn't know the extent of the danger you put yourself through—really."

Clint appraised me and patted my shoulder. "It's okay. Sorry if I sound gruff. I don't mean to. It's that this new breed of mountaineers is all about fancy tricks. If you're not focused on safety every moment you're on this mountain, you die. It's that simple. I can't seem to pound it through the thick skulls of some of these kids."

"You mean like Ben Tyler?"

Clint clenched his jaw. "Ben and I didn't always see eye to eye. He wanted to get as many people up to the summit as possible. If you want to write anything in this story of yours, you write about the danger this team itself is going through—willingly every day. That's a story that needs to be told."

I closed my notebook and stuffed the pencil into the spiral spine. "Thanks so much. That really helps, and don't worry, I'll do justice to the work you do."

Clint looked like he wanted to say something else, but at that moment the team returned. They wore genuine smiles on their red, wind-kissed faces. Danger or no danger, these guides clearly loved the mountain.

Before we ascended to begin the first round of training drills, Clint leaned in and whispered in my ear, "Remember what I said. The mountain is one dangerous place."

A shiver ran down my spine as he barked out orders to the team. I'd learned a few things. He had another funding source. That was new news. His attitude made more sense, too. He wanted to make sure the guides were in tip-top shape, up to date with the latest technology and gear, and, most importantly, that both they and their clients make it back alive. Something about his words left me feeling the same about myself. I'd be happy when this day was over and I could return to sea level.

TWENTY-SIX

I followed the Rangers to the first training station, below the Silcox Hut in the tree line where they'd be working on building snow caves. The bruise on my head pulsed in rhythm to my footsteps through the knee-deep snow. This was going to be a long day.

Clint stood in the center of a circle and mapped out instructions for building a snow cave. He numbered everyone off in groups of three and sent them to begin constructing their shelters.

"Let's spend about an hour on this task. What's the one thing you *cannot* do?" Clint bellowed.

"Cheat?"

"Knock over someone else's cave?"

Clint folded his arms across his chest. "I'm serious, troops. What is the one thing that will absolutely kill you if you're stuck up here?"

"Hypothermia!" someone shouted.

"That's right." Clint gave the team member a half salute. "Never, ever sweat."

I flipped my notebook back open and quickly jotted down

more notes. "Sorry, quick question." I raised my hand. "Why can't you sweat?"

Clint motioned to Jackson. "Do you want to answer that question, Doctor?"

Jackson stepped forward. "Sweat is your body's natural cooling mechanism. Normally we appreciate the fact that our body has an efficient and effective way of cooling itself, but if you're exposed to the elements, sweating equals death. Not only does it cool you down, which for obvious reasons we don't want to happen in cold weather, but also the moisture stays on your skin and clothing, continuing to lower your core body temperature. When climbing in cold weather where there's a bigger risk of exposure, it's imperative to minimize your level of exertion."

"Couldn't have said it better myself." Clint clapped Jackson on the back. "All right, troops. No sweating. Break into teams. Start building. You have to be prepared to survive in subzero conditions…" He trailed off and looked at his watch. "You've got one hour. Get to it."

The team scattered in all directions, leaving trails from their boots in the snow. I removed the camera from my neck and adjusted the setting to outdoor mode. The viewfinder revealed that the summit, shrouded by a wall of sturdy clouds, wasn't in the mood for a photo shoot. I clicked off a couple shots anyway. Maybe I could use these eerie images alongside brilliant, sunny ones to highlight Clint's grave warning about the danger the mountain possessed—the beauty versus the beast.

I followed the path through the snow to where the teams worked on their snow caves. At each stop I took multiple photos and chatted with the guides as they compacted the powdery snow.

When I found Henry's team, I pulled him aside to answer my questions about the process. He wiped his nose with the back of his sleeve and took a second to catch his breath.

"Thanks for giving me a break. It's pretty gnarly work."

"Is this your first time building a shelter?" I positioned him so that the camera could zoom in on his ruddy face with his other teammates in soft focus in the background.

"Nah, I've made them before. Never had to crash in one, but I know how to build them."

"Can you explain the steps?" I let the camera slack on my neck and opened my notebook.

Henry waved his arm out to the wide-open sea of snow. "First you have to find a large open area with a lot of snow. Obviously that's not a problem for us today. See how level our spot is?" He pointed to where his teammates were on their knees rounding a huge pile of snow. It reminded me of kids building a snowman. "You also have to make sure you're not in an avalanche zone."

"How can you tell?"

"Sometimes you can't, especially if the weather's a mess, you know."

I wrote as Henry continued. "What they're doing now is packing down as much snow as they can into a big pile. You want it as firm as possible. You really have to make sure the snow is packed, otherwise you run the risk of having the cave collapse on you."

"Really?" I grimaced.

Henry socked me in the shoulder. "You want to volunteer to test it out when we're done?"

"Uh, no." I shuddered. The thought of being stuck inside a snow cave made me worry that I'd have a full-blown panic attack. I tapped my pencil on my notebook. "Okay, so after you pack down the snow, what's next?"

Henry grinned. "Dude. Meg, chill. It's not that bad."

I wrinkled my nose and stuck out my chin. "I'm working on an important story here. Can we please focus?"

"Right. I'm totally dragging you in there, though. Just wait."

He winked. "The next step is you try to let the cold air harden the snow. That helps further reduce the risk of collapse. We won't do that today, because there's no time, but if you're ever in a real-life survival situation, you want to make sure to let your snow pack have some time to really firm up."

He motioned to the team again. "Now they're shoveling a tunnel. It helps if you bring a shovel. We're required to carry them in our packs, but a lot of climbers don't. If you don't have a shovel, you can dig with your hands or try to makeshift one out of branches or something. Like Clint was talking about, you have to be really careful about not working too hard. It's easy to overdo it.

"After you dig a tunnel up to your snow pack, you hollow out a dome in the pack. Usually we try to make them tall enough so that you can sit up inside it."

I bit my lip. My irrational fear of tight and small spaces made my fingers clench as I tried to take notes. I couldn't imagine anything worse than being trapped in a snow coffin.

Henry shook his head at my look of horror. "If there's space, you can carve sleeping benches in the cave. The higher you get, the better, because then the cold air will sink beneath the bench and keep you warmer."

As much as I didn't enjoy the subject, I was impressed with Henry's knowledge. I knew he was an expert boarder, but he definitely didn't fall into the category of those who only wanted to do tricks on the slope. He knew his stuff.

"Then you cover the ground with any padding you may have, and the most important step is to create a hole in the roof of your cave. It should be about an inch or so wide. Otherwise you could suffocate overnight."

I pounded my notebook on his head. "Seriously, Henry, are you trying to freak me out?"

"No, I'm dead serious. You have to be able to breathe in

there." For effect, he let out a long breath. It looked like steam pouring out of his mouth as it hit the cold air.

In the distance, Henry's team crawled into the cave. "Once they're in, they'll block the entrance with their packs. That helps keep as much heat as possible inside, and, of course, you use each other's body heat, too. Depending on how big the shelter is, you have people rotate positions throughout the night. That's pretty much it."

"That pretty much ensures that I'm going to have night-mares about sleeping inside a snow cave tonight. Thanks. Thanks a lot."

Henry rolled his eyes. "Come on. Come inside with me. Check it out. I think you'll see it's not that bad. If you were ever trapped out in weather, it's funny how quickly your body will override your mind and do anything it can to survive."

He yanked me through the powder to the cave.

"No, Henry, please," I protested, digging my boots into the ground to try to slow him down.

It didn't work. His arm, chiseled from hours spent on the slopes, pulled me with ease through the flaky snow. Something about him shifted. My normally lackadaisical friend had a hard-ness to him that I hadn't seen before.

A few feet from the entrance to the cave he stopped abruptly. I froze in fear. I thought maybe he was going to pick me up and shove me headfirst into the structure. Instead he released his grasp and took a step back.

"Meg, sorry. Are you really scared?" His face relaxed.

"A little," I admitted, scrunching my face.

"Dude. Sorry. I was just messing around. I didn't mean to freak you out."

"It's okay. I knew you were kidding," I lied. I didn't like this side of Henry.

Before he could say anything else, the sound of a booming voice made us both snap our heads around.

"Time's up, troops." Clint lumbered up the gentle slope to the clearing. "Let's see what you've got."

He spent the next five minutes circling the mounds of snow, rapping the tops of the compacted shelters with his cane and bending over to inspect the inside of the structures.

"Climb on in," he ordered each team after he finished his external assessment. They dutifully dropped their packs and crammed into the shelter.

I took the opportunity to snap a shot of them piled up inside their snow cave. They reminded me of newborn puppies lounging on one another to keep warm. This photo was going to go viral on our social media pages. That should make Greg happy.

"Not bad." Clint held out an arm as the team squeezed free of the shelter. He pounded the roof with his cane. "This could be a bit tighter, but otherwise not half bad."

After the last team member had been extracted from the cave, Clint directed them to the next task. Everyone scattered. Clint pulled Henry aside. I watched as they hung back while the rest of the team disappeared into the tree line. I couldn't hear what they were saying, but from Henry's rigid stance and Clint's grip on his cane, it didn't look like either one of them was happy.

Was Clint angry with Henry's performance? If so, he was mistaken. Henry clearly knew his stuff. Or had he heard the rumor about Henry's Ten-Eighty deal? I'd have to find an opportunity to ask Henry what Clint had said, I thought as I stepped carefully through the worn footprints in the snow. We'd been outside for a little over an hour, and my body was beginning to feel the chill. Maybe I could sit out for the next round of training and warm up in the hut and work on outlining my story.

A cup of coffee or hot chocolate sounded like heaven right now. My nose dripped and tingled. The tips of my fingers felt numb. I guessed I hadn't realized how cold I'd gotten.

As I stepped out from the evergreen trees heavy with snow, I knew that skipping the next training activity was not in the cards for me. My boss, Greg, stood balanced on thin skis, next to the crew of Rangers. Damn.

TWENTY-SEVEN

"Greg! You made it." I clomped over to greet him.

"Hey, there's my star writer. How goes the story?"

"Good. Really good." Okay, fine, that might have been a little white lie, but hey—he was my boss. What else could I do? Plus, thanks to my interview with Clint, and Henry's instructions on building a snow cave, I finally had some material to work with. Stories didn't just appear in thin air. They took time to develop.

Greg kicked his boots free from his bindings and stepped out of his skis. He nodded his head in the direction of the hut. "Walk with me?" It wasn't a request. He picked up his skis and tucked them under his arm.

"I didn't think you were coming." I trotted behind him.

He rested his skis on the side of the hut. "I had to." He raised an eyebrow. "I heard there's been a murder. You're two for two on big assignments so far. I send you out on a story and bam—there's a murder. Do you want to tell me what's really going on?"

"You make it sound like I'm a suspect." I winced internally, trying to put on a brave face as I pulled my notebook from under my arm and flipped it open. "Look, I promise I'm working on the piece, but I don't know if I have the exact story I pitched you. It's going to be pretty lame to do a write-up about a guiding team that doesn't exist, but I've got a lot to work with in terms of everything else that's happened."

"And?" He folded his arms.

"And what?"

Greg gave me a skeptical look. "Ben's murder. You've left that completely alone—right?"

I bit my lip. That was an odd reaction. Why wouldn't he want me on the story? This was huge news in the world of extreme sports and beyond. "Well, it's been a distraction for sure. In fact, this morning's the first time the team's done any actual work."

"Mm-hmm. Listen, Meg. We've been through this once before. I can't quite wrap my head around how it's happened again, but I want you to stay as far away from the murder investigation as possible. You're here on assignment. Is that understood?"

I nodded.

"Good. Because if I hear one word about you snooping around—"

"Yeah, but listen—"

Greg held up his hand and halted me in midsentence. "Not another word. This isn't up for debate. I hired you to write a story about the Ridge Rangers. Figure out if you can do that and get it done." He whipped around and stormed into the Silcox Hut.

Wow. Why the shift? Greg was usually a pretty laid-back boss. Why was he acting like a dictator and treating me like a student in detention? Come to think of it, how did he know about Ben's murder? Had one of the Rangers called him and told him I wasn't doing my job?

Could this weekend get any worse? With Greg breathing

down my neck, I couldn't afford any distractions from my story. On one hand, I understood Greg's side. After involving myself in a murder last spring, I'd put myself in a dangerous position. He knew that. But I couldn't let Ben's murder go that easily.

The next training exercise involved ice climbing. Clint gathered the team together and explained we'd be climbing the base of the glacier where the Rangers would practice with crampons and ice axes. He gave everyone a ten-minute break to make sure they had the appropriate gear and to grab a quick drink or snack.

Time to get serious, Meg. I squared my shoulders and followed him inside.

I decided this was my chance to warm up my hands and try to calm my mounting fear of trekking even higher on the mountain. Lola had stoked the fire and set out trays of fruit, cheese, crackers, and warm cookies on the main dining room table. I helped myself to an oatmeal-raisin cookie and an apple and poured a cup of cider.

"Want one?" Lola handed me a napkin as she circled the room with a tray of sausage rolls. "How's it going out there?"

I declined. "Good. It's chilly, though." I scooted closer to the fire.

"I bet. I wish I could get out there myself. I hate being stuck inside."

"Do you want to trade?"

She chuckled. "In a heartbeat. If it wouldn't get me fired."

I took a bite of the chewy cookie. "Me, too. I'm really screwed. My boss just showed up."

"Greg?"

"Yep."

"Lucky. He's a hottie. I don't think I'd be able to concentrate if my boss looked like that." She held out the tray to a couple team members, who grabbed handfuls of sausage rolls.

"I'm in trouble at the moment," I confessed. "I don't have a choice. I have to concentrate."

She placed the empty tray on the table. "Why are you in trouble?"

I finished the cookie and took a sip of the cider. It burned my tongue. "He thinks I'm distracted by Ben's murder."

"Aren't we all?"

"Exactly."

Lola stuffed the extra napkins in her apron pockets. She grabbed the tray. "I better go refill this before you all need to hit the slope. By the way." She turned. "You had some visitors here looking for you about thirty minutes ago. They said they'd come back."

"Visitors?"

"Yeah, a really pretty woman—tall, skier—and a cute guy. Both about your age."

Matt and Jill had come to see me. Too bad I'd missed them and probably would again. Every time it felt like Matt and I were about to take things to the next level and maybe finally admit that we had feelings for each other, something got in our way.

It was like the Universe was conspiring against us.

I sighed heavily and glanced at the clock on the wall. There wasn't much I could do about it now. Time to get back out there.

TWENTY-EIGHT

Following the Rangers up the steep slope took every ounce of energy I had. My short legs struggled to match their pace as we broke through the heavy snow. Greg joining our expedition cramped my style and my quads cramped from the climbing. I grinned through clenched teeth when he turned to check on me.

"How you doing back there, Meg?"

"Great!" I waved. I didn't attempt to say more. Breathing was a struggle.

"Hey, you want to hop on my back?" Henry caught up with me, slowing his stride to match mine.

"N—no. I'm—I'm fine," I said between gasps for breath.

"Come on, Meg. You're like half the size of everyone here. Let me give you a ride." Henry stuck out a gloved hand.

"No, I can't. Really, thanks." I paused to catch my breath. "I can't. Greg has to see that I can keep up. Otherwise he'll fire me."

Henry repositioned his snowboard under his arm. "Dude, I'm pretty sure Greg knows what's up."

I halted. "What?"

"Chill." Henry patted my shoulder with his free hand. "It's cool."

"B—but," I sputtered. The cold numbing my lips, lack of oxygen to my brain, and the realization that Greg and everyone else on the mountain knew that I was a fraud made me want to turn around and not stop until I arrived in Portland.

Henry chuckled. "Meg, come on—chill. Greg would never fire you. Your stories are awesome. I've read every one and you're a great writer."

"Thanks, that's sweet." It was but I wasn't sure Henry's opinion of my work would have much sway.

One of the Rangers hollered to Henry. He patted my shoulder again. Before he took off to join his friend, he tried to reassure me one more time. "Meg, you're fine. See you up there."

I continued trudging upward. *What are you doing, Meg?* I thought. Was I that obvious? Was I just a big joke? Did everyone sit around making fun of the fact that I had no athletic talent? Maybe that explained Greg's shift in attitude—he was fed up with my lack of skill and planned to fire me. Great. That should be a perfect end to an already crummy weekend.

As I climbed higher on the mountain, every muscle in my legs quaked. I panted and pushed my way forward, determined to show everyone that I could climb, too. Greg helped lead the pack and didn't bother to check on me again. I became lost in my thoughts.

I'd spent the last nine months trying to convince him (and myself, for that matter) that I could do this job. Why? I mean, the obvious reason was because when I had my chance encounter with Greg last January, I was desperate for a job. After months of living on Jill's couch, I would have probably taken a job writing for the *National Enquirer*. Okay, maybe I wouldn't have stooped that low, but I'd applied to every newspaper and magazine in town without any luck. When Greg came along—a chance encounter at a coffee shop—it felt like divine intervention.

Sure, I wasn't exactly an intrepid adventurer and I might not have possessed the same natural talent as Greg, but I knew I could do one thing well—write.

What I didn't know, I quickly learned. That was where I shone. I might not have been able to slalom down the mountain in record time, but I could describe it to our readers. I could make them feel like they were on the exposed ridge, with a biting wind gusting behind them and nothing but pure powder in front. I spent hours researching slang, interviewing experts, watching freestyle boarding videos online. Wasn't that what a good journalist was supposed to do?

And the truth was, I had come to love this job.

I could feel my heart rate climb as I forged onward. I was starting to get angry. If Greg wanted to fire me, *fine*, but I'd done the job he'd assigned me to, and along the way I'd really begun to find myself. Without this job, I never would have pushed myself to hike to the top of a cliff or spend a weekend stranded on the summit of Oregon's highest mountain. I might not have been the most athletic member of *Northwest Extreme*, but I could easily argue that I was challenging myself the most. That was the motto Greg lived by—push your limits. I was doing that.

There was something else, too. Pops.

Being out in nature, researching a story, made me feel connected to him in a way I'd lost since he died. I could have easily pulled the covers over my head and hunkered down on Jill's couch indefinitely. Instead, writing for the magazine had given me a new purpose and allowed me moments of quiet in the forest where I found my memories of the father I adored. I'd bottled them up when he died. Gam said it was a natural response to grief. I couldn't lose that connection to him now. It was the only thing I had left.

Onward, Meg. I commanded my feet to keep moving. Forget feeling sorry for myself. It was time to climb up this mountain and show Greg that I had grit.

This was easier said than done as the slope became steeper. For every two steps I took forward, I slid another four backward. My boots filled with snow. The tips of my gloves were covered with ice. I could feel my fingers tingle inside, but I soldiered on. The mountain was not going to get the better of me.

After a few minutes, I spotted the Rangers a hundred feet or so ahead. They'd stopped to put on their crampons. Now the climb was going to get interesting and treacherous.

"Meg, there you are." Greg extended his hand and pulled me up the steep ledge onto a flat surface where the team assembled their gear.

"Careful. Watch your footing. It's dicey," Greg cautioned as he lifted me up.

Ropes, crampons, ice axes, and the Rangers' black rescue packs were spread out on the ledge. The team tied off ropes and adjusted their crampons. Clint called everyone together.

"Okay, troops. As you know, a number of novice climbers get themselves into trouble every year as they attempt to summit the South Side. The most popular spots are the Old Chute and the Pearly Gates. We're going to work on technical terrain, rope systems, and self-arrest, so make sure you have all the necessary gear."

I removed my notebook from my pack and took notes while he explained the dangers of Oregon's most iconic peak.

"This is one steep and exposed climb. Many people underestimate how difficult and technical an ascent can be. That's what gets them into trouble and that's when we're called in to help."

"Do people climb it this time of year?" I looked up at the steep icy ledge caked in layers of snow.

"Yeah, some do," Jackson replied.

"Only if they have a death wish." Clint grunted. "Climbing here happens in the spring and summer. Did you know this is the second-most-climbed glacier in the world?"

I nodded. "Yeah, second to Mount Fuji—right?"

Clint looked impressed. He handed one of the Ridge Rangers a bundle of rope. "Here's what happens. Climbers ride up on the snowcat, like you did. Once they get dropped off, they have to shoulder their packs for the hike up and then decide which route to take to the summit. Even in good weather, there's no guarantee. Assuming all goes well, it should take anywhere from five to seven hours on the ascent and another three or four on the way down. It's doable in a day. A long day, and a lot can go wrong—you take a fall, break something, weather closes in and you're stranded. You have to be prepared. It takes an extremely high level of physical fitness to summit any of the routes." He pointed to the cliff face. "As you can see, it's not easy to execute a recovery mission from up there."

I inhaled through my nose. "That's an understatement."

Clint continued to direct the team as they pounded the ice with their axes and practiced how to safely assist an injured climber off the mountain.

I clicked a round of photos. Clint continued to fill me in on what the team was doing in between ordering them around.

"I want our troops to be able to handle any situation they come across. Imagine if your rope is too short. Or maybe it gets stuck. That's happened before. Or your partner gets injured as you're climbing. We are the guides so we have to know how to rescue someone else and *ourselves*."

He surveyed the team and continued. "Anyone who's climbed long enough has a story of getting in a jam. It's how you get out that counts. What they're working on now is using the gear they have to get themselves out of a jam. See that?" He pointed to Henry, who was working with two other team members knotting ropes. "They're working on hauling systems, setting up the anchors so we can belay. You have to be able to improvise and use whatever you have.

"Next, we're going to work on how to transition on multip-itch snow." He called the group together again.

I watched in amazement as team members hammered their axes into the steep face and shimmied up. Then they swung back down on the rope with ease. Greg joined them. I made sure to keep myself busy with note-taking and snapping as many photos as I could. No way was I going to participate.

Clint seemed satisfied that the Rangers had demonstrated the skill he was looking for. He told us all to break for lunch. The team scattered on the ledge and began to devour the sack lunches that Lola had packed. Greg hung back with Clint.

I found a patch of icy snow open next to Henry and plopped down. "What's for lunch?"

Henry held a sandwich. "Egg salad."

I opened my brown paper bag and removed a turkey sand-wich. "Beat you. Turkey."

"Dude, mine's so much better." He bit off a hunk and chomped it down. His mood seemed lighter. Maybe being out on the slope had helped ease his mind about Ben's murder.

"That was some impressive climbing." I zipped my coat. It was starting to get chilly.

Henry shrugged. "That? Nah. You should come back in the spring when we can really climb this beast."

"Right." I took a bite of sandwich. The bread felt frozen on my teeth. "That's not going to happen."

Henry started to laugh, but stopped. I watched his eyes follow Jackson, who stood shoulder to shoulder with Clint. Jackson whispered something in Clint's ear, and then they both stared directly at Henry.

"What's going on?" I looked from Henry to Clint and Jackson.

Jackson said something else to Clint. A look of shock

washed over Clint's face. Jackson hauled through the snow in our direction.

Henry sighed. "No idea." He stuffed his empty sandwich wrapper in his paper bag, threw on his pack, and started down the mountain before Jackson made it to us and before I could say any more.

TWENTY-NINE

Jackson kicked snow in his wake as he raced over to me. "Where'd he go?"

"Who?" I played dumb.

"Henry." Jackson wasn't amused. He peered down the slope. "Did he tell you where he was going?"

"No. Why? What's the problem?" I folded my lunch sack and tucked it into my day pack. "Is something wrong?" I asked, pushing to my feet and scanning the mountainside for Henry.

Jackson ignored me and started down the steep terrain. Why the sudden panic over Henry?

I gathered my things. Thanks to Clint, I should have plenty of material to work with for my story. Before I started my descent, I checked my footing. It had been hammered in by every guidebook that I'd ever read and every training session I'd attended that the way down was always more dangerous than the way up.

Would I look ridiculous if I opted to sit on my bum and scoot down the ledge? *Yeah, Meg, don't even think about it.*

Or maybe I could flip onto my stomach and slide down the

hill like Jill and I used to do when we were kids. *Nope, not an option.*

I was going to have to climb down like a grownup. Bummer.

"Heading down?" Greg's long legs lunged over a foot-wide gap in one easy move.

"I think I have everything I need." I looped my pack on my shoulders.

"Good. Good." He eyed me and then craned to see Jackson sprinting through the heavy snow twenty feet below. "You're going to be able to piece something together for the feature, right?" His tone made me feel like I'd been caught in a lie.

"Yeah. What else would I be working on?"

"Meg, give me a little credit. I know what you're up to, and I'm going to tell you one more time to knock it off. If you can't focus on your assignment, I'm sending you home tonight."

I fiddled with the straps on my pack. A gust of wind whipped the top layer of snow. "I promise. I got a ton of material from Clint. It's taken me a little while to find my way into the story, but I'm close."

Greg scrunched his brow. He paused. "What am I going to do with you?"

"What do you mean?"

"Never mind. Be careful on your way down." He leaped back over the crevasse, leaving me feeling like I'd gotten a final warning before being sent to the principal's office. Was I that obvious? I really was working on the story, but I couldn't change my inquisitive nature and my need to solve the puzzle. Of course, now I thought of a hundred things I could have just said to Greg. Like "Isn't my tenacity for following a story what makes me a good journalist?"

Whatever. Obviously, I was going to have to watch myself around Greg. I didn't want to lose this job. Although being sent home didn't exactly sound like a punishment at this particular moment.

I inched my way along the side of the mountain, making sure I didn't look down. We'd only been out in the elements for a little over an hour, but the cold was starting to seep through all my layers. I shivered. Time to get moving. My head spun.

Once I made it back to the base of the glacier, it was a straight shot to the Silcox Hut. I found our tracks from the route up and stepped in them, so that I didn't have to exert as much effort plowing through the snow.

I could hear the hum of the Magic Mile ski lift rotating and the sound of skiers on the groomed slope. Clint had given us a break before the next round of training. I decided I'd better hightail it to the hut and start typing up my notes. That way I'd have tangible proof for Greg that I was working on my assignment.

The Silcox Hut sat buried in snow as I approached it from above. A cheery billow of smoke rising from its chimney was the only evidence that there was anything hidden underneath.

I stopped at the entryway to stomp caked snow from the bottom of my boots. Voices in the dining hall echoed. Someone was fighting.

Leaving my boots to dry, I crept on my tiptoes down the hallway toward the dining room. The sound of shouting became clearer. One of the voices was Henry's.

This was getting out of hand.

I leaned against the wall and cupped my hand over my ear to get a better listen. I didn't want to get too close and risk having Henry and whomever he was fighting with see me.

"Dude, I don't know what your problem is." Henry's usually low-key voice sounded on edge.

"*Dude*, yes, you do." Jackson's voice mimicked Henry.

"Ten-Eighty? Take it. I don't care, bro."

"This isn't about Ten-Eighty, *bro*." Jackson's voice was laced with fury.

"Then I have no idea what your deal is. I'm over this."

"You know what I'm talking about. Don't move. You're not leaving until we finish this," Jackson commanded.

"There's nothing to finish. I've told you a million times it wasn't me."

What wasn't him? Ben's murder?

I couldn't hear what they were saying. I took two small steps forward, keeping my back tight against the wall. There was the sound of something crashing and then Henry laughing.

"I'm not fighting you." Henry's voice sounded closer. If he left the dining hall he'd see me right away.

Time to get out of here.

I whipped around to run toward the entryway and smacked into Lola. I let out a little scream and threw my hand over my mouth.

She held a stack of folded dish towels in her arms that went flying when I bumped into her. Clutching one towel tightly to her body, she bent over to pick up the rest.

"Oh, my gosh, I'm so sorry. I didn't see you." I bent to help her.

"Stop." She cradled the towels. "I got this." Lola stood. "I could say the same thing about you. What are you doing?"

"Me?" I snuck a glance toward the dining hall. "Nothing. I was just looking to see if anyone was back yet."

"Sure." Lola gave me a skeptical look and placed the last dish towel on the top of her stack.

Henry huffed past us. He stopped in midstride. "Oh, hey. What's up?"

Lola held up the stack of towels. "Off to put these away."

I pulled my pack off my shoulder. "I'm off to write up my notes." I scanned the hallway to make sure Jackson hadn't followed him.

"Is everything okay?" I kept my voice low.

Henry rolled his eyes. "You don't even want to know."

"I do. Do you want to talk?" I motioned toward the dining room and whispered, "Things are crazy. Someone hit me at the pool last night."

"What? Are you okay?"

I showed him the bump on my head. "I'm fine. What were you and Jackson fighting about?"

"That's gnarly." Henry looked concerned. "You're sure you're cool?"

"I promise. Do you want to talk outside?"

Henry shrugged. "There's nothing to say. I'm quitting. This is messed up. I need to ride. The longer I'm on the snow, the more my board connects. Time to hit it. As long as you're sure you're cool?"

"Go ride. I'm fine."

Inside the dining room, Jackson stood near the fireplace, his gaze focused on the snow-encrusted window. There was nothing to see outside except for snow, but he held his eyes on the window as if he had X-ray vision and could see through it. Lola stood next to him, the dish towels still stacked in her arms.

They hadn't noticed me yet. I considered whether I should approach them. If Jackson had just threatened to fight Henry, maybe it wasn't such a good idea. On the other hand, I was dying to know what he and Henry were fighting about.

"Hey!" I called brightly.

Lola grimaced. She gave Jackson a funny look and returned to the kitchen.

Jackson shook himself out of the trancelike stare. "Is it time?"

"Time for what?" I approached him with small steps.

"Ski training."

I glanced up at the clock. "I don't think so. Clint said three o'clock, right?"

Jackson nodded. He brushed imaginary dust from his shoulders and took a long, slow breath.

"Is everything okay?" I came closer.

He acted like he didn't hear me.

I asked again. "I'm worried about Henry. Is something wrong?"

Jackson scanned the room. I turned to see Lola eavesdropping. She pretended to polish a fork when we caught her.

"You're a reporter, right?" Jackson slicked back his hair with his fingers.

I nodded. "Yep, in the flesh."

He hardened his eyes. "I'll tell you this. You have a story with your friend out there that would make the tabloids jealous."

"The tabloids?"

"That's what I said."

"You mean about Ben's murder?"

He looked confused for a minute. "You're the reporter. You figure it out." He sauntered past me and out of the dining room.

My reporting and investigating skills were being put to the ultimate test this weekend. I had no idea what Jackson had alluded to, but I got the distinct impression he wasn't referring to Ben's murder. Could it be that he and Henry were simply battling it out for an endorsement gig? But Henry told Jackson he didn't care about the Ten-Eighty contract and Jackson kept pushing.

I had to talk to Henry before he quit and left the mountain. However, before I did anything else, I had to type my notes. Clint said they'd start the next round of training in a little under an hour. That should give me plenty of time to pull a rough outline of my story together.

I headed toward the bunk rooms to grab my laptop. On the way out, Lola stopped me.

"Can I give you a little feedback?" She grabbed my sleeve.

"Sure. What's up?"

"You know, you're acting kind of weird." She dropped my sleeve.

"I am? How?"

She tapped her fingers on the countertop and inspected me. "Why are you so interested in Ben's murder all of a sudden?"

"I'm not."

"Please." She looked skeptical. "We're friends, right?"

"Yeah. I've enjoyed getting to know you." I reached my hand out and squeezed her arm.

"Look, I know you're young and kind of naïve." She gave a half smile. "Don't take this the wrong way, okay?"

That was the second time I'd been called naïve this weekend. I huffed internally, but waited for her to continue.

"You remind me of my little sister. I don't want to see you hurt."

"Hurt?"

"Forget it." Lola opened a drawer and took out a tube of ChapStick. She twisted the tube.

"What do you mean about getting hurt?"

She ran it over her lips. "Don't sweat it. Just be careful. Okay? You never know who you might accidentally piss off."

"Okay?" I tried to catch her eye, but she twisted the tube up and down. "Well, thanks for thinking of me. I appreciate it."

I left her to go get my laptop. Was she being thoughtful? Was she really worried about me? Her response seemed strange. First she seemed annoyed that I'd been listening in on Henry and Jackson's fight. Then she was trying to hear my conversation with Jackson. Now she was acting like a concerned older friend.

Could there be a more sinister reason for her concern? Could Lola have something to do with Ben's murder? Maybe she wanted me to stop meddling because she was worried that I'd find something that pointed to her.

One thing was for sure—I had to gather my notes. I plopped onto my bunk and spent the next forty minutes pounding out my thoughts on the keyboard. By the time I'd finished I had a much better idea where the guts of my story were. As to who might have killed Ben? I had no idea.

THIRTY

After I finished typing my notes, I pulled on my damp snow gear. I wondered if avid skiers minded constantly getting in and out of wet pants. This wasn't exactly my idea of fun. The inside of my sleeves were soaked with melted snow. I considered hiding out by the fire and skipping the ski-training portion of the afternoon, but I was already skating on thin ice with Greg. Not showing up would definitely earn me a one-way ticket back to Portland.

Ignoring my soggy sleeves, I headed outside to meet up with the team. Light snow began to drift from the low-lying clouds. It looked dainty and delicate, the complete opposite from the storm two days ago.

There wasn't any sign of the team nearby. I guessed in my hurry to catch up with Henry, I'd forgotten an important detail —to ask where we were supposed to meet next.

I circled back to the clearing where we'd gathered earlier. When I arrived, the Rangers were nowhere in sight, but their snow caves were still intact. It reminded me of a miniature snow village. I could almost imagine a magical frozen town coming to life here with families tucked tightly in their snow caves and a community bonfire burning in the center.

I was mesmerized by the cozy thought and decided to take this moment alone to capture the makeshift abandoned village for *Northwest Extreme.* The action shots that I'd taken earlier of the team at work in the snow were pretty standard. Maybe I could impress Greg with a more artistic interpretation of the snow shelters.

I dropped my day pack on the ground and shot the clearing from a bunch of angles. Who knew if the photos would translate once I uploaded them, but I figured it was worth a try. Before I left to find the team, I opted to take a few more shots of the inside of each structure. Thanks to Greg tasking me with managing our social media, I'd gotten pretty good at adjusting the camera settings to create an artsy shot. I bent onto my knees and angled the camera up inside each shelter. They were all solid. The cool air and new layer of snow had helped to firm them. Each was quite impressive.

As I was about to leave, something caught my eye. Sticking out of the floor of the last structure was something that didn't look natural. Was it a stick? It didn't look right. There was a long, thin branch—or something—on the floor near the far wall of the cave. I inhaled and crept inside.

I reached up and gently tapped the ceiling to make sure it wasn't about to cave in. It felt solid, but I could feel panic rise in my body. I crawled farther into the cave, continually checking the snow wall above me. The object came into sight. It wasn't a branch or a stick. It was the barrel of a gun.

I froze in the snow cave. This wasn't just any gun. This was Henry's historic hunting rifle that he'd been bragging about at dinner the first night. The night that Ben was shot. What if this was the murder weapon?

What should I do? I'd never seen a gun close up before. Could it go off?

How could I tell if it was loaded?

No way was I touching it. I backed out of the cave.

Think, Meg. Think.

My phone was in my day pack. I'd call Sheriff Daniels and tell him what I'd found. I ran through the snow to where I'd left my pack and pulled out my phone. I waited for the sound of the line ringing on the other end. Nothing but silence.

I checked the home screen—no bars. There must not be cell service this high on the mountain. I'd have to call him from the satellite phone at the Silcox Hut. I didn't want to take any chances that whoever killed Ben (and it was looking worse for Henry by the minute) would come back and retrieve the gun, so I cinched my gloves on again and scooped a handful of snow from the front of the cave. I'd bury the gun in snow.

Why would someone hide a gun in one of the snow caves? Sheriff Daniels had searched the Silcox Hut yesterday. Maybe the murderer needed a temporary place to keep it until they could find a more permanent hiding spot?

Is that why Henry took off so quickly? Could that be what he and Jackson were fighting about? Maybe Jackson found the gun, but why wouldn't he have called the sheriff?

I finished covering the gun with snow and went to grab my pack. As I was turning to head to the Silcox Hut, a figure on skis emerged from the tree line.

Malory startled and nearly fell over on her skis when she saw me. She was outfitted in sleek turquoise pants, a cream ski coat, and a visor beanie cap. I thought I'd seen an exact replica of her outfit in one of our ad campaigns last month.

"Malory! What are you doing here?" I couldn't contain the surprise in my voice.

She checked behind her, and skied over to me. "Where is everyone?"

"I'm not sure. I came out here to look. They're supposed to be training."

Malory punched her feet free from her bindings with her ski pole. She ignored me and scanned the clearing. Was I just imagining things or did her gaze linger on the snow cave where the gun was hidden?

"Where did you come from?" I asked. Come to think of it, where had she been all day? She wasn't here when the team built the snow caves and I didn't see her when they were practicing belaying either.

She bent over and adjusted her bindings. "I've been skiing."

"Out in the *trees*?" I pointed to the forest behind her, which was in the opposite direction of the Silcox Hut and the groomed runs.

"Tree skiing." She gave me a nasty look and clamped her boots back into her skis. Without another word she skied away, leaving me staring after her.

What was Malory doing skiing in the forest? It was a well-known fact that I wasn't a ski expert, but this was the first time I'd heard of it. How could anyone ski *up* the mountain?

I had to talk to Sheriff Daniels, but if I left to call him now, what if Malory came back for the gun? It might be the only solid piece of evidence in the case. I weighed my options. I could either hurry to the Silcox Hut as fast as my short legs would allow or I could stand guard in front of the snow cave and hope that someone else would come along.

I decided on option one. Grabbing my pack and camera, I trudged through the snow, following Malory's ski tracks back to the Silcox Hut. The place was empty. I didn't bother to remove my coat. I just banged the snow off my boots and slid on my socks to find the satellite phone.

"Lola? Are you here?" I called.

The dining hall sat empty. It didn't look like the fire had been stoked for a while. A single log smoldered.

I found the phone in the kitchen and punched in the sheriff's number. He answered on the first ring. "Sheriff Daniels here."

"Hey, it's Meg. Where are you?"

The phone crackled. I could hear music in the background, but our connection wasn't great.

"Sorry, what's that?"

"It's *Meg!*" I shouted. "Where are you?"

"Margaret?"

Hearing the sheriff call me by my full name made me hold the phone away from my ear. He'd always treated me very formally, calling me "Ms. Reed." Gam called me Margaret.

"Are you there?" he yelled on the other end of the line.

"Yeah, where are you?"

"Timberline."

"Can you get up here?"

The line cut out for a second. I thought I'd lost him. "Sheriff, are you there?"

"I'm here. What did you need?"

"I asked if you can come up here."

"To the hut?" he grunted.

"Yes! I found something."

There was a pause. A long pause.

"You found something, Ms. Reed?" There we were, back to formality. I could tell from his tone he didn't approve.

"Yes. I found a gun."

"A gun?"

"I think it's the murder weapon. I didn't know what to do and I didn't want to touch it, so I buried it in the snow and came inside right away to call you."

He let out a sigh. "I'll be there as soon as I can. Don't touch it."

The phone went dead. Sheriff Daniels didn't sound happy. Not only was I going to have to face the wrath of Greg for not being there for the ski training, but now I was going to have to face the wrath of Sheriff Daniels, too. It wasn't my fault. It wasn't like I intentionally went digging in the snow. All I was trying to do was get a great shot for the magazine. Never did I imagine I might find the weapon used to shoot Ben.

I returned the phone to its charging base and planned to wait for the sheriff by the front door. I let out a scream as I turned around.

Lola stood blocking the exit with one arm. Instead of her normal apron, she wore latte-colored ski pants and a neon yellow coat. Her braids hung from her knit cap.

"Oh! You startled me." I smiled and let out a sigh of relief.

"What are you doing in there?" She didn't return my smile. "Who were you talking to?"

"The sheriff." I could feel the hairs on my neck rise.

She pursed her lips. "Why?"

"No biggie. He's just coming up to check a couple things out." I tried to sound casual.

"You know, after we talked I thought you were going to listen to my advice."

"I did. Really, it's no big deal." I started to move toward her. She kept her feet planted in the doorway and her arms crossed.

"Rumors are swirling that you've been involved in a murder investigation before." She gave me a hard look. "Are you working with the police or something?"

Her stance unnerved me.

"No. Not at all. The sheriff is a friend of my grandmother's. That's all. Honestly, it's no big deal."

She didn't respond.

"I need to grab my laptop and get a little work done while I wait for him." I took a step forward.

She didn't move. "I'm going out to get a run in. Don't mess with anything; I've got a casserole baking in the oven."

"Okay." Weird. What would I touch in the kitchen? I moved closer. "Can I sneak by you?"

She held her stance a moment longer and then stepped to the side for me to pass. I could feel her eyes burning into me as I walked by.

Was she angry with me? Could she have been the one who hid the gun in the snow cave? She'd been alone in the Silcox Hut all day. She'd have had plenty of opportunities to go hide it.

Was it possible that she could have murdered Ben?

THIRTY-ONE

When I returned to the dining room with my laptop, Lola was gone. I plugged it in and waited for it to boot up. I knew I was missing the training, but honestly, what else was there to cover? My feature wasn't going to write itself.

While I waited for my laptop to come to life, I thought about Lola's comment. Why would she tell me to stay out of the kitchen? Unless she had something to hide?

I left my laptop and snuck into the kitchen. I didn't have any idea what I was looking for, so I started opening drawers and cupboards randomly. Everything seemed to be in place.

Meg, what are you doing? I shook my head. *Seriously. You're a mess. Stop snooping and get back to work.*

Just one last drawer, I thought to myself, pulling open a deep drawer filled with canisters of flour, sugar, and baking supplies. I pushed the canisters to the side and removed a box of baking soda. Underneath sat another thin, narrow box. Not a box used for cooking. It read: AMMUNITION.

I gasped. *Oh, my God!*

Keeping one hand on the drawer handle, I pushed onto my

tiptoes to check and make sure no one was nearby. Nope. The coast was clear. I reached into another drawer and found one of the dish towels Lola had brought in earlier. As I wrapped it around my hand, I thought back to bumping into Lola in the hallway. I'd offered to help her with the towels and she'd forcefully refused. What if that was because she'd been hiding the box of bullets inside the stack of towels?

I'd learned that it was important not to contaminate evidence, so I carefully removed the box of bullets, making sure my hand stayed inside the towel. That way I wouldn't leave any fingerprints on the box. With my free hand, I wrapped the towel around the box and placed it on the counter. Then I put everything back where I'd found it.

I couldn't risk Lola returning to find me with the bullets. I crept to the door with the towel behind my back. Checking all directions, I scooted to my bunk room.

Where to hide the evidence? As soon as Sheriff Daniels arrived, I'd give him the bullets and show him where the gun was hidden. But if Lola (or whoever had hidden the bullets in the baking drawer) came back and found they were missing, I had to play it cool and make sure they didn't find them. I stuffed the towel into the bottom of my sleeping bag. Nope. Too lumpy.

Next I tried cramming it under my pillowcase. Good. But if anyone came looking and felt my pillow, they'd spot it immediately. Finally I opted to squeeze the box into one of my tennis shoes and bury them under all of my clothes in my suitcase.

How long would it take for Sheriff Daniels to get up here? I didn't know how often the snowcat ran, and I didn't want to wait to find out. Turning off the lights in the room, I hurried back to the dining hall.

Greg and Clint sat in deep conversation when I returned to the dining room. They were thumbing through a stack of old newspaper clippings and photos.

"Meg." Greg held a black-and-white photo in his hand. "Where have you been?"

"Working on my story." I pointed to my open laptop at the far table. "What are you looking at?"

Clint spread the photos out like a fan of cards. "Walking Greg through the Crag Rats' past."

I dragged a bench to their table and joined them. "Wow, these are amazing." I picked up a photo, yellowing around the edges, showing five men in baggy wool pants, flannel shirts, and ankle boots. Skiing attire had come a long way. No wonder Henry wanted to land the deal with Ten-Eighty.

"Careful. Careful." Clint cradled his photo, barely touching the edges with the tips of his fingers. "These are on loan from the Mount Hood Museum."

"Wouldn't it be cool to run some of these with the feature?" I asked Greg. Greg clicked his jaw and shot one finger at me.

"Cool."

I felt my cheeks warm with heat. You'd think I'd be used to him by now. "Are their skis wooden?" I asked, pointing to one of the photos.

"Yep." Clint rested his photo on the table. "Most men made them by hand. Have you checked out the museum yet?"

I shook my head.

"You should. It's down in Government Camp. Timberline has a nice little history of the mountain, too."

"Yeah, in fact I was planning to head down there soon. I took a quick glance at it yesterday, but I want to spend some time walking through it. And someone said there's a video of the lodge's timeline that they run?"

Clint gathered the photos and clippings together. "Yep."

Greg rested his elbow on the table and scratched his chin. "You're going to the lodge, huh? I can ski with you."

"Oh, no. No. That's fine. You don't have to. I'm cool."

There was the word "cool" again. What was wrong with

me? I prided myself on my vocabulary. Apparently whenever I was around Greg I had to sound my age.

"Megs, Megs, are you here?" Jill and Matt called in unison as they peeked into the dining hall.

Ah. Saved by my besties. Thank you, Universe.

I jumped to my feet. "Yay! You came back."

"We had to find our favorite reporter." Jill brushed snowflakes from her jacket. She caught Greg's eye and flashed a grin. "Sorry, are we bothering you?"

Greg waved her and Matt in. "Not at all." I noticed him appraise her. It would have been hard not to. A simple black headband held her hair away from her face, which was gently tanned from the sun. Her full lips were coated with a simple gloss. She smiled with ease.

"I don't think you've met. Greg, this is my best friend, Jill. Jill, this is my boss."

Greg extended his hand. "Delighted. Any friend of our Meg is a friend of mine."

Jill didn't blush at his compliment, or when Clint stepped forward and lavished her with equal praise. "Have I seen you on the cover of *Downhill Magazine*?"

"Not me." Jill laughed. Her ski suit in monochrome black made her appear even taller.

"Clint, good thought, my man," Greg said, clapping him on the back. "You could model for me. Have you ever thought about it?"

Jill shook her head. "Uh, no?" She gave me a look to help her.

"Greg, you remember my friend Matt. Matt, this is Clint. He's one of the Ridge Rangers."

Clint stepped forward to shake Matt's hand, but, awkwardly, neither Greg nor Matt acknowledged one another.

"Are you up here to ski?" I asked.

Jill smiled. "Yeah, we're going to head up to Palmer."

Matt glared at Greg. What was up with those two?

"Let me walk you out." I yanked Matt by the sleeve of his green and yellow parka toward the front door.

Jill politely exited, saying how nice it was to meet them both. Matt's body stayed rigid all the way to the entrance.

"How's your head?" he asked, holding the door open.

"Better." I tried to read his body language. His jaw looked tense. "Did you hear that Ben's death is officially a murder?"

Matt shook his head and scowled. "You're being smart, right?"

Jill made a big production of fiddling with her bindings. I could tell she was trying to give us space.

I nodded.

"Okay. Take it easy, Megs." He whispered under his breath, "We'll talk more later."

"You're going to ski the glacier?"

"As long as Matty here is up for the challenge." Jill staked a ski pole in the snow.

"First one down buys the beer." Matt winked.

"I'll meet you at the lodge later. I've got a few things to finish up."

They agreed and skied off toward the Palmer chairlift. I felt lonely watching them leave. They were my connection to sanity and the real world.

My phone buzzed. Maybe service was better outside?

"Ms. Reed?" Sheriff Daniels greeted me on the other end of the crackling line.

"Yeah?"

"I'm going to be a bit delayed."

"That's okay. I'll come to you," I said. The connection went dead before I could hear his response. It didn't matter, I had to get out of here before Greg decided to follow me down to the lodge. No way was I skiing. Or taking the chairlift, for that matter. I'd take my own sweet time and walk—that's right—walk down to the lodge.

My snow gear, hanging in the front lobby, was still damp. I yanked on my pants. *Please, please, don't let Greg follow me.* I said a silent prayer to the Universe as I zipped my parka. He'd fire me for sure if he learned I couldn't ski.

I slid on the packed snow outside the Silcox Hut's front doors. I avoided falling flat on my face by waving my arms in large circles to keep my balance. Hopefully it wouldn't be this slippery all the way down to the lodge.

The Mountaineer Trail, which connected Timberline Lodge and the Silcox Hut, would take me down 1,000 feet in elevation. For the record, it was the highest trail on the mountain. Walking was going to be enough of a challenge. I couldn't imagine descending it on skis. The thought sent a shiver through my body. The weekend's blizzard left the main trail impassable. I decided my best route would be to follow the groomed ski trail, being sure to stay off the actual runs.

Boarders and skiers whizzed past me. I watched as a snowboarder launched his body over a jump, catching huge air and perfectly executing a grab twenty feet off the ground. Snowboarding culture had the best slang.

Henry taught me some of it. It was like speaking another language—the crail, cross-rocket, Japan air, slob, roast beef, and the squirrel, just to name a few. Those were just the grabs. Slides, spins, flips, and rotations all had their own slang. I needed a cheat sheet with photos, or better yet—videos.

I loved watching the boarders' tricks and the skiers' expert maneuvers as I continued my descent. Even though I had no interest in attempting anything similar myself, I was totally amazed with the athleticism, raw talent, and utter lack of fear on display. There were a handful of families and more novice skiers about, but for the most part the upper runs of the Palmer Glacier and Magic Mile attracted advanced snow lovers.

Every few minutes someone would flash by me as I struggled to keep my footing on the way down. It was hard to keep my focus forward. I felt like I had a front-row seat at the Winter Olympics. I kept getting distracted by the acrobatic moves and the shouts of fellow boarders cheering on their friends. The snow on the side of the trail was thick and heavy. It felt like I was moving through molasses. The air smelled fresh and the clouds had stopped spurting out showers of snow.

I'd probably gone about a quarter of a mile when someone plowed right into me, knocking me face-first into the snow.

The skier twisted sideways on her skis and came to an abrupt stop, spraying powder all around. I brushed snow off of my face and shook it from my hood. My face stung.

I pushed myself onto my knees and assessed my body. Almost automatically I reached for the bump on my skull. It didn't feel great, but it didn't feel any worse. My back was another story. The skier had nailed me right in the middle of my spine.

"Hey!" the skier yelled. "Stay off the run!"

I stretched from side to side. My back cracked. I hated that sound. It didn't even hurt that badly. It just felt tight, but the sound of it cracking made me cringe.

"Did you hear me? This area is only for skiers!" the woman shouted again.

"Sorry," I said, as I twisted my back again and stood.

My eyes made contact with the skier yelling at me. It was Lola.

Had she followed me? Did she knock me over on purpose? I stood with my nose crinkled and my outerwear coated in snow. I probably looked like I was auditioning for the part of a snowman.

"Meg? Sorry. I didn't know that was you." Lola sounded surprised to see me.

"Lola?"

She positioned herself toward Timberline, crossing her skis. "Be careful. You have to watch where you're going. It's dangerous up here. People have died."

With that she waved, bent her knees, and slalomed down the slope. I'd be more careful for the rest of my descent. Her parting words made me shiver. *People have died.* I didn't want to be one of them.

THIRTY-TWO

It took another half hour to get down to the lodge. I felt relief knowing that Gam was nearby. I hoped I'd have a chance to talk to Jill and Matt. They always help me feel better and could lend some insight into the past few days' events. First I had to find Sheriff Daniels.

I stomped snow from my boots and shook free from my wet coat as I entered the temporary tunnel in front of the lodge. It looked like no time had passed. The fire roared with skiers gathered round and Timberline's Saint Bernard ambled over to greet me.

Neither Gam nor Sheriff Daniels was near the fire. I circled it once, just in case. Then I checked the Blue Ox and headed upstairs to the Ram's Head. No sign of them. I checked my phone, but it only had one bar. I asked the woman at the front desk if she could call either of their rooms or page them. No answer.

Where could they be?

What if they'd headed up to the Silcox Hut? It would be just my luck to have passed them on the way down. I asked the woman at the front desk if the snowcat was en route. She said no. It wouldn't be leaving for another hour.

They must be here somewhere.

I decided if I hung around the lobby for the next hour or so, I could catch the sheriff on his way out to the snowcat. I guessed I might as well follow through and work on my feature. Except there was one small problem—in my haste to leave I'd left my laptop in the dining room.

Good move, Meg.

Hopefully Greg wouldn't notice. Or worse, go through it. There wasn't much I could do about it right now.

Adjacent to Timberline's massive fireplace was a mini historical museum of sorts. Glass cases on the wall contain artifacts, the original loom used to weave the lodge's blankets and rugs, and a pictorial timeline.

I meandered through the space, making notes on a pad I borrowed from the front desk and studying old photos of work crews pounding recycled railroad ties and telephone poles into the ground. The process of constructing the lodge was truly a marvel, resulting in a structural design that was a work of art.

I learned that in the 1950s the lodge was shut down by the U.S. Forest Service. The management company controlling the lodge at the time didn't pay its bills and let prostitution and gambling run rampant. Timberline was in complete disarray and in desperate need of repair.

If it hadn't been for New York social worker Richard L. Kohnstamm, who had no experience managing hotels, Timberline would have been demolished. Kohnstamm convinced the U.S. Forest Service that he could return the lodge to its original glory, and when he was awarded the role as new operator in 1955 he began the process of renovating and restoring the property to the gem it was today.

A Forest Service ranger explained this to a group of tourists.

"Who would have thought some twenty-nine-year-old social worker from a wealthy family in New York would be able to accomplish this?"

I listened in as he continued. "The R.L.K. Company still maintains the property today with a focus on its roots and historic preservation. We're really lucky to have had such a visionary at the helm."

From Ruin to... XXX. I made note of a potential headline or photo caption on my notepad. I could use something like "repair" but that sounded too predictable. If I left it alone for a while I knew the right word would pop into my head.

As I jotted notes and followed the tour into the screening room, where a documentary of Timberline's evolution ran, I wasn't paying attention and bumped into a woman standing near the loom.

"Sorry." I looked up from my notes. "Guess I should watch where I'm going."

"Don't sweat it," she replied.

I almost dropped the notepad when my eyes focused on her face. This was the woman Will had been chatting with at the Blue Ox. My palms started to sweat. Should I say something? What?

How did I always end up in situations like this? Gam said nothing was a coincidence. She believed the Universe (and our own free will) led us to exactly where we needed to be.

Did I need to be here now?

She appraised me. "Reporter?"

"How did you know?"

"Notepad. Pencil. Studious, eager face." She twisted a diamond-studded earring in her ear. "I'm guessing you're pretty fresh on the job."

"I'm Meg." I reached out my hand. "Yep. You pretty much nailed it. I'm on assignment for *Northwest Extreme* magazine."

"Charlotte." She pressed her hand into mine.

"What about you? Are you here for business or pleasure?" I asked. Was this actually happening?

"A little of both." She gave a coy smile.

"Are you a writer, too?"

"No. I work with a lot of writers, though. I know the type."

While her demeanor was friendly, there was something about her guarded attitude that I didn't trust. And not just because I suspected she was having an affair with my best friend's boyfriend.

The tour group had moved into the next room. "Are you on this tour?" I nodded toward the guide.

"Hmm?" She glanced behind her. "No. I'm waiting for someone."

Yeah. I had one guess who.

I debated whether to catch up with the tour group or try to get more information out of Charlotte. She didn't seem to be overly chatty. But if I could keep her talking for a little while, maybe Will would show up.

"Hot date?" I winked.

She furrowed her brow and gave me an odd look. "What makes you say that?"

I stammered. "Well, I—it's just that you're not dressed for skiing." She wasn't. She wore black tailored pants, a low-cut red silk blouse, and stilettos. "You know, it's so romantic here," I rambled on. "I thought maybe you were meeting a date or something."

At that moment, Will appeared. He certainly wasn't dressed for skiing either, in a three-piece black suit with a red tie.

"There you are." He kissed Charlotte on the cheek. "I've been looking everywhere for you. I thought we were going to meet at the Blue Ox again."

Charlotte raised her eyebrows. He didn't notice me.

"Will, this is Meg." She gave him a look I couldn't decipher. Was she nervous? Trying to carefully remind him that they weren't alone?

Will threw his shoulders back as if he were ducking from a punch. "Meg! What are you doing here?"

Charlotte's face froze for a moment. She looked at Will and then back to me. "You two know each other?"

Will cleared his throat and adjusted his tie. He didn't fool me. I could tell he was trying to regain his composure. He hadn't expected to find me here. I was also no good at disguising my body language. I was sure Charlotte could feel the negative energy pulsing out of me.

"Meg, this is my colleague Charlotte." Will's usually refined speech sounded rushed. "Charlotte, this is my friend Meg."

"We've met." Charlotte didn't look at me. Her tone was cool.

"Good." Will straightened his tie again. There was no need. His tie, like every hair on his well-groomed body, was perfectly centered. "Charlotte, we should go look over the, uh, case." He motioned toward the Blue Ox Bar. "See you later, Meg." He hurried away.

Charlotte turned and waved with her fingers. She smiled broadly. It wasn't a kind smile. It was sickeningly sweet. She flipped her head back around and looped her arm through Will's.

She knew that I knew, but did she know that Will was in a relationship? What was I going to do? I hated Will. Not that I'd ever liked him, but now I could have killed him. How could he cheat on my best friend? How could anyone cheat on Jill? She was literally the most gorgeous woman I knew. Not to mention the nicest.

I forgot about the tour and plopped into an empty chair by

the fire. This was the worst possible position to be in. I knew I had to tell Jill, I just didn't know how.

Damn you, Will Barrington. You're going to make me break my friend's heart.

I dropped my head in my hands. Every time I thought things couldn't get worse, they did.

THIRTY-THREE

I wasn't sure how long I sat feeling sorry for myself as the crowd of skiers and guests ebbed. Lost in my own thoughts, I barely took notice when someone sat in the chair next to me.

"Penny for them," Gam's gentle voice said.

I collapsed into her shoulder. "Am I ever glad to see you."

She enveloped me in her arms. Her skin felt warm to the touch, and she smelled like jasmine and honey.

"Gam, are you wearing perfume?" I sat up a little.

She removed her arm from my shoulder and placed her hand on my knee. "I may have dabbed the back of my ears with some essential oils." She smirked.

"Gam! You are totally smitten with Sheriff Daniels!" I poked her in the ribs.

She squeezed my knee and giggled. "Don't you just love him in his jeans and cowboy boots? He's like an old-fashioned Western star. I can see him smashing up all the bad guys."

I liked to tease her about her affinity for Westerns and action flicks. She didn't mind. She claimed that seeing the "good guys" win helped her restore her faith in the world every once in a while. I kept telling her she should host an action-flick weekend at her spiritual bookstore, Light and Love. It would be hilarious to see all her energy-healing clients gathered round to watch "shoot-'em-up" flicks.

"Where is he? I need to talk to him."

Gam pointed down the stairs. "He's working. They're letting him use one of the empty rooms downstairs as a temporary office." She pressed her hand into my knee. "Although I think he already left for the hut."

"Oh, no. I can't believe I missed him."

"Let me give you a little zap of Reiki. You look stressed."

Within seconds, the warm energy from her magic hands spread down my leg and pulsed in my toes. I felt my heart rate mellow.

"Thanks, Gam. That already feels better. Can you do a little work on my head?"

She clapped her hands together. "Good! I love it when it works like that. Don't you?" She moved her hand to the back of my head. "Is this the spot?"

I nodded and filled her in on running into Will and Charlotte. She listened, keeping her hand gently resting on my head the whole time.

When I finished, she brushed her hands together, clearing the energy. A soft smile tugged at the corners of her lips and she stared into the fire. I knew she was tapping into "all that is." She went into almost a trancelike state when she connected with her spirit guides. Just watching the transformation was always enough to make me believe.

"Mm-hmm." She nodded, speaking to the fire. "That's what I thought." She returned her attention to me. "They're telling me to remind you that this isn't your journey."

"I shouldn't tell Jill?"

"You should do whatever feels like it's the highest and best for you and your friend."

"What if I don't know what that is?"

She placed her hand on my arm. "Margaret, I know this is a terrible position to be in and that you don't want to hurt your friend, but this is the path she's choosing."

I started to protest.

She continued. "Even when it doesn't feel like it at the time, great spiritual growth can come from painful experiences. It's not what happens to us but how we respond that makes a difference in our outcomes."

"You should tell that to Mom."

She took a deep breath. "Have you spoken to her lately?"

"No. Why?"

Gam folded her hands in her lap. "It's not my story to tell."

"What do you mean?"

"You're learning so much about yourself through your grief. I know it may not feel like it in this moment, but you'll be able to reflect on this experience in the years to come and understand that it absolutely helped to shape who you are. I can see that you're frustrated." She rubbed my arm. "I'm sorry."

"It's okay." I didn't meet her eyes.

"Margaret, look at me." She cradled my chin in her hands. "I only want to help you have a deeper understanding of the fact that we're all—each and every one of us—on our own unique life path. I know in my heart that Jill, just like you, will be okay. Some parts of our journey are challenging."

I nodded, fighting back tears.

She studied me for a moment. "Shall we go see if we can find some of those delightful oatmeal-chocolate cookies for a little treat?'

I agreed and followed her upstairs to the Cascade Dining Room. I knew she was right. But I didn't want to have to tell my best friend that her boyfriend was cheating on her.

THIRTY-FOUR

After Gam and I polished off three oatmeal-chocolate cookies each, she left me in the Ram's Head to go change for dinner. I didn't have time to craft my words carefully before talking to Jill.

She snuck up behind me and covered my eyes with her hands. "Guess who?"

She tucked her hair behind her ears and sat down. "Why the sullen face?"

I blew out all the air in my lungs. "We have to talk."

Jill gave me a quizzical look. "That sounds bad. Did someone else die?"

"No. I wish." I rubbed my eyes.

She raised her eyebrows. "Meg, come on. What's up? You can tell me anything."

"Exactly. That's what makes this so hard."

She shook her hair free. "Is this about *me*?"

I nodded.

"What?" Her eyes widened. I hesitated.

She pleaded. "Meg! Tell me."

"Okay, but before I tell you, please know that I love you and

I'm here for you. You've been so good to me, I just want you to know that it's my turn."

"Seriously. Enough. Start talking."

"It's about Will."

Her face registered my words with a look of what Gam called "a knowing."

"Last night, after I got hit at the pool, I went down to the Blue Ox to have a beer while you were getting ready. I saw Will with another woman."

She took in the news, gazing past me.

"I don't know what it means. They just looked pretty cozy last night. He had his arm around her. I didn't see them do anything else, but then this afternoon when I was working on my story I bumped into the woman—her name's Charlotte—and she was waiting for Will."

Jill studied her nails. I noticed they were polished with a pale pink shimmer.

"Then Will showed up. He said she's a colleague from work. So it could be nothing. I could be worrying for no reason. But I had to tell you. I couldn't keep it a secret. If it were me in your position, I'd want to know."

Her fingers looked like they'd been expertly manicured. It was a hobby of Jill's. Maybe because she didn't get to express her art by painting, she used her fingernails as her canvas. The way she inspected them now made me think she was examining a famous piece of artwork.

"Jill, are you okay?" I tried to get her to meet my eyes.

She kept her eyes on her nails for a moment. When she finally looked up, her face was completely neutral. I had no idea what she was thinking. Was her heart ripping apart or was she being aloof? Part of me wished I could keep my emotions buttoned up like Jill, but then another part of me realized this self-protection strategy didn't allow her to open up. It was one of the reasons she wasn't pursuing her art. At that moment, I wondered if it was also one of the reasons she was dating Will. He was an easy choice—handsome, successful, her parents approved—but did he make her happy?

"I know Charlotte," she said, looking toward the doorway.

"You do?"

She nodded. "She's a lawyer at our firm."

"Oh, whew!" I clapped my hands together. "See. Never mind, then. I was just overreacting. You know me and my imagination. That makes sense. She and Will were probably going over work stuff. I'm sorry I said anything."

"Stop." Jill chuckled. "You're so transparent, Meg."

"What?"

"Come on, I know you. Whenever you're nervous, you do this." She motioned with her hand.

I threw my hand on my heart. "Me? I'm not blabbering. I just had a moment of clarity and was trying to explain."

Jill rolled her eyes. "Right." She got quiet. I thought I might have to prod her to go on, but after a moment she continued. "Thank you for being worried about me. Really." She smiled.

"Of course. You know I love you."

"I do. I don't really want to talk about Will right now, okay? I need some time."

"Jill, really, I didn't mean to put doubt into your head. I'm sure I misinterpreted what I saw."

She frowned. "You didn't."

"Oh." I couldn't think of anything else to say. If Jill suspected that Will was cheating on her, why hadn't she said anything? One thing I'd learned about her through the years of our friendship was that pushing her wouldn't work. That was probably one of the reasons we worked as friends. We balanced each other out. I had a tendency to jump into things too fast whereas Jill took her time and considered everything before she moved ahead.

I'd have to tread carefully. Baby steps.

Changing the subject felt like a good first step. "Where's Matt? Did he ski down with you?"

Jill sat up a little straighter. "He should be here any minute. What about you? Did you learn anything new about Ben's murder?"

"Hold that thought." I held up my finger. "There's Matt and Will now." I waved to them.

Matt strolled in wearing a pair of faded jeans and a navy pullover sweatshirt. Will looked completely out of place in his suit at the casual restaurant where most of the diners wore ski pants and layered long johns. As they passed by a group of forty-year-old women drinking cocktails, I watched Matt ignore their flirtatious waves and chatter. Will flashed them a dazzling smile and popped a maraschino cherry from one of their drinks into his mouth.

Gross. If only Jill would come to her senses and kick him to the curb.

Remember what Gam said—this is Jill's journey, not yours, I told myself as they joined us.

When Will went to plant a kiss on Jill's lips, I noticed she turned away at the last minute. The kiss landed on her cheek. I hoped I could interpret this as a sign.

Will recoiled slightly and shot me a nasty look. I smirked in return. So much for playing nice. That lasted all of two seconds. Oh, well. We'd never been close, but after seeing him with Charlotte I knew things were going to be icy between us from now on.

"No drinks?" Matt commented on the empty table. "What gives? It's happy hour."

"Right. Drinks." I smiled sweetly at Will. "Jill and I were just so wrapped up in conversation we totally spaced on ordering drinks."

Will snarled at me. He stretched and wrapped his arm

around the back of Jill's chair. Without missing a beat she picked it up, like a dirty sock, and removed it.

"I'll go order at the bar." She pushed back her chair and ignored Will's puppy-dog eyes.

"Thanks a lot, Meg." Will glared at me. Matt kicked me under the table.

Will scooted his chair back and ran after Jill.

"What was that all about?" Matt watched Will hurry to catch up with Jill.

"Don't ask." I blew out a breath and shook my head. "I hope Jill's finally had it with him, but who knows."

Matt looked thoughtful. "That's one thing I'll never understand about women. Why do you always go for the bad guys? Nice guys like me never get any love. It's always the dudes who treat women like dirt who you fight over."

"Not me." I made a gagging face. "I'd rather be single forever than date Will Barrington."

"Sure, that's what you say now, but I've seen you with your boss. You're no better than Jill. Whenever he's around you act like a completely different person."

"Hey!" I slugged him in the arm. "That's not fair. Greg's a nice guy."

Matt scoffed.

"He is. Plus, he's my boss. If I act differently around him it's because I'm trying to be professional. You know, do my *job*."

"Sure." Matt nodded in disbelief.

"How did we get on this topic anyway? I thought we were talking about Jill?"

"We were." Matt glanced toward the bar. Jill's back was to us, but Will was motioning wildly in an obvious attempt to appease her. I couldn't tell if it was working.

"She'll figure it out. Don't worry," Matt assured me.

"Anyway, we got off topic earlier. You mentioned that this whole thing with Pops has something to do with my job?"

Matt tugged on his sweatshirt strings. "I don't think we have time to get into it now."

I let out an exasperated sigh. "You can't do that to me. I've been thinking about it all afternoon."

Matt nodded toward the bar. "I know, but they're going to be back with drinks in a minute, and like I said before, we're not discussing this with anyone else right now."

"Can't you at least give me the quick version?"

Matt wrapped the strings of his hood together. He checked on Jill and Will. "There's too much to tell, but I'll give you one thing to think about, okay?"

I urged him to continue.

"Have you ever thought about how you got the job at *Northwest Extreme*?"

"Yeah. Fate. I ran into Greg at a coffee shop, remember?"

"I remember." Matt seemed to take notice that he'd wound his sweatshirt strings together. He dropped them. "Have you ever wondered if there was more to it than that?"

"No. Why?"

"Doesn't it seem a little too convenient to you? Think about it. You 'happened' to bump into an editor of a major magazine who just 'happened' to have the perfect position that you were... well, if I'm being honest, completely unprepared for and wrong for."

"Hey!"

Matt held his hand in the air. "I'm not saying you aren't a fantastic journalist—you are. But writing for *Northwest Extreme* isn't really your beat, Meg. You've done a great job and come a long way. But don't you find it more than a little curious that Greg would hire you on the spot for a position that requires tremendous knowledge and expertise of extreme sports?"

"Jeez. Is this 'Attack Meg Night' or something?"

"Not at all. I'm not questioning your skills as a writer. I'm suspicious of Greg's motives. That's all."

"Oh, that's all." I rolled my eyes.

He dropped the subject because Jill returned with a pitcher of beer. Will was nowhere in sight. I crossed my fingers, but it was clear she didn't want to talk about it. She handed over menus and Matt poured three pints.

My head buzzed. I had so many more questions for Matt. He was suggesting that my "accidental" run-in with Greg wasn't an accident. Why? I thought back to the fateful rainy morning when I'd literally fallen flat on my derrière and Greg came to my rescue. Our conversation had been light. We clicked over our mutual distaste for umbrellas and—and... he knew Pops. I felt like my jaw must be on the floor. What did that mean? Could Matt be right? Had Greg faked our chance meeting? If so, why?

THIRTY-FIVE

Jill tried to keep her tone chipper, but I could tell that she was distracted.

She kept looking over her shoulder.

I didn't bother to ask where Will had disappeared to. I had a pretty good idea, and I didn't want to make her feel worse.

"Fill us in on what you've learned about Ben's murder." Jill sipped her beer.

Ben's murder was the last thing on my mind. Between having to tell Jill that I'd seen Will with another woman and Matt putting doubt in my head about Greg, I'd forgotten all about the day's crazy turn of events.

I told them about Henry running off, Jackson chasing after him, finding the gun hidden in the snow cave, Malory showing up nearby and claiming that she'd been skiing. Pausing to catch my breath, I continued on with my suspicion that Lola had hidden the bullets in the flour drawer, and how she skied right into me and left with a cryptic comment how I needed to watch where I was going.

"Not a very eventful day, then?" Matt teased.

"When I repeat it all back, it does sound kind of overwhelming, doesn't it?"

Jill perked up a bit. "Okay, it's just like on *Masterpiece Mystery*. We have to figure out which clues are legit and which ones are red herrings."

"Yeah, good luck with that. I'm utterly confused." I leaned back in my chair.

"Let's start with Henry." Jill looked to Matt for support. "None of us think he could have done it, right?"

I shrugged. "I don't want to think he could have done it, but I have to admit I'm starting to have my doubts. I've seen another side of him the last couple days that I never knew existed. He's been really angry and bitter. Not at all like him."

Matt tugged off his sweatshirt. "Am I the only one sweating in here?" He stripped down to a charcoal-gray T-shirt with a bundle of bright green hops in the center. It read: GET HOPPY.

"I'm kind of warm, too." Jill fanned her face.

Matt stuck his sweatshirt on the empty chair. "Maybe Henry's worried about being a suspect. We should give him the benefit of the doubt. What would his motivation for murdering Ben be?"

"Money," I replied.

They exchanged a look.

"I'm serious. There's big money at stake. Ben wanted him to sign a non-compete and didn't want any of the team to do endorsements on the side. How much do you think a deal with Ten-Eighty would pull in?" I asked Matt.

He thought for a moment. "Fair enough. Endorsement money could be a chunk of cash." He held his beer to the light.

Jill laughed. "What are you doing?"

"See how clear this is? That's the goal. Unless you're brewing a stout you want to be able to see through your beer."

"I'm glad you approve." I smirked.

Jill tapped her index fingers on the table. "Now, can we focus? We have a murder to solve."

"I love you two." I held up my glass and clinked both of their pints. "Yes. We do have a murder to solve. Anyway, as much as I hate to say it, Henry did have a motive. With Ben out of the picture he was free to take the deal with Ten-Eighty. The other weird thing is that he and Jackson have been fighting. I overheard Henry say something about Ten-Eighty. Could Jackson be trying to land a deal with them too?"

"Are you writing this down?" Jill interrupted.

"No, but I can." I grabbed the Timberline notepad.

Jill motioned with her finger. "Ten-Eighty. How much cash?"

I noted Jill's suggestion. "I know, but Jackson's a doctor. Why would he need endorsement money?"

Matt set his pint glass on the table. "Maybe he's not making that much? Doctors have to pay a ton in malpractice insurance these days."

Jill shook her head. "He has family money."

I made a list of suspects on the notepad. "There's one thing I know. Lola told me last night that she saw Malory and Ben making out. If Jackson learned that Malory was cheating on him, that would be some serious motivation to murder Ben."

Jill's body tensed.

Stupid. Why don't I think before I talk?

"Then there's Clint," I said, resting my pencil on the table. "He's acting like nothing's changed. He implied that he has another funding source. With Ben out of the way, he has full control of the direction the Rangers take. But he has trouble just walking around. I don't know if he could have physically done it."

Matt refilled my pint.

"And Malory." I took the glass from him. "What was she

doing out in the woods? She said she was skiing, but where? Maybe she came back for the gun."

Matt considered this for a moment. "Yeah, I can see that. From what you've said, she sounds like a social climber. If Ben threatened to tell Jackson about their affair, that could have spurred her to murder him."

"They could have had a lovers' fight." Jill's fists clenched. "Maybe she got pissed at him and shot him."

I made a couple notes next to Malory's name. "Where'd she get the gun and why hide it in the middle of the woods?"

"Where were you exactly?" Matt asked.

"Out in the clearing. She showed up right after I found the gun. Kind of convenient, if you ask me."

Jill unclenched her fists. "Wait a minute. What clearing?"

"I don't know." I shrugged. "Maybe a few hundred feet from the Silcox Hut, but away from the ski runs—on the other side. She said she was *tree skiing*—is that even a thing?"

"It is." Jill made a clicking sound. "Too bad. She's a good suspect. Alas, people do it all the time. There are all kinds of trails that shoot off from the Silcox Hut. In fact, you can ski from Meadows to the summit."

"You can?"

"Yeah, I've done it many times."

"But she was wearing downhill skis."

Jill moved her head from side to side. "Probably back-country skis with skins."

Matt agreed. "She could have skied from Palmer."

I tapped my pencil on the table. "That leaves us with Jackson and Lola. Jackson said he's been to Vermont and they've been weird around each other. Malory told me to stay away from Lola. Do you think she could know something?"

"It almost sounds like Lola could have been trying to set Malory up." Jill paused as a group of men passed by the table.

She lowered her voice. "Think about it. Why would she tell you about seeing Ben and Malory together?"

"Because we bonded? Am I really that oblivious?" I halted. "Don't answer that." They both laughed. "No, really. I thought we were friends. You know, that she was confiding in me."

"Don't sweat it, Megs. She might have been." Matt tried to help.

"Or she played you." Jill grinned. "Either way, what's her motivation for killing Ben?"

"He kept hitting on her," I suggested.

"That's a stretch," Matt said.

"I agree." Jill frowned. "Don't get me wrong. I don't enjoy being hit on either, but to murder someone for that? Not likely."

"She did mention that he reminded her of her stepdad. It didn't sound like they had a very good relationship."

Matt shook his head. "That still isn't going to translate to murdering someone, though."

I sighed. "You're right. What about the bullets? Who else would have hidden them in the kitchen? She's the only one who spends time in there. If someone else hid them, they'd run the risk that Lola would find them. Plus, she told me to stay out and basically warned me to stop snooping."

"Maybe she has another reason that we don't know about?" Jill offered.

"This is hopeless." I rested my chin on my hands. "There's one other critical clue we're missing—who hit me at the pool?"

Jill patted my hand. "I forgot to ask you how your head is feeling. We got so wrapped up in the details."

"It's okay." I rubbed the lump. "A little tender. I wish I knew who did it. Jackson, Malory, and Clint were all here last night. It could have been any of them."

"Did you ask the sheriff to check with the lodge?" Jill asked. "They might have a security camera at the pool."

"I'll ask him. I need to go find him. I don't want anyone else to get the bullets or the gun before he does." I gripped my hands together, feeling the weight of the pressure to figure it all out and deliver a story to Greg by the end of the weekend.

Matt frowned. "You have to be careful. Remember your last experience with this? You almost ended up a corpse."

"He's right." Jill tapped her nails together.

"Wait a second." I twisted my mouth into a frown. I knew they were worried about me. I was worried, too, but I was all in at this point. "You two have been sitting here encouraging me to think through all the clues I've assembled so far and now you're telling me to stop? What gives?"

Jill refilled Matt's beer. "No, we're not saying that you have to stop, but you do have to be careful, Meg. I didn't know you'd hidden evidence. That's not a good idea."

"What else was I supposed to do? I couldn't leave it there and let the killer destroy it permanently." My tone sounded slightly pitchy. I knew I was defensive, but I couldn't help it. I could already hear Sheriff Daniels scolding me in my head.

Matt took a swig of beer. "Make sure the sheriff gets that tonight, okay?"

Jill checked her copper watch. It sparkled in the candlelight. "Did you know it's almost ten? When's the snowcat's last run? I think they shut down the lift soon."

"Is it really?" I jumped to my feet and shoved the notepad into my coat pocket. "I need to run. I don't want to miss my ride or Sheriff Daniels."

"Megs—wait!" Matt called after me.

I froze. "What? I really have to go."

"Do you want me to come with you? What if they've already shut everything down for the night?"

"I'll be fine." I plastered on a bright smile, wishing I fully believed that was true. "I'll see you tomorrow, okay?"

"He's right, Meg. Come back if they've closed the lift. You

can always crash with me," Jill hollered as I raced down the stairs.

"Has the snowcat left yet?" I asked the desk clerk between breaths.

She motioned to the clock above her desk. "Last run was twenty minutes ago."

"What about the lifts? Are they still running?"

"For five minutes. If you want to make it, you're going to have to hustle."

I thanked her and flew out the door. I didn't have time to think about the fact that the Magic Mile lift was thirty feet in the air and I'd be riding it in the pitch blackness of night.

"Runs are closed," a kid in a Timberline jacket and knit cap said as I approached the chairlift.

"I'm staying up at the Silcox Hut and missed my ride. Is it too late to take it up?"

He studied me for a moment. "Gonna be a cold and lonely ride."

Maybe I should have stayed, but I had to get back to the Silcox Hut and talk to Sheriff Daniels. And despite the fact that I didn't want to ride the lift, I really wanted to make sure the bullets were still safe in my shoes. Not to mention this was my last night with the Ridge Rangers. If I didn't show up for their final meeting, Greg would fire me for sure.

"No problem," I lied.

"All righty. Hop on, then. I'll radio up and let them know we have one last rider. Tell the guy at the top so he knows you're it. Cool?"

"Cool." I swallowed as he motioned for me to stand on the marked platform and wait for a chair to swing around and scoop me up.

My knees shook as the base of the chair made contact, forcing me backward. I fell into the chair. My feet dangled below me.

I closed my eyes and tried channeling Gam's calming energy. A wave of dizziness came over me. Okay, eyes open. Closed was a bad idea.

I clutched the bar that ran through the middle of the chair and attached to the cable above me. *Hold on tight, Meg. You're going for a ride.*

THIRTY-SIX

If I could stomach heights, it would have been a beautiful ride. Moonlight reflected on the brilliant snow. A wisp of clouds hung low on the horizon. Stars flashed in the distance. My heart felt as if it were trying to beat free from my chest.

Relax, Maggie. Breathe, sweet one. I could hear Pops's voice in my head as I tried to concentrate on keeping my legs as still as possible.

The rickety chair swung and creaked as I started to ascend the slope.

The ground was getting farther and farther away.

Don't look down.

How was it that I always ended up in precarious positions like this? Gam would probably have told me that I attracted situations that pushed me past my limits and helped me expand into a deeper sense of myself.

Uh. No. At that moment, I preferred to have my feet firmly planted on the ground.

A small gust of wind sent the chair rocking from side to side. I tightened my grasp on the bar. How long was this ride? Five minutes? Ten? Why hadn't I asked before I got on?

The cool wind on my face made my cheeks tingle. Every sound made my heart pound faster. The forest below my feet was eerily quiet and deserted, unlike earlier in the day when the busy run had been full of noise, laughter, and flashes of color as skiers flew by. Everyone had returned to the lodge or cozy cabins farther down the mountain. I imagined the skiers gathered in front of crackling fires, swapping stories of their time on the slopes. Meanwhile, I was riding an empty chairlift suspended 1,000 vertical feet in the air. Alone, in the dark.

Not my wisest choice.

It didn't help that the chairlift creaked and groaned, convincing me it could snap and fall from the sky at any moment. I gripped the bar tighter as the metal chair rail grated along the cable. How sturdy were these things, anyway?

Even through my thick gloves, I could feel my fingers beginning to go numb. I wasn't sure if it was from my death grip on the bar, or exposure to the bitter nighttime air.

Could this thing go any faster? It felt like each inch forward on the thin cable took hours. What was I thinking? Why hadn't I just stayed with Jill? Every time I felt like I was starting to mature and follow Gam's advice of listening to my inner guidance, I did something like this to set me back.

A bright light twinkled on the black horizon. Was that the Northern Star?

Maybe it had appeared to help guide me forward.

Maybe not. At that moment, the chairlift screeched to a halt. I was pretty sure I screeched, too. The chair lunged in response. I couldn't clutch the bar any tighter. What was happening?

I took a quick peek below me. *Ah! I must be forty feet in the air.* I mean, dangling in the air.

Please help, I prayed internally. I forced air through my nose, trying to use any of Gam's relaxation techniques without letting go of the bar. They weren't working.

Why wasn't the lift moving? What was taking so long?

I rolled my shoulders forward slightly and quickly checked my surroundings. No one was in sight. All the chairs in front of me sat completely empty, reminding me how stupid I was to take this ride. It took every ounce of courage I could find to rigidly turn my shoulders to see if anyone was behind me by chance.

The empty lift to the south looked even creepier in the moonlight. The chairs behind me swung from side to side in the gusting wind, mocking me. Had the lift broken down? Or what if the kid manning the Silcox station hadn't received the radio call? What if they thought the lift was empty and had closed it down for the night?

Oh, my God. I could die up here. A wave of involuntary shivers erupted from inside my parka. How long could I survive the elements out here? I frantically tried to remember what I'd learned in my training. A few hours? There was no way to stay warm on a chairlift forty feet above the tree line. What was I going to do?

I was on the brink of having a full-blown panic attack. I could feel it in my muscles as they twitched in response to each thought my brain triggered.

Relax, Maggie. There was Pops's voice again. *It's probably a glitch. Sit tight. It'll be all right.*

It'll be all right. It'll be all right. Like a crazed person, I kept repeating the mantra. Maybe if I repeated it with fervor, I could will it to be true.

My body temperature was starting to plummet. Shivers came in steady rhythm—one right after the other. My nose dripped, but I didn't dare loosen my grasp on the bar to wipe it. I'd probably develop an ice mustache above my upper lip in a few minutes.

Besides the sound of an occasional gust of wind and the bar

swinging on the cable, the mountain was devoid of sound. Gam's wise words came rushing to mind.

"The route to inner peace, Margaret, is as simple as quieting the noise in your head."

Nothing about the silent forest felt calming. I wondered if I should scream.

Who would hear you, Meg?

Was it a bad sign that I was talking to myself? Probably. But if I couldn't connect to my inner calm, then I'd have to settle for connecting to my inner journalist. *Think, Meg. Think.*

Okay. I took a deep, open-mouthed gasp of air. I could do that.

My rational brain ran through the situation. Like thought bubbles in comic strips, I could see each option pop up in my head.

My phone! I kept one hand clutched to the bar and pried the other free. Reaching into my pocket, I tried to move as slowly as possible. I pulled my phone from my pocket and clicked it on.

No service. Not a single bar. Next plan.

If the lift was broken, someone would have to come by to help. The kid at the bottom knew I was up here. He'd send someone up. Right? So that meant my first option was to do nothing. Well, maybe not nothing. I could keep focusing on staying calm and staying put with the knowledge that help was on the way.

As much as I liked that scenario, I knew there was another, which unfortunately was equally as likely. Let's say the radio communication hadn't gone through and that the lift operator thought the chairs were empty and had shut it down for the night. Even as that thought passed through my brain, I could feel energy surge.

Chill, Meg.

The lift operator still had to get down the mountain, right? That meant he or she would likely be skiing right underneath me soon. I just had to keep my eyes down—ahhhh—and as soon as they skied past me, I'd yell like crazy.

Okay, you do that, Meg.

I wiggled my toes. They felt like they were starting to swell. Bad idea. The slight motion sent my chair swinging again.

My brain refused to exit out of survival mode. A new thought bubble popped into the forefront. What if I'd missed the ski lift operator? How long had I been suspended in midair? Two, five, maybe ten minutes? I wasn't a good judge of time under normal circumstances. But under stress, forget about it. My watch might offer a clue. However, that meant removing an arm from the chair rail and there was *no* way I was about to do that.

What were my options, if the operator had already skied past me? Well, the obvious answer was to wait it out until morning. Was that really an option, though? No. I wouldn't survive the night in a parka, snow pants, and gloves. If the wind picked up or it started to snow, I'd be a goner.

You could jump.

I wanted to smack myself. What was my brain even thinking? Jump? Uh, no.

Think it through, Maggie. Consider all possibilities. Pops's voice sounded commanding in my head.

I wanted to fight back and yell at him to stop cramming my brain with insane ideas. I knew it was futile. I'd be fighting with myself. Plus, this *was* me trying to survive. Maybe I did have some more guts than I gave myself credit for.

Keeping my hands wrapped around the pole, I craned my neck forward.

Quickly I pushed it back. Taking a few short breaths, I tried again.

Beneath me lay a blanket of snow as far as I could see. The ridgeline to my right was heavily forested with frosted evergreen trees. Farther to the left was the groomed ski run. If I dropped straight down, I was pretty sure I'd only hit snow.

I gulped. *What are you thinking, Meg?* I gauged the distance from the chair to the ground below. Maybe I'd exaggerated. It could be closer to a thirty-foot drop. Who was I trying to fool? I couldn't tell, especially in the dark. Thirty feet or forty feet—it didn't matter. It was a long way down.

Could I survive that fall? And if I did, could I survive it without injury? If I fell and broke my leg, that wasn't going to put me in a better spot than dangling from the chair.

Gam always told me to focus my intention on the positive—that what we put out was what we got back. Of course she sounded more eloquent than me.

"Margaret, if you want more love, joy, and peace in your life, focus on thoughts that are aligned with those qualities. Life reflects back to us what we focus our energy on the most."

Reflecting positivity four stories above the ground was proving to be a difficult task. I scanned the trail for any signs of the lift operator. No one was in sight. How long would it take them to shut down the upper lift? Not this long. I must have missed them.

I wondered how long I should wait to see if the lift started moving again. It felt like hours had gone by, but I chalked that up to stress. It was more likely that only minutes had passed.

What I did know for sure was that I was cold. Really cold. My body trembled. Circulation to my legs had been cut off. Blood must have been pooling in my toes. The snot above my lip had frosted over and my cheeks burned with cold.

I was going to have to make a decision soon.

Out of the corner of my eye, I saw a flash of movement below.

Thank God. It must be the lift operator. I hadn't missed them after all.

"Help!" I yelled. "Up here!"

The skier shifted direction, dug their skis in the snow, and came to an abrupt stop.

"Help! I'm stuck!" The chair swung with my cries.

The skier, dressed in all black from helmet to ski boots, turned in the direction of my voice.

I pried one hand from the pole and waved. "Help! Please!" They waved in response and skied in my direction.

Thank God.

Relief flooded my body with warmth. Okay, so maybe I should practice Gam's suggestion of focusing on the positive. Miracles did happen.

It took a minute for the skier to ski from the groomed run to the area underneath the lift. The snow was too thick to ski through. He stopped to remove his skis.

"I'm so glad you're here!" I yelled. "I thought you'd forgotten me."

The skier took his skis and staked them in the snow. Then he removed a pack and placed it on the ground.

I wasn't sure if my eyes were having trouble seeing in the dark, but the pack looked like one of the Ridge Rangers' emergency survival kits. Why would a chairlift operator have one of their packs?

I didn't have to wait long for the answer. The skier beneath me removed his black helmet and tossed it on the snow.

"Clint! What are you doing here?" I couldn't contain my surprise and joy.

Thank goodness. Clint would know what to do. I was saved for sure.

He didn't return my smile. "Following you."

"What?" I clutched the chair with both hands.

For a minute I thought I must have been hallucinating or losing my vision. Clint ignored my question, bent over, and removed something from the pack.

I squinted down and with a jolt of horror realized he was aiming Henry's hunting rifle directly at me.

THIRTY-SEVEN

"Clint?" I gripped the chair tighter and scooted backward, as if that would help. "What are you doing?"

"Cut the crap." He aimed the rifle at me.

"I don't understand—you? *You* killed Ben?"

He waved the rifle. "Catch on quick, don't you?"

"Why?"

"Look, missy, I don't have time to chat. You're going to take a nasty little fall. Another casualty of the mountain. Shame, isn't it?"

"Clint, please. Really, I don't understand. I didn't even think it was you." They said in times of stress that your senses sharpened. Mine didn't. My head was being bombarded by questions, but I knew from my experience last spring that I had to keep him talking. Sheriff Daniels commended me on doing just that when I'd been cornered by a murderer on a bridge. Here I was again. *Seriously, Meg.*

Clint didn't strike me as the talking type. More like the shoot-now, ask-questions-later type. But I had to try.

"Wait, Clint. Why me?"

He stepped closer. Even in the moonlight I could see that

he wasn't limping. Hey, wait. He'd skied perfectly down the mountain.

"Nothing personal, kid. I kind of like your tenacity, but I can't risk you going to the sheriff. My plan has been executed perfectly. Now I clean up this one little loose end and ski off into the sunset, as they say."

"I'm not going to the sheriff. I didn't even think it was you. I thought Lola killed Ben."

"Lola? That little skinny stick? Ha! She couldn't even hold this." He positioned the rifle on his shoulder.

"Why? If you didn't like Ben, why'd you agree to work for him?" I had to shout over the wind.

"Ben Tyler was a pompous, entitled showboat."

I understood how much Clint cared about the Ridge Rangers and maintaining a high level of professionalism, but I still couldn't understand why he killed Ben.

Clint answered my thoughts before I could form them into a question. "Ben never worked a day in his life." I could hear the disgust in his voice. "I've worked my fingers to the bone, literally to the bone, from the time I was twelve years old. Everything I have in this life I've worked my butt off for. Ben was going to ruin that. I couldn't let him."

As he spoke, his shoulders slumped a little. *Keep him talking, Meg.*

"What was Ben going to ruin?"

Clint looked up at me. "What's that?"

"Ben. What was he going to ruin? The Ridge Rangers?"

"Stop talking!" Clint barked as he straightened his shoulders. "I know what you're doing. I wasn't born yesterday. Here's how this is going to go down. You have two choices. We can do this the easy way or the hard way."

He planted his feet in a solid stance and pushed out his chest. "The easy way is you go ahead and take a little tumble from the lift; that'll save me a bullet."

Blood rushed in my head. I could hear my heartbeat pound in my ears. "What's the hard way?"

"Take a guess." Clint waved the gun in the air. "Either way you're not going to make it back to the Silcox Hut tonight. I've made sure of that. The lift is shut down. When they find your body tomorrow—*if* they find your body tomorrow—it'll be a tragic accident. Happens more than you think, actually. Did you hear about that kid in Colorado who was horsing around, throwing a snowball at his buddy, and fell to his death?" Clint made a tsking sound.

I quickly weighed my options. What had Henry said about the hunting rifle? It wasn't great at long range. Clint was thirty to forty feet below. How good of a shot would he be from that distance and aiming upward? This was the one moment in my life that I wished I knew more about guns.

Clint was a decorated war veteran. He probably knew his way around a rifle. He'd killed Ben outside in a blizzard, after all.

My only other choice was to jump. Was there a way to choose neither?

Okay, Meg, think.

I closed my eyes and visualized how I might fall. Roll in a ball, like doing a flip turn in the pool. The snow was soft. There was plenty of it. As long as I avoided the trees and any rocks, I had a chance, right?

Except assuming that I survived the fall, all that Clint would have to do was walk over and shoot me at close range. That was no good.

Taking slow, forceful breaths, I kept my eyes closed and tried to focus on centering. There had to be another solution. I felt like I knew what it was but couldn't access it.

"What are you doing up there?" Clint shouted.

I didn't answer.

"Stop messing around. Either jump or I'm going to shoot."

The word "shoot" exploded in my head. *That's it, Meg!*

"There's one major problem with your plan, Clint. If you shoot me, it's not going to be a 'tragic accident,' as you put it. I think the sheriff will be able to tell the difference between a gunshot and an accident."

Clint flinched. Had he not thought this through? Maybe this was my opportunity. Or maybe he was completely insane.

"That's why you're going to jump." He motioned with the rifle. Was he bluffing?

He wasn't going to shoot me. What had he said about being a poker player? He was trying to scare me into jumping.

"I'm not going to jump, Clint. If you want me to come down, you're going to have to shoot me." My voice sounded much more confident than I felt.

"Nice try." He let out a shot in the air. The sound echoed on the empty slope.

I screamed and nearly fell from the chair. It rocked wildly from side to side. Maybe he wasn't bluffing after all.

"Take your pick. You can jump, I can shoot you, or I can also leave you here to freeze overnight."

Crap. I'd forgotten about how cold I was until this moment. In response, my body shuddered.

I tried one last attempt to keep him talking. "Hey, how are you going to ski out of here? I thought you injured your knee."

Clint patted his knee with the barrel of the gun. "This old thing? It's a bit creaky every now and then, but I've still got it. That's what Ben thought, too. Got him killed, actually. Kind of like you. You should have left well enough alone. I wouldn't have to do this if you weren't such a snoop."

"That's what I don't understand. I didn't find anything that incriminated you. Why come after me?"

"You found this!" Clint patted the gun. "I saw you in the clearing. Went back there to get this, and lo and behold, who's snooping around but the little reporter? I heard your dad got himself killed for snooping, too. Must run in the family."

How did Clint know that? My pulse was fast and my feet were most likely frostbitten. I had to make a decision soon.

"Enough stalling. Time to jump," Clint ordered.

My head might have been playing tricks on me, but I thought I heard a rumbling sound in the distance. Could the lift be chugging back to life? Up ahead it looked like the chairs came closer to the ground. I'd have a better chance of survival if I didn't have as far to fall.

"I said, 'jump'!" Clint shot again. This time he didn't shoot straight up.

He aimed in my direction.

It all happened so fast. I could hear the bullet whiz by and the awful shattering sound of it ricocheting off a tree.

I ducked in response, but the motion was enough to make me loosen my grip on the chair and fall forward.

Before I had time to react, I was plummeting toward the ground.

THIRTY-EIGHT

I didn't think I'd ever had an out-of-body experience until now. Everything in front of me appeared in shades of white or black, like I was being pulled into the light or darkness and had seconds to choose.

Curl in a ball, Maggie. Now! Pops's voice commanded in my head as my body hurled toward the ground, faster and faster.

It's too fast. I can't do it. This is it. This is the end.

No, Maggie. Curl up. NOW!

My arms flailed. I kicked my legs like I was swimming through the air.

This was bad, really bad.

ROLL! Pops sounded like he was right here next to me.

I tucked my head and tried to pull my knees into my chest. The white ground before me looked like it was rising up to catch me. I braced myself for the impact, trying to keep my body as tight as I could.

The next thing I knew, I hit the ground with a thud. Snow exploded in the air like fireworks as I slammed down. Instantaneously, pain shot up my left arm. The ground wasn't so soft after all.

I froze. Was I alive? Had I blacked out? I didn't think so. It just all happened so fast.

Buried in a blanket of snow, I wasn't sure what to do next. Should I try to move?

I'd landed on my left side, not in a nice, tight ball as I planned. Somehow I'd avoided a giant rock protruding from the snow a few feet away. I brushed snow from my face and tried to wiggle my toes. They responded. That was a good sign.

Next, I gently swiveled my neck from side to side. It moved too. Another good sign.

However, pain seared from my left shoulder down to my fingertips. I tried moving my arm slightly. It felt like someone was jabbing a hot needle through it.

I winced in pain. It had to be broken. My fingers felt like they were going to swell through my glove.

Where was Clint? How much time had passed? A minute? Seconds? I had to get out of here—now.

I pulled my left elbow in as close to my ribs as I could. The pain was almost more than I could bear. I thought I might throw up.

With my injured arm glued to my chest, I rolled onto my other side. My shoulder made a popping sound unlike anything I'd ever heard.

Oh, God, Meg, don't pass out. Concentrate.

I swallowed back vomit and pushed onto my knees. Keeping my left arm immobile wasn't working. The pain came in waves —pulsing through my arm and rippling through my entire body.

The rumbling sound that I heard before I jumped was getting closer. Unless I was going to faint, I thought I caught a glimpse of lights flashing in the sky. Was the snowcat coming?

You have to get out of here now, Meg.

I rocked from my knees to standing, trying to ignore the intense pain in my arm. The stars spun above me as I made it to my feet. My eyes must have been playing tricks on me. I was going to pass out.

Another deafening bang shook the ground and threw me forward into the snow.

Without even thinking I stuck both hands out. Big mistake. If my left arm wasn't broken before, it definitely was now.

I pushed up on my right arm and wrapped my left arm close to my body. A whooshing sound muddled my hearing. My ears rang. The shot must have been close.

Where was Clint? I was disoriented from the pain and the weird sound of blood rushing in my head.

Something flashed in my peripheral vision. Clint. He was running away from me. Why?

I tried to stand. My knees buckled. The pain in my arm forced me back to the ground. I watched as Clint raced toward his skis. His silhouette was illuminated by a moving ball of light. Was I losing it?

No! The snowcat came into view as Clint snapped his boots into the bindings and glided off into the darkness. He was getting away. I had to get to the cat.

Taking a deep breath, I summoned all my strength. *Just do it, Meg. It's going to hurt, but it'll be like ripping off a Band-Aid. Do it and do it quick.*

I dug my left arm into my side and used every muscle in my short legs to stand. It worked, but the snowcat was chugging up the slope. I had to hurry.

Limping through the snow, I waved my right arm frantically in the air and called out, "Help! Help!"

It was no use. The operator couldn't hear me.

The cat continued upward, leaving me abandoned on the trail. Now what?

I had two choices. I could follow the trail back down to the lodge or continue up to the Silcox Hut. I tried to gauge the distance. Unfortunately I was smack in the middle. My natural inclination would be to take the easy route—down. That was the direction Clint headed. So up was my only option.

There was a strong possibility that Clint had disappeared from the main run long enough to avoid being seen by the cat, but as soon as it was out of sight, he'd come back after me. For all I knew, he'd skied to the opposite side and was waiting with his gun ready to take me out.

I decided to stay hidden in the tree line. As long as I kept the chairlift in my line of sight I could follow that all the way up to the hut.

The going was slow. My arm throbbed. The 1,000-foot vertical slope would have been a challenge to navigate without a broken arm, hypothermic body, and the threat of a madman nearby. There was a reason people skied *down* the slope. Not climbed up it.

Any slight sound made me skittish. The snowcat finally disappeared, leaving me in complete darkness. My only light was the moon, which kept fading in and out as clouds passed in front of it.

Each step forward felt like a small victory. My breath came in quick, short bursts, like trying to breathe underwater. At least expending this kind of energy was warming me up.

My thoughts returned to Clint. What did he mean about Ben ruining everything he had worked for? The Ridge Rangers? That didn't make sense. There had to be more to the story. Unless he'd completely lost it.

I counted the chairlift poles as I trudged up the mountain, telling myself I could rest every ten. When I stopped to catch my breath and reposition my arm, I checked behind me to make sure Clint wasn't following. I'd been wrong before—obviously. I figured he could have easily caught up to me. He was probably halfway down the mountain.

Ten more, Meg. Just do ten more.

I had to be getting close, right?

After another fifty chairs, the Silcox Hut came into view. I was almost there. *You can do this, Meg. Forge ahead.*

I made it to the Silcox Hut, out of breath and soaked with sweat. Did you sweat more when you were in pain? It felt like it. My hat was drenched and sweat fell from my face like tears.

Ten more steps.

I pushed through the door.

"Help!" I yelled as I stepped inside. Then everything went dark as I collapsed on the floor.

THIRTY-NINE

"Ms. Reed, Ms. Reed, are you with me?" Sheriff Daniels patted my cheek.

I blinked open my eyes and tried to sit up, momentarily forgetting about my arm. The pain felt like an assault. I started to fall backward. Sheriff Daniels caught me.

"Easy, easy." He cradled my head in his hands. "Stay right here with me. I've got help on the way."

"What happened?"

"You passed out."

"Clint!" I sat up a little.

"Careful, Ms. Reed." Sheriff Daniels shifted his hands to support my neck. "Why don't you lie back down? I want Dr. Hughes to take a look at you before you move."

"I'm okay." I brushed him off and sat all the way up. Another wave of pain came over me.

"You look pretty green."

"It's my arm." I grimaced, cradling my arm to my side. "I think it's broken."

"All the more reason not to move." Sheriff Daniels motioned Jackson over. "Here's the doctor now."

Jackson dropped to his knees next to me and removed a blood pressure cuff from his emergency bag.

He started to move my left arm in order to place the cuff on it. I yelped.

"Sorry." Jackson looked surprised. "Did that hurt?"

"Mm-hmm." I whimpered. "I think it's broken."

"Let's take a look, okay?" Jackson's demeanor lost all its pompousness. "Sheriff, will you hold her right hand?"

Sheriff Daniels nodded. He kept one arm behind me to support my back and wrapped the other over my hand.

"I've got to get your glove off. It might hurt. I want you to squeeze the sheriff's hand, okay?"

"Okay." I took a big breath.

"That's it. Relax. Keep breathing. I'm going to be as careful as I can. Are you ready?"

I nodded.

Jackson tugged the glove.

"Ouch." I winced.

"Squeeze my hand, Ms. Reed." Sheriff Daniels clasped my hand tighter. I squeezed back and held my breath.

Jackson tried again. The glove wouldn't budge.

"It's no use. Too swollen." He placed my arm on my leg and searched through his bag. "I'm going to have to cut the glove off."

Jackson pulled a pair of industrial scissors from his bag. "Actually, this will be better. I'll be able to keep your arm stable. Hold it tight on your lap there, okay?"

I closed my eyes as Jackson moved my hand slightly to slice into the glove.

"All done. That wasn't too bad, was it?"

I opened one eye. "Yikes."

"That's what I'd say about your hand." Jackson moved his eyes down toward my arm.

I opened both eyes and followed his gaze. My hand looked

like something from Willy Wonka. It reminded me of Violet Beauregarde, the competitive gum-chewer who expands into a giant human-sized blueberry after snatching a piece of Wonka's newest gum.

"Is it broken?"

Jackson laughed. "Uh, yeah. It's broken. I'll splint it now, but we are going to have to get you down to get an X-ray. It's a bad break and you could have multiple fractures. What did you do? Decide to jump off the top of Magic Mile or something?"

"How did you know?"

Jackson looked from me to Sheriff Daniels. "What? I was kidding."

"I had to. Clint was after me."

"Clint?" Jackson placed my destroyed glove on the floor and searched his bag for more supplies. "Sheriff, can you help me get her coat off? I can't splint her arm over that."

Sheriff Daniels carefully freed my right arm from my parka.

"Hold as still as you can. I'm going to do this quick." Jackson stretched my arm away from my body at an angle. "Okay, ready?"

I gulped. "I guess."

Jackson slowly tugged my jacket off my arm. Sheriff Daniels grabbed my right hand again. "Give me a good squeeze, Ms. Reed."

I turned to Sheriff Daniels. "Thanks." Maybe if I focused my attention on something else, it wouldn't hurt as much. "Clint's the murderer. He stopped the lift and stranded me up there. He came after me with a gun. Tried to shoot me down."

Sheriff Daniels squeezed my arm. "Easy there, Ms. Reed. Why don't you let the doctor finish splinting your arm and then you can fill me in."

"But... but... he's out there. He's getting away. Who knows how far he's gone by now?"

"Did you bump your head out there?" Jackson finally freed my arm from my coat. So much for doing it quickly.

He positioned my arm across my waist and wrapped an ACE bandage from my shoulder to my wrist. "This is going to be a bit loose, but I want to make sure there's a little room for the swelling. You're probably going to keep swelling for the next twenty-four hours or so. Even if we had an X-ray up here, I wouldn't cast you for a day or two until the swelling goes down."

"I didn't hit my head. It was Clint." The sling made the entire left side of my body immobile.

Jackson filled a syringe. "I'm going to give you a shot for the pain. Are you okay with shots?"

"If it takes away the pain, then yes, I'm totally cool with that."

He came around to my other side. Sheriff Daniels let go of my hand and moved so that Jackson could take his spot.

Jackson pushed up my sleeve and stuck the needle in my arm. "This should work pretty fast. You might feel a little light-headed or dizzy. I'm going to give you an anti-inflammatory to help with the swelling, too."

As soon as the needle pierced my skin I could feel the cold medicine running through my veins.

"Let me know when that starts to work. I can give you more in"—he paused and checked his watch—"another six hours."

Sheriff Daniels extended his hand. "Let me help you up, Ms. Reed."

He lifted me with ease. Jackson put a plastic cap over the needle and handed me ibuprofen from his bag. "Take these with some water."

"I'll see to it that she takes them." Sheriff Daniels grabbed the medicine from Jackson's hand and guided me toward the dining hall. "Why don't you come with me and get warm?"

"Thanks for your help, Jackson," I said. "My arm already feels better in the sling."

"No problem. It's what I do."

"You're really good."

He smiled. "Thanks. This is what I love."

Sheriff Daniels ushered me to a bench in front of the fireplace. The dining hall was quiet. A couple of Rangers played cards and another read a book. Everyone looked up when Sheriff Daniels led me past them.

He placed me on the bench. "You wait here. I'll get you a glass of water. Then we'll talk."

I agreed. The less I had to move, the better. I wondered if I'd be able to sleep tonight. Hopefully Jackson's painkiller would take effect soon. So far I didn't feel anything.

Sheriff Daniels handed me a glass of water.

Working with one hand was going to be difficult. I placed the water on the table, grabbed the medicine, popped it in my mouth, and then grabbed the water to wash it down.

He studied me for a minute. "All right, Ms. Reed. You feel up to talking now?"

My mind returned to Clint. How much time had passed? He could be back in Portland and headed to the airport by now, for all I knew.

I nodded. "Yeah, it's Clint. He's the killer. You have to go after him or call for help. Whatever it is you do."

Sheriff Daniels held up a hand. "It's under control, Ms. Reed. Why don't you start from the beginning and fill me in on your statement?"

"He's getting away. Right now."

"I can assure you, Ms. Reed, he's not."

FORTY

"I don't understand. I saw him ski down the mountain."

Sheriff Daniels removed a toothpick canister from his breast pocket. He untwisted the cap and took out a wooden toothpick. "Want one?" He offered the canister to me.

I declined. This was one of the things about the sheriff that drove me crazy. Whenever he knew something, it was like he took great pleasure in withholding that information from me, stretching it out and waiting as long as he possibly could before speaking.

He chewed the toothpick.

"Are you going to tell me how you know he's not getting away? Why aren't you going after him?"

"Because I already have the killer in custody, Ms. Reed." He chomped on the toothpick and winked.

"What? How?"

"You seem to forget sometimes that I've done this more than once or twice." He frowned.

"I don't. I mean—"

His face was solemn. "I am a sheriff. I do know my way around a murder investigation."

"Sheriff, please, you're killing me. What happened to Clint?"

"Killing you. Good one, Ms. Reed." He chuckled. "Has anyone ever told you how much you look like your grandmother, especially when you crinkle your nose like that?"

Now I could tell that he was intentionally playing with me.

"Sorry, I shouldn't tease." He twisted the toothpick. "Clint Shumway was apprehended at Timberline Lodge. My deputy is transporting him to Sandy as we speak to book him for the murder of Ben Tyler."

Sandy sat at the base of the mountain and was the closest town with a police station.

"But how did you know it was Clint?"

"Call it a hunch." He sounded like Gam. Maybe she was rubbing off on him.

Sheriff Daniels looked thoughtful, before a thin smile spread across his lips. "I can see that I've thrown you, Ms. Reed. Not to worry. I haven't adopted your grandmother's abilities. Forty years in the field has taught me a thing or two. When someone is overly eager to help, it's a red flag for me. As soon as we were able to establish an Internet connection again, I had my deputy run checks on all the suspects. It turns out Clint had an outstanding warrant."

"He did?"

"He's wanted on multiple accounts of fraud and attempted murder." He cleared his throat. "I hate to admit it, but we have you to thank in part. If you hadn't lured him to the ski slope, he might be halfway to the border by now."

"What, really?" I couldn't believe I'd actually helped the case. "But he's a major commentator. He's well-known in the skiing world. How could he have a warrant out for his arrest?"

"Conundrum, isn't it?"

The pain medication was kicking in. My head felt heavy. I struggled to hold it up.

"Ms. Reed, are you okay? Maybe we should continue this in the morning. You need to sleep."

"No, no. I'm fine. Please, continue. I won't be able to sleep until I know exactly what happened."

Sheriff Daniels looked doubtful. "If you're sure?"

"I'm sure." I tried to nod, but my head flopped. "Go on."

He removed the toothpick from his mouth and flipped it in his hand. "Clint was on borrowed time and he knew it. His past was about to catch up with him and he was ready to bolt. That is until you came in."

Until I came in... I hadn't expected that my run-in with Clint on the ski lift had played even the slightest role in his arrest. I felt a bit lighter, like a weight had been lifted from my shoulders. "He mentioned he saw me in the clearing. He must have known I found the gun. Do you think that's why he was trying to make a break?"

"Seems that way." He tipped his head in acknowledgment. "Hopefully my deputy will be able to get that information and more out of him. What we know in the short term is that Ben Tyler learned about Clint's past and threatened to go public with it. Clint snapped. Made a rash decision. Ben should have come to us instead of confronting Clint. That mistake got him killed."

The medication had definitely taken effect. It sounded like the sheriff was speaking underwater. I wiggled my toes under the table, trying to keep focused. "What did Ben learn?"

"Clint isn't who he says he is. He's not a decorated war veteran. In fact, he had a nervous breakdown after one tour in Vietnam and was dishonorably discharged from the military."

"How did he end up as a national broadcaster for winter sports, then?" I stifled a yawn, forcing my eyes to remain open as I took everything in.

"He created a new identity, became a real-life war hero—reinvented himself."

I stretched, slowly moving my head from one side to the other, considering this. "Wouldn't the media have figured that out? Wouldn't they have looked into his records before they hired him?"

Sheriff Daniels shrugged. "Define 'looked into his records.' They didn't have any reason not to trust him. It would have been easy enough to provide a fake résumé and have a couple of buddies act as references. You of all people should know how much the media love a good story. Clint's story was too good to pass up. War veteran and world-class skier. They ate it up."

"What does this all have to do with Ben?"

"Ben did his due diligence, learned the truth about Clint when he hired him." He shook his head.

"So Clint killed Ben to keep him silent?" Everything felt like it was finally snapping into place like the pieces of puzzle. I wished I had seen it sooner, but I was relieved to know the truth and felt a tiny glimmer of pride that I'd played a small role in bringing Clint to justice.

"In part. He was in financial trouble, too. It appears he'd been trying to secure funding for his own guiding team before Ben came along." He paused. "Ms. Reed, it looks like your head is about in your lap. I think it's time for bed."

His tone reminded me of Pops. When I was a kid, I used to stay up late reading with a flashlight under the covers. Pops would catch me. "Maggie, it's almost midnight. You have school in the morning."

"Just one more page, Pops?"

He'd duck into my room, kiss me on the forehead, and whisper, "One more page, dear one."

Sheriff Daniels eyed me with concern. "I'll bring your grandmother up first thing in the morning and then we'll drive you to Sandy."

As much as I wanted to protest, I didn't have the strength. It was a struggle to keep my eyelids open. Whatever Jackson gave me was pulling me under.

"Let me help you to your room." Sheriff Daniels lifted me from the bench and wrapped his sturdy arm around my shoulder.

Maybe it was the pain or my subsiding anxiety and relief that I'd escaped Clint, but my eyes welled with tears. The sheriff was being so sweet and kind to me. So much like Pops.

"Am I hurting you, Ms. Reed?"

"No, not at all." I brushed a tear from my eye.

He helped me into the bunk room. "You be sure to check in with Dr. Hughes when this wears off."

I smiled and leaned my head into his chest for a moment. He smelled of aftershave. Not at all like Pops. "Gam's lucky to have you."

"Thank you. I'm lucky to have her." His gruff voice caught for a moment. "Now get some rest. That's an order." Then he nudged me toward my bunk and disappeared from the room.

Even with the numbing medication pulsing through my veins, finding a comfortable position to sleep was challenging. I tried lying flat on my back. That didn't work, so I flipped onto my stomach and finally landed on my right side.

Visions of the chairlift and Clint aiming the gun at my head flashed as I tried to fall asleep. Jackson tiptoed in to check on me. He thought I needed more pain medication, but really my restlessness had more to do with all the questions that needed answering.

FORTY-ONE

When I woke the next morning, I felt like I'd hit the ground from four stories up. Oh, wait, I had. I'd slept through the night, which was good, but that meant the pain medication Jackson gave me had worn off hours ago. My arm throbbed. My head felt like it was a tangle of cobwebs. My mouth felt dry, and I felt nauseated. Yep, I was in great shape.

I took my time getting out of bed, moving with intention, trying not to bump my arm on any part of the bunk. There was no point in changing clothes. I'd slept in them last night and until I saw the real doctor I didn't want to disturb Jackson's sling.

Passing in front of the mirror on my way to breakfast confirmed that while I might have narrowly escaped death last night, my body hadn't. The color in my cheeks matched the snow outside. Puffy, purple circles surrounded my eyes. Ugh. No amount of lip gloss or pinching of the cheeks could hide the beating my body had taken.

The short distance from the bunk rooms to the dining hall felt almost insurmountable. Not only was my arm on fire, but my legs ached from the climb last night.

I shuffled into the rustic room where everyone was lounging near the crackling fireplace and around the dining table.

Lola scurried over to me with a bottle of ibuprofen in one hand and a cup of coffee in the other. "Oh, Meg! I heard the news last night. I'm so glad you're okay. Here, come with me. The sheriff ordered me to set you up in a comfy chair by the fire. He'll be here soon. I moved this nice, plush chair over to a private corner by the window for you and brought in some pillows. Let's get you situated. You don't look good."

"Thanks." I tried to smile, but even that hurt.

She ushered me to the chair, moving everyone aside as we passed by.

"You sit tight. Drink this coffee. I'm going to bring you breakfast, okay?" She practically ran to the kitchen without giving me a chance to respond.

I wasn't sure I could stomach breakfast yet. I'd rather wait and see how the coffee went down. Breathing in the nutty scent made the cobwebs in my brain stretch apart a little. I took a sip.

Lola left the bottle of ibuprofen on the table next to me. I picked it up and then realized I couldn't twist off the childproof cap with one hand. What would that mean for writing? Typing with one hand was literally going to cramp my style. My feature was due in a few days. I was going to have to get moving soon if I wanted to get it in on time.

"Here's breakfast." Lola set a plate of hash browns, sausage links, and fruit salad next to me. She paused and looked at the bottle. "You want me to open that?"

"That'd be great." I raised it up to her. "Why are you being so nice this morning?"

She cracked open the bottle and shook a couple of tablets in my hand. "What do you mean?"

"Well, you seemed upset with me yesterday about snooping." I popped the medicine in my mouth and swallowed it down with a swig of coffee. Probably not the recommendation on the bottle—oh well.

"Sorry. I wasn't upset. At least not with you." She glanced around the room. "You mind if I sit?"

She lowered her voice. "I'm sorry if I seemed short yesterday. It wasn't about you." She checked around us again. No one paid any attention. The early risers were focused on chowing their breakfast as fast as possible to hit the snow.

"I didn't tell you the whole truth."

"About what?" I stabbed a sausage link. It matched my swollen fingers on my broken hand. I passed it over for a bite of fruit.

"Well, Jackson and I met a while back in Vermont."

I chewed the sweet pineapple, maintaining eye contact with Lola. "Oh?" I remembered Jackson saying that he'd spent time in Vermont. I should have connected that they'd met before.

"Yeah, we kind of had a thing."

"You and Jackson?" I said through a mouthful of fruit.

She blushed. "He's a really good guy, Meg. I know he likes to act the part of rich doctor when Malory's around, but he's not like that. At least, not with me."

I thought about Jackson's tender bedside manner with me last night.

"Anyway, he came out for the winter season last year and we hit it off right away. When he left, we kept in touch, but I didn't really think much about it. Then he called this spring and told me he heard about this job opening up. He's the one who helped me get the position."

"Oh." I couldn't think of anything else to say. My face probably conveyed that, too.

"I know what you're thinking—Malory, right?"

"Uh. I—I..."

Lola reached out and patted my hand. "It's okay. It's not what you think."

"It doesn't matter what I think. You don't need to explain." I took a bite of Lola's eggs.

"No, I want to explain." Lola looked over her shoulder. Satisfied that our conversation was private, she leaned in and continued. "Jackson never wanted to get engaged to Malory. He was pressured into it by his family. The only thing is Jackson doesn't love Malory. He loves me."

The cobwebs in my head felt like they'd been dusted away.

"Jackson doesn't even want to go for chief of staff. He wants to travel around the world—ski, climb, work in underserved communities where there's little access to healthcare."

I reached for my coffee. Stretching hurt.

"Are you okay?" Lola handed me the cup. "I don't think you're supposed to be moving." She checked the entryway again. "Jackson should be up soon. He'll give you another shot."

A reprieve from pain sounded good, but my head was starting to clear. I wasn't sure I wanted to cloud it with drugs.

"So Jackson broke it off with Malory?"

Lola nodded. "I told him to wait until the weekend was over. I begged him in fact, but he said he couldn't wait any longer."

"How did she take it?"

"Not well." Lola rolled her eyes. "It's not like she's in love with him. She and Ben were having a fling. Jackson knew. She just wanted the name, the position, the money. She totally freaked out when he told her the wedding was off."

In another moment of clarity I thought back to their fight at Timberline. Could that have been when Jackson broke things off? But then they were all lovey-dovey on the snowcat ride back to the hut.

"I didn't want anyone to know, at least not yet. I wanted to give it a little time, but Jackson told Malory about us. Not surprisingly, she's been awful to me. That's why I was short with you yesterday. I thought maybe she told you, and you were going to tell everyone."

"Why would I do that?"

She shrugged. "I don't know. I guess I've been paranoid. Since Ben's murder, I've been skittish. Malory cornered me, and told me she knew that Jackson killed Ben in a fit of rage. She claimed Jackson found out about their affair and was distraught. I knew that she was trying to get under my skin, but..." She trailed off.

I finished my coffee and rested it on the table. I couldn't believe how much I'd missed. Never would I have predicted that Jackson and Lola were a couple. It all made sense. The Vermont connection. Jackson's total lack of interest in Malory. Lola's shift in attitude when she thought her secret was in danger of being revealed.

"When the sheriff showed up last night to let us know that Clint had been arrested, I can't even begin to tell you how relieved I was. Now Jackson and I can focus on our future together." A smile tugged at the corners of her lips.

"Did I hear my name?" Jackson appeared behind her with his medical bag. He planted a kiss on the top of Lola's head and grinned at me. His style matched his casual demeanor. He rolled up the sleeves of his relaxed dress shirt. "How's my patient this morning? Sling looks good."

Lola moved for Jackson. "Here, you take a look. I think she needs another round of pain meds."

She pointed to my coffee cup. "You want a refresher, Meg?"

"That'd be great, thanks."

Lola grabbed my cup and squeezed my knee. "Thanks for the chat. I've really loved connecting with you. I hope we'll be able to keep in touch."

Jackson examined my sling. He tightened it across my shoulder and gently tested my fingers. Watching him work confirmed everything Lola told me. He clearly had a passion for medical care, and without snooty Malory observing his every move, he fell into a calm and gentle manner.

"You're still pretty swollen. Did you take more ibuprofen?"

I pointed to the bottle.

"How long ago?"

"Maybe like fifteen minutes or so."

Jackson checked his watch. "How's your pain? Do you want another shot?"

"It's okay," I lied.

"Rate it on a scale of one to ten."

"Maybe like a seven." I scowled.

"You sure about the shot? Trust me; you want to stay in front of the pain."

I waved him off. "No. I'm good. I don't like how fuzzy it makes me feel."

Jackson smiled. "Yeah. I get that. Better than half my patients at the hospital who come in to dull the pain of their everyday lives." He opened his bag and removed a bottle of Tylenol. He shook a few out and placed them in my hand. "At least take a couple of these. You can double up with the ibuprofen. It won't be as strong as what I gave you last night, but at least it'll take the edge off."

"Thanks." I swallowed the pills. "I'm glad to hear about you and Lola. She's pretty amazing."

He turned back to me. "She's amazing, isn't she?"

How was he ever with Malory? He and Lola were perfectly matched. I thought they had a really good shot at making it work and I told him as much.

As Jackson and Lola left to go ski, I was feeling pretty pleased with myself. That was until Greg walked into the room.

FORTY-TWO

He stormed over to me. "Meg Reed, what am I going to do with you?" His brow furrowed as he studied my splinted arm. "When are you going to learn?"

I cleared my throat. "Sorry, I know what you're thinking, but I swear I did leave it alone."

"Yeah, right." Greg leaned closer to examine the sling. My pulse rate quickened in response. He smelled like he just stepped out of the shower, like Irish Spring soap and mouthwash. Anytime he was this close to me, I couldn't help but react. He was even more gorgeous close up.

"Jackson did a decent job on this. How are you getting down the mountain?" Greg appeared to be completely oblivious to the fact that his proximity had me sweating.

"I, uh, I..."

He stepped back and chuckled. "Left it alone, huh?"

I guessed the silver lining was that he didn't realize my stumbling had more to do with his dreamy looks than with ending up in the middle of a murder investigation—again.

"No. I'm just fuzzy from last night. I didn't sleep much.

Sheriff Daniels or my friends will help me get my car back to Portland." I faked a grin as he sat down next to me. "No problemo."

I thought I had some sort of nervous speech tic when it came to Greg. No problemo? Where did that come from?

He raised an eyebrow and ignored my comment. "How do you intend to write with one arm?" He fiddled with the zipper on his ski coat.

"Uh, I—um—"

"Exactly," Greg interrupted me. "Exactly my point. You go get yourself injured and can't complete your assignment."

This was it. I braced myself for the impact of his words. He was going to fire me. I held my breath. It felt like my face was turning blue. What was Greg waiting for?

He pursed his lips and shook his head. "You leave me with just one option."

Just get it over with.

I placed my good hand on my heart and patted my chest in an attempt to keep from crying. If I was getting fired, I wanted to retain a tiny piece of dignity and this time I was going to at least fight to keep my job.

Greg sighed.

"Just say it." I let out my breath.

He looked confused. "Say what?"

"I'm fired, but let me explain."

He hung his head, shaking it in disbelief with a half chuckle. "Oh, Meg. Please. Not this again. I thought we were past this."

"What do you mean?" I sat straighter.

"I mean this dance about getting fired. You're a great writer. When is that going to sink in?"

"But my arm." I removed my hand from my chest and motioned to my injury.

"It sucks. That's why I'm going to have to assign Angie to help you for the next few weeks."

"Angie?" My mouth hung open. "From finance?"

Greg nodded. "Yeah, it's a slow time of the year. She's a meticulous typist. You can dictate your story to her."

Not Angie, my bunkmate from Collins Lake. If I didn't fit in at *Northwest Extreme* with my affinity for pink and vintage fashion, Angie certainly didn't fit in with her outdated nylons, frilly blouses, and sneering personality. As the resident finance director (granted, she was a department of one) she worked part-time, and on days that she was in the office, the writing staff was paper thin.

My colleagues warned me about her highlighter when I started. She was notorious for highlighting any clerical errors in neon yellow and calling you out in team meetings. Angie seemed to take a particular dislike to me. I didn't know if it was just the way she acted with all newbies or if I'd done something horrid, like miscalculated my mileage rate, to end up on her bad side. I couldn't imagine she'd take kindly to the idea of typing my story.

"Are you sure?" I asked Greg, crinkling my nose. "I don't think Angie likes me."

He scoffed. "That's her thing. She likes you just fine."

"You haven't seen my expense reports," I mumbled under my breath.

"Listen, Meg. I'm headed out of town. I need your completed story on my desk by the end of next week if it's going to run in the next issue. Is that doable? It's a fairly fast turn-around with your injuries and all."

I nodded. "Yeah, I'm on it. No problem." Honestly, I had nothing else slotted for the week and finishing this story would be a good way to bring closure to Ben's death.

He patted my knee and stood. "Good. I'm hitting the slopes. See you in about a week."

"See you," I called halfheartedly after him.

Great. Now what had I gotten myself into? Greg sounded confident that Angie would be thrilled to help me with my feature. I knew better.

My mind launched into a foot-long to-do list. Maybe I should have taken Jackson up on that shot after all.

FORTY-THREE

Malory stalked into the dining hall. She made a point of throwing an extended death stare Lola's way before proceeding over to me.

"Meg, I'm so, so sorry about your arm." She gave me a half hug.

"Thanks." I gave her a smile, but kept my shoulders squared, not trusting her saccharine sweetness.

She whipped her head in Lola's direction. "I suppose you've heard?" She tapped her fingers on the table. I noticed her engagement ring was absent from her finger.

I wasn't good in situations like this. Was I supposed to play dumb? Was their breakup official news?

She gave me an expectant look.

I decided to follow Gam's strategy—honesty. Man, honesty sucked sometimes.

"Yeah." I tried to make my face look serious. "I'm sorry it didn't work out with you and Jackson."

She clapped her hands together. "Don't give it a thought. There are plenty of *bigger* fish in the sea, if you know what I mean."

"What will you do now?"

"Do?" She looked confused.

"I mean, are you heading back to Portland?"

She shrugged. "We'll see. I'm in no hurry. The powder's great. And there's a rumor floating around that the state bar association is coming up for a conference today. I may hang around for a while and see if any eligible lawyers show up."

It must have been nice not to have to worry about minor details like going to work on a Monday. Malory's socialite status would be perfect for a legal retreat.

"Meg, I feel like we've really gotten to be friends this weekend." She gave me a sickeningly sweet smile.

That wasn't quite my assessment of our relationship. I let her continue. "I'm wondering if you might do me a tiny favor."

There it was. I knew she was putting on an act. "What's that?"

"It's about your story."

"What about my story?" I couldn't keep the mistrust out of my tone.

"I just wonder if Jackson really deserves to be featured, you know, given all that's happened."

"All that's happened?"

Malory's narrow jawline tightened. "Yes, you know. The scandal with Ben's murder and Clint."

I knew Malory couldn't care less about the scandal. "What does that have to do with Jackson?"

"You know he and Clint were very close. Which I'm sure you understand is one of the reasons I had to call off our engagement. Can you even imagine what sort of play that story would get in the society column?"

So Malory's story was that *she* broke off their relationship? Wow. That was rich. I didn't have the energy or interest in setting her straight.

"I still don't understand what this has to do with my feature."

"All I'm saying is that you should consider Jackson a liability. I think it would be a huge mistake to include him in your feature."

For someone who claimed to have called off the relationship, she sure had a personal vendetta. I decided my only tactic was to change the subject. "Hey, speaking of Clint. The other night, down at Timberline, remember how I got hit in the pool? You said that you found Clint in the hallway when you came to help me. Where was he?"

Malory considered this for a moment. "Come to think of it, he was in the lobby. He must have followed me down the hallway. He kind of startled me when he asked where I was going. I told him and he tagged along."

"I can't figure out why he hit me. I didn't know anything at that point. I mean, later on in the weekend I found some evidence that ultimately incriminated him, but honestly, I never really suspected him."

"Weird. Maybe it wasn't him." Malory's eyes were like ice. "I guess this means you're not going to listen to my advice and keep Jackson out of your story?"

I shook my head. "Even if I wanted to, I can't. I'm a journalist, Malory.

I'm bound to uphold a code of ethics."

"Please, you work for *Northwest Extreme* magazine." She flipped her hair with both hands. "You can't play the 'I'm a journalist' card when you write for an adventure-junkie magazine."

What I wanted to tell her was where she could go. Instead I forced my lips into a smile and grimaced through the pain as I stood. "Thanks for the feedback, Malory. I need to pack."

I left her in front of the fireplace, where I was sure she was shooting glares my way. *Go ahead, let her*, I thought as I headed for the bunks. Jackson and I both dodged bullets this weekend.

There was something unsettling about her response to that night at Timberline. It didn't make sense that Clint would have attacked me. I tried to think back to what had occurred before that night, and there wasn't anything I knew at that point in time. I found the gun and bullets the next day. Could Malory have been the one who hit me? Why?

I'd witnessed Jackson breaking up with Malory that night. Could she have come after me to stop me from telling anyone?

No, Meg, stop, I told myself as I rolled a pair of socks in a ball. Then again, Malory had already worked out a lie about her breaking things off. Could she be unstable enough to have done something drastic?

I wasn't sure, but it wasn't out of the realm of possibility. I wouldn't put it past her. Yep, going home sounded like a great plan. I was definitely ready to get off the mountain.

Henry knocked on the door as I finished attempting to create order in my bag. Packing with one hand was hard.

"Dude, what's up?" He entered the room and knelt beside me. "Nice packing job there, gimpy."

"Gimpy?" I scoffed, giving him my best attempt at a furrowed brow.

He ruffled my hair. "Every boarder needs a nickname."

"Aw, does this mean I'm officially a boarder now?"

Henry stuck out his tongue. "Did you even get on a board this weekend?"

"No." Although that was perfectly fine by me.

He did the "hang loose" sign with his hands. "Enough said. Next time, try taking a ride and then we'll give you a real nickname."

"What's yours? I don't think I've heard it." I changed the subject, hoping he'd drop the idea of getting me out on the ski slope.

"Sure you have—The Kid."

"I thought they just called you that because you're young."

"Nope, it's my move."

"Your move?" I scrunched my brow. That was news. Did Henry have a signature move?

He nudged me in the waist. "Scoot over, I'll help you get this mess shut. Now, this looks like a boarder's bag."

"I can't believe you have your own move and you never told me."

"Sure, everyone does. It's what makes the sport great. You know, everyone brings their own style."

"Thanks," I said as Henry zipped my bag shut.

"What's 'the kid'? Can I see it?"

He grinned. "Nope. It's top secret."

"What?" I punched him in the arm.

"I'm kidding. You're not in good shape today." He nodded toward my arm. "Come up when you're better and I'll show it to you."

"Deal." Although the next time I was on the mountain it was going to be with a hot chocolate in hand and a comfy spot in the lodge.

He pushed to his feet and lifted my bag onto the bunk. "Is the cat coming to get you? I'll take this out."

I followed him toward the front door.

Henry checked outside to see if the snowcat had arrived. "Not here yet." He ducked back inside. "I'll wait."

"Are you staying to board today?" I noticed he wore Ten-Eighty-branded gear from his helmet to his boots.

"Dude, it's killer out there. I can't pass it up."

I pointed to the Ten-Eighty patch on his parka. "Are you still in talks with them about a partnership?"

He grinned. "It's done. I'm in."

"Henry, that's great! Congratulations." I leaned forward and kissed him on the cheek. "I'll be able to say 'I knew you before you were a major Olympic star.'"

He flashed peace signs with both hands. "Nah. I'm an old man compared to the kids out there now."

"I thought you were *The Kid*."

"Funny."

I could hear the distant rumble of the snowcat. It would be here soon. I had to ask Henry about Jackson. Moving so that my body blocked the door, I lowered my voice. "Since we're alone, what happened with Jackson? Why were you fighting?"

"You're not going believe this."

"Was it because of Ten-Eighty?"

"Huh?"

"Wasn't Jackson telling you that you couldn't take the endorsement deal?"

Henry looked confused. "No."

"What was he so upset about then?" I couldn't contain my anticipation, so much so that my foot tapped on the hardwood floor.

"Chill, Meg."

I looked down at my leg. "I know. It's like a disease."

Henry laughed.

"Tell me! Put me out of my misery."

"He was pissed about Lola."

"Lola?"

"Yeah, he thought I had a thing for her."

"Oh! Of course." Why hadn't I put that together sooner?

"Of course, what?" Now Henry looked at me with anticipation.

"They're together."

"Who?"

"Lola and Jackson."

He looked confused. "I thought he and Malory were engaged?"

"Nope. He broke it off with her."

Henry let out a whistle. "Didn't see that coming."

"Tell me about it."

The snowcat hummed to a stop outside.

"Wait. One more thing before I go," I said, blocking the door.

"What, you're not letting me out?" Henry chuckled. "All ninety pounds of you and your one arm?"

I punched him with my good arm, and immediately regretted it as it sent a wave of pain ricocheting through the other one.

"What were you doing outside that night and how did Clint get your gun?"

"You don't let things go. You should really take up boarding. It's like meditation when you connect with the snow."

"Enough on the boarding. You know me, Henry. It's never happening, like ever."

"It could." He checked the hallway behind us. "I think Clint planned this for a while. He's the one who told me to bring up the gun. Said he was going to do a whole demo about the history of rescue training and stuff. I asked him about it that first night and he blew me off. Said we'd do it later. After I left the meeting, I went back to my bunk and noticed the gun was gone. That's why I went outside."

"So you knew it was Clint? Why didn't you say anything?"

Henry shook his head. "I didn't know. I just knew my gun was missing. Later I thought it might have been Clint's but I didn't have any way of proving it and he was throwing all suspicion at me. Jackson, too."

"I have to tell you, you had me worried for a while there. You were acting so angry. I've never seen that side of you."

"Yeah. I'm usually pretty chill, but Jackson was following me around everywhere I went. I was like, 'Dude, back off.' He wouldn't. It got old, you know?"

The snowcat driver rapped on the door. He peered inside. "Heard I have a med-evac?" He paused and stared at my injured arm. "You again?" He grinned. "I knew you were trouble. Come on, let's get you down."

Henry loaded my bag onto the cat and then helped me on board. "Thanks for sticking by me, Meg." He took a step back and ran his fingers through his hair. "You want to grab a beer or something next week?"

"Of course." I planted another kiss on his cheek.

Was I imagining things, or did he turn a brighter shade of pink?

The driver warned me that the ride back to Timberline was likely going to hurt. "I'll take her as slow as I can, miss, but it's about to be bumpy."

He wasn't kidding.

FORTY-FOUR

The rest of the day was a blur. Matt, Jill, Gam, and Sheriff Daniels were all waiting for me at Timberline.

Gam embraced me and refused to keep her hands off my body. "Stay however you're comfortable. I'll give you a zap. Your friends want to take you home. If they do, I'll stay and ski. As long as you're okay with that?"

"For sure. You're going to ski, Gam?" I nodded to her petite teal ski jacket and purple ski pants.

She winked. "You know me. I love speed. I talked Bill into it."

Sheriff Daniels's eyes widened. He tried—unsuccessfully—to hide a grin. "Don't know how the old back will hold up, but you only live once, right?"

Gam swatted him on the arm. "Bill, you'll be just fine." She gave me a final squeeze. "Love you, darling. See you back at home."

They departed hand in hand. My heart felt full. At least someone had found love this weekend.

Jill and Matt had worked out a plan to get me and my car down the mountain. I didn't remember much of the drive. Jill tried to keep the conversation light as she easily maneuvered the winding road. I winced over every bump and sharp turn. That's what I got for not accepting a painkiller.

Matt followed us in my car.

The route home was almost unfamiliar. Where the mountain streets had been bare a few days ago, snow piled on the median and compacted on the asphalt. The evergreen trees were coated in white, and the purple sky threatened to unleash another round.

Once we made it to Portland, Jill drove me straight to the hospital, where the emergency room doctor confirmed that I'd shattered the bones in my hand and broken my arm in three places. The X-ray made me sick to my stomach. He splinted my arm and sent me home with a bottle of pain medication and a referral to an orthopedic surgeon for the next day. Maybe that deadline was going to be tighter than I realized. Or I was going to have to quickly master voice dictation.

"You want me to sleep over?" Jill asked, unlocking the front door to my apartment. Mail piled near the steps. She scooped it up. "I can't believe you still get a hard copy of the paper. Why don't you read it on your tablet?"

I made a beeline for the kitchen, poured a glass of water, and swallowed the pain medication. At this point feeling a little woozy was worth "staying in front of the pain," as Jackson put it.

"Never." I plopped on the couch and picked up the Sunday paper. "This is like my Bible. I'm not giving it up. The smell of the newsprint, the feel of thin paper on your fingers. It's a sensory experience."

"Right." Jill lugged my bag into my bedroom. "Seriously, you want me to stay?"

"I think I'll be okay. Matt said he'd hang out and I'm sure Gam will come check in on me."

"If you're sure?" She watched out the window as a group of kids passed by on scooters. "I don't have anywhere I need to be."

"What about Will?" I asked, placing the paper on the coffee table.

"He's still at Timberline." She kept her gaze focused outside.

"Oh."

"There's a bar association meeting going on."

I remembered Malory telling me as much, but wondered if there was more to Will staying than Jill was letting on. She didn't expand the conversation.

After staring out the window for a couple minutes, she clapped her hands together. "Hey! I have something I want to show you. Stay right there. I'll be back in a flash."

I pointed to my splint. "Where am I going?"

"Good point. Sit tight." She floated out the front door.

I wasn't sure how much to push the subject of Will. Jill was tricky. If I gave her space, I figured she'd eventually confide in me, but I didn't want to give her too much space. With enough room to retreat, she might completely close in. It was something I knew all too well.

Breezing back in the room with a canvas tucked under her arm, Jill's face didn't reveal a hint of worry.

"I took you up on your offer." She removed the canvas from under her arm. "That space downstairs is perfect."

She held the canvas for me to see. "What do you think? Be honest."

I drew in a breath. Jill's artwork tended to be modern—with angular lines, geometric shapes, bold colors. She dabbled in a variety of styles and approaches when we were in college. There was a black-and-white phase when she only painted in monotone colors, a sketching phase, and a minimalist phase.

This painting was none of those. It made me understand for

the first time what people said about art being revealing. I felt like I understood Jill in a new way as I studied the canvas. She'd painted a spring landscape with a touch of whimsy and an edge of mystery. It reminded me of billboards around town displaying advertisements for Cirque Du Soleil's upcoming show.

A young woman stood in a sea of brilliant wildflowers. Her arm extended toward the sun, offering up a blooming purple flower as her body drank in golden light.

I stood to get a closer view. Jill gave me an eager look. "Well, what do you think? Is it horrible?" She frowned.

"It's amazing." I noticed how Jill's brushstrokes made each flower come to life and how the woman's face held a balance of hope and hunger. "It's not like anything you've ever done."

"That's what I'm worried about."

"You shouldn't be. It's captivating." I wasn't exaggerating. I couldn't tear my eyes away from it. Every inch of canvas contained a new detail.

"Jill, I would pay big money for this." I met her eyes. "Big money."

She blushed. "But you're broke."

"Fair point." I shrugged.

We laughed.

"Plus, you have to say that. You're my bestie."

"No, I don't. I swear. This is really good. I can't quite figure out what it's like. I mean, on the one hand it's a beautiful sweeping landscape, but then there's this other layer, something a bit darker that makes it intriguing. I want to know her story. The woman—what's she after?"

Jill smiled. "I call it 'Breaking Free,' if that helps."

"It's you?" I asked softly.

"Maybe."

I squeezed her arm. "Does this mean you're going to paint more?"

She tucked the painting back under her arm. "We'll see."

"You have to! Are you going to sell this one? I bet an art gallery is going to snap it up."

Jill rolled her eyes. "You're the best, Meg. The art scene is really competitive in Portland, though."

I wanted to push her more, but I knew she had to figure it out on her own. "The basement is always here for you."

She made sure I had "the essentials" within arm's reach. In other words: bags of candy, my phone, and medication nearby before she left. "You call if you need anything, okay? I'm only ten minutes away." She planted a kiss on my head and left.

The pain medicine started to kick in and I nodded off on the couch. A knock on the door startled me awake.

"Come in," I called, sitting up. "It's unlocked." I knew it must have been Matt.

Before the door was completely opened, I knew I'd made a mistake. One whiff of the perfume wafting through the door announced who had arrived. It almost made me wish I were back on the mountain.

Emphasis on *almost*.

I arched my shoulders completely upright and squared my jaw as my guest stepped inside.

"Mom. What are you doing here?"

FORTY-FIVE

"Darling, now what kind of greeting is that for your dear mother?"

Pleez.

She marched in with an armful of grocery bags from one of the upscale markets. Her outfit was perfectly coordinated, from her dangling opaque earrings right to the tips of her pointed pumps. I had to admit for fifty she looked good, but I suspected she'd had some help. Her face had been wiped free of age spots, and the lines around her eyes seemed to have vanished. I supposed it could be good genes. After all, Gam looked amazing for a woman in her seventies, but she also looked her age.

Mom took one look at the piles of candy on the coffee table and shook her head. "Oh, no. This won't do." Searching for a space to drop her bags, she decided on the nearby chair and then proceeded to scoop all the candy away.

"Your grandmother called me, darling." She placed a bag of seaweed and kale chips on the coffee table. "I brought you some special snacks. Your body needs healing food, doesn't it?"

"Thanks, how kind." I forced a smile through my gritted teeth.

"Now, darling, don't use that tone with me. You need to keep your energy up, and these will help." She continued emptying the contents of her grocery trip onto my coffee table: chicken soup, orange juice, and mushroom tea.

"Oh, you'll love that." She noticed me eyeing the tea.

I bit my lip.

"Don't bite your lip, dear." She didn't miss a thing. "Mind if I sit?" She sat down next to me before I could decline.

"To what do I owe the pleasure?"

"Sarcasm isn't becoming to you, Margaret. It makes your face too pinched." She adjusted the silk scarf around her neck. "I'm worried about you." Her tone shifted. She dropped the affected quality of her voice.

"Thanks, but I'm fine. Really. They're sending me to a surgeon tomorrow."

"Who?"

"I don't know." I shrugged and pointed to the coatrack near the front door. I found the coatrack at one of my favorite vintage boutiques on Belmont Street. "His card's in my purse."

Mom jumped to her feet and removed my purse from the iron rack. "Shall I look inside?"

"Go for it."

She rifled through for the card. "Ooh. Dr. Meyers. Good. I hear he's wonderful. One of the best."

I didn't bother to ask how she'd heard this. One guess—her gossip-hungry friends who met for lunch.

"Your grandmother mentioned you were involved in another murder?" She returned to the couch.

"You make it sound like I was part of the murder. I was a witness."

"That's not what I hear from your grandmother. She said you were helping Detective Daniels with the case."

"Detective? I think he's a sheriff."

Her gold bracelets clinked together as she waved me off.

"Sheriff. Detective. It's all the same thing. And, frankly, I think 'Detective' sounds more official."

I sighed. "Anyway, regardless, I wasn't part of the investigation."

Mom scooted closer and rested her hand on my knee. I was surprised to see that she wore her wedding ring on her left finger.

She looked down. "Oh, that. I can't seem to take it off."

"I thought you took it off when you walked out on him," I spat out without thinking. My words made her flinch.

"This?"

"Why didn't you take it off when you deserted him?"

She let go of my knee and leaned back on the couch. Her body deflated, like a balloon losing its air. For a moment I thought she might cry, but then she regained her composure.

"I can't do this anymore, Margaret."

"Do what?"

"This. Us." She motioned between us with her hands. "I'm done trying to protect... I—I don't even know what I'm supposed to be protecting."

I couldn't remember a time in recent history that Mom had appeared rattled. She was notorious for maintaining a stiff upper lip.

"Protecting?"

"Margaret." Her piercing eyes challenged me.

"Seriously? How many times are we going to do this? Why can't you just give me some space? That's all I'm asking for. I loved Pops so much. Maybe it's grief. Maybe it's misplaced anger. I don't know. But I can't forgive you yet. I'm sure someday I'll be able to do it. But not yet."

"Margaret, your father's death was not my fault." She twisted her wedding finger and lowered her voice. "I loved him, too."

I sprang from the couch. Pain swelled in my arm. "You left

him!" I was yelling now. "You left him when he needed you most. When everyone else had given up on him, you—*you*... walked out!"

She jutted out her stiff bottom lip and forced her index finger toward the couch with such violence I thought she might snap it in half. "S*it*."

"No, I'm not a little girl anymore."

"Margaret Mary Reed, sit down this instant." She held her finger in position.

I hung my head and slid down the couch. "Fine. I'm sitting."

"Good, because you need to hear what I'm about to say."

"Nothing you can say is going to change the way I feel right now."

"This is."

"What?"

"I didn't leave your father." She spoke so softly, I had to lean closer to hear her next words. "He left me."

FORTY-SIX

The pain in my arm disappeared. The room spun. I buried my head in my hand. "What?" I blew out a long gasp of air, keeping my hands on my temples. "Pops left you? No! No way. That can't be true."

She tried to place her hand on my knee. I flinched. "It's true."

I refused to look at her. "No way. Pops would never leave you. Never. He loved you." She started to respond. I pushed to my feet and started pacing around the living room. "No, don't even talk. I can't do this right now. My brain isn't even functioning with the pain medication."

"Margaret, listen." Her eyes welled with tears.

"No. Not today. Can you just go?" I walked to the door and held it open.

She picked her black leather purse off the floor, looped it over her arm, and walked toward me. "Fine, but, darling, we do have to talk about this. We can do it when you're a little calmer."

I held the door open, keeping my eyes on the floor.

Mom paused on the threshold. "Maggie, I thought I was

doing the right thing. You're so stubborn, just like your father. Please forgive me."

I didn't meet her eyes. She walked out.

How could she do this to me? She must be lying. She had to be lying. If she weren't, then that meant that Pops had lied to me, which wasn't possible.

A tsunami of tears spilled from my eyes. The stress of the weekend—Ben's murder, Will's wandering eye, Pops—all of it came flooding out. I'm not sure how long I sobbed on the couch, not caring whether or not my neighbors could hear me. I could hear that life went on as usual outside my front door, kids zooming up and down the tree-lined sidewalks on scooters and neighbors raking leaves and chatting to one another in the late-afternoon November sun. But it felt like I was alone in a bubble of my own sorrow, worlds apart.

I heard the sound of Matt arriving sometime later, and he came to the couch at once and joined me. "Megs? Are you okay? Is it your arm?" He sat beside me and wrapped his arm around my shoulder.

I shook my head and fell into him. He let me sob on his shoulder until I was parched.

Did I trust anyone? What did Mom mean that I was stubborn like Pops? He wasn't stubborn. He was kind and wise and calm. She was the stubborn one.

Matt propped pillows behind my back. Then he disappeared into the bathroom, returning with a warm, wet washcloth, tissues, and a glass of water.

"You want to tell me what happened?"

I let the damp washcloth soak into my skin and blew my nose in the tissue. My breath had steadied but my body convulsed every few minutes, like it was trying to rid itself of my final sobs.

He waited while I dabbed my eyes and drank the water. He kept his arm around my shoulder, carefully so he didn't touch the splint. Having him so close to my body was an instant relaxant. Was that a bad sign? Whenever Greg was in close proximity, I fumbled my words and felt my heart beating out of my chest. With Matt it was the opposite. I could feel the tension I'd been holding in my body melt away in his arms.

I told him about Mom. Matt held my back as I spat out the story. When I finished, he crossed one leg over his knee and took a deep breath.

"She could be right, Megs."

"That's what I'm afraid of. Why would Pops lie to me?"

Matt tapped his fingers on his lips and sighed. "If he did, I'm sure he had a good reason. Didn't you say your mom said she was 'protecting' you? Maybe it had something to do with the meth case."

My brain couldn't take it all in. "Let's let it be for tonight."

He removed his arm from my shoulder and cradled my face in his hands. We sat suspended in the moment. His eyes searched mine. For what, I wasn't sure. A sign that I returned his affection? To see if I was stable?

I take back what I said about feeling calm in his arms. Matt's body shifted. I could feel the heat between us, like a palpable force. *This is it. He's going to kiss me.* I tilted my chin. He leaned closer. At the last minute, he planted a quick kiss on my cheek and released his grasp.

Matt reached for his iPhone. "Are you hungry?" The moment was lost.

"Actually, I am."

"Cool. I'll order a pizza." He scrolled on his phone for the number to our favorite pizza shop and placed an order for a Count Basie—barbecued chicken, red onions, and cilantro.

He slid his phone into his pocket and turned to face me head-on. "Megs, you discovered a dead body, got knocked out in the cold, fell off a chairlift, and just had it out with your mom. Let's call it a day. We can revisit the meth case later this week once your arm is back in one piece."

I gave him the look.

He placed his finger on my lips. I had to resist the urge not to kiss it. "Megs, I promise. I'll come over with the files and we'll go through everything I've been able to piece together so far."

Matt looked resolved. He had a point. My body felt like it might implode at any minute. The pain in my arm had returned and my blow-up with Mom had left me rattled.

I agreed that we could table the conversation for the night, but after Matt left I wondered if I'd made a mistake. I spent the entire night replaying every snippet of conversation I'd had with Pops before he died. It didn't make me feel better.

FORTY-SEVEN

At the orthopedic surgeon's office the next day, I learned that—thankfully—my arm didn't require surgery. The swelling had gone down enough to cast it. And guess what? They had *pink*!

I rolled into *Northwest Extreme* late in the morning with my new cast and pages full of notes from the weekend that I was going to have to decipher and shape into a story.

My colleagues stopped by my desk to check in and sign my cast. Hey, if you had to have a cast, you might as well have some fun with it, right? I kept my collection of colored Sharpies on the corner of my desk so they were accessible when people came by.

Everyone wrote such nice things about me, I'm pretty sure that my cheeks matched the cast. My coworkers offered to make a coffee run and help me with the copy machine. I could have got used to being pampered like this every now and then, if the price weren't a broken arm.

The morning breezed by. I updated our social media sites with one hand, and couldn't resist taking a selfie of my cast to post. None of our followers needed to know that I'd fallen off a chairlift. Posting a photo of my broken arm after a weekend of training with Ridge Rangers led to an epic online chat with many of our followers. I felt like a real adventurer. So maybe I omitted a few minor details.

The afternoon took an unpleasant turn when Angie appeared at my desk. Without looking up from my laptop screen, I said, "Do you want to sign my cast?"

She cleared her voice and folded her arms across her chest. "No."

"Oh, sorry, Angie. I thought you were someone else."

Angie pursed her pencil-thin lips so tight it looked painful. She was by far the most senior member on staff both in age and attitude. Her current locked-lip stare made her face look even older. I'd seen her smile once at Greg, and when she relaxed she was actually quite pretty. This wasn't one of those times.

"I was told that I'm to help you with your story." She reminded me of an uptight librarian, the kind they always portray in the movies (not the real-life amazing kind), with her straight skirt, tucked-in shirt, nylons, and reading glasses resting at the tip of her nose.

What was the opposite of *chipper*? Who knew? I didn't have the energy to pull up the thesaurus, but whatever it was, that was Angie.

Smiling broadly, I tried gushing out my thanks.

"I'd prefer to do this in my office." She scowled and walked away.

Great. I flipped my laptop shut and piled my notes together. I wasn't ready to dictate to her, but she hadn't given me a chance to explain that. I wondered if Greg had her on strict orders to report my progress to him. Time to get creative.

For the next hour Angie groaned, sighed, and tapped her fingers on the keyboard, waiting as I'd start a thought and then change my mind.

This wasn't going to work.

"Angie, can we take a ten-minute break? I want to do a

quick little walk outside to see if I can kind of center my train of thought."

She looked at her watch. "I have an errand I have to run since I had to come in on my day off to help you. Take your walk and please try to get your thoughts together. I don't have time to waste."

"I understand. I'm sorry. I've just never tried to write a story out loud. It's a totally different experience."

Did she just roll her eyes at me?

"Meet me back here in thirty minutes sharp." Angie gathered her things and left me sitting in her office.

I started to push my chair back. Maybe fresh air would trigger my creativity. The fall sunshine had returned to Portland, and outside Angie's window I could see joggers and groups of walkers enjoying its rays.

My cast bumped a stack of files on Angie's desk as I stood. Maneuvering with this thing was going to take some getting used to. I bent over to pick up the files and restack them on Angie's desk.

One of them was labeled: MEG REED.

I know what you're thinking, but I couldn't help myself.

Placing the other files back on Angie's desk, I sat down again and opened my file. It contained copies of my expense reports, the paperwork, a non-compete that I signed when I first got hired, and all the usual human resources stuff. I was about to put the file back in the stack when something caught my eye.

Clipped to the back of the file folder were press clippings of Pops's meth madness story—every single one.

A sick feeling rose in my stomach as I leafed through the old news features. Behind the clippings I found a photo of me and notes about my routine, dating to last November.

Matt was right. My chance encounter with Greg at the coffee shop last January had nothing to do with chance. He'd planned the meeting for two months before he ever "accidentally" bumped into me.

I threw the folder on Angie's desk and ran out of the office. My heart pounded in my chest and my fingers shook as I slid my phone on and scrolled through my contacts to Greg's name.

He answered on the second ring. "Meg! How's it going? How's your story coming together?"

"Greg. Stop. We have to talk."

"Okay. What's up? Why so serious?"

"I just found my personnel file."

The line went quiet.

"Greg, are you there?"

He cleared his throat. "Listen, Meg. It's not what you think."

"Here's what I think. I think you knew that I was Charlie Reed's daughter and you planned on hiring me the entire time. Why? To keep tabs on me?"

Greg coughed. "No, Meg. To keep you safe."

A LETTER FROM THE AUTHOR

Huge thanks for reading Meg's story! I hope you felt like you were off on an adventure with her. If you want to hear about my new books and bonus content, you can sign up for my newsletter!

www.stormpublishing.co/ellie-alexander

If you've enjoyed Meg's adventures—or perhaps misadventures—I'd love it if you would take a minute to share your review so other readers can grab a mocha and hang with Meg and her friends!

I am so grateful you picked up this book. I know there are so many distractions these days, and the fact that you spend your time in the pages of a book makes my heart happy. Here's to more armchair adventures from the comfort of your couch!

Ellie Alexander

https://elliealexander.co

facebook.com/elliealexanderauthor
instagram.com/ellie_alexander

MEG'S ADVENTURE TIPS

Rule One—Slope style. Braving the winter elements requires more than style on the slopes. Meg's fingerless gloves might have looked cute, but they did little to protect her digits from the extreme and biting cold that assaulted her right outside the Silcox Hut. Frostbite can occur in minutes in freezing temperatures and with low wind chills. Exposed extremities like fingers, toes, and the tip of the nose are at the highest risk. When heading out into winter weather, it's critical to dress the part. Outdoor experts recommend layering. Look for a coat with a fleece lining, down insulation, and a removable waterproof outer layer. Always be sure to choose boots that are insulated, waterproof, and rated for below-freezing conditions. Pack a hat, or better yet, a balaclava—a ski mask that shields the entire face. And most importantly, don't forget your fingers! A good pair of waterproof ski gloves is a necessity for any mountain outing. Meg escaped frostbite this time, but next time she might not be so lucky.

Rule Two—Know before you go. "Know Before You Go" is the motto of the U.S. Forest Service, and perhaps one that

Meg should adopt. While she's slowly starting to improve her outdoor prowess and beginning to realize the importance of always being prepared, she still has a long way to go and much more to learn. Meg made some rookie mistakes again, like venturing outside in a raging blizzard. Don't be like her and get left out in the cold. Whether heading out for a leisurely afternoon on cross-country trails, or into the backcountry for a more intense adventure, be sure to check conditions before you go. The Northwest Avalanche Center (NWAC) is a great resource in Meg's neck of the woods. Their professional meteorologists provide forecasts and avalanche warnings for slopes across the Pacific Northwest. You can also learn more about avalanche safety from the Forest Department: https://www.fs.usda.gov/visit/know-before-you-go/avalanches

Rule Three—find a guide. The Ridge Rangers, despite their internal conflict, helped Meg learn essential winter survival techniques. When attempting to summit a new peak, it's imperative (especially for novice climbers) to find a qualified guide who is familiar with the terrain and understands its challenges. A professional mountain guide could be the difference between a successful summit and disaster. To find a certified guide, visit the American Mountain Guides Association. They train and certify expert guides who can help you accomplish your dream of summiting with a focus on safety. Not only will a professional guide ensure your safe return from elevation, but they'll also make the experience enjoyable and fun. As for Meg, she's glad to have her feet planted firmly on lower ground for the moment.

MEG'S A SLAYING AT THE SKI LODGE
SCENIC TOUR

Follow along on Meg's adventure on Mount Hood. If you're feeling ready to brave the elements, bundle up and bring your skis. Or if you're more like Meg, you can cozy up in front of the fire with a steaming drink and watch the snow fall outside.

Stop One—Government Camp. Start your day at Government Camp by following Highway 26 east from Portland for 55 miles. This alpine village boasts a variety of shops and restaurants where you can gear up or grab a bite before hitting the slopes. If you visit Government Camp in the summer months, you're likely to spot several world-class skiers and boarders in town to train on Palmer Glacier. Ski Bowl, the mid-mountain ski resort nearby, features a summer adventure park with alpine slides, bungee jumping, a zip-line, mountain biking, and much more. In the winter, Ski Bowl transforms into America's largest night skiing area, and offers plenty of adventures for novice and expert skiers. Meg's a fan of some of the tamer winter options at Ski Bowl, like coasting down the tubing hill or tucking in under a warm blanket on a horse-drawn sleigh ride.

Stop Two—Collins Lake Resort. Collins Lake Resort is located on the Government Camp Business Loop, just off Highway 26. Take advantage of night skiing at Ski Bowl, and extend your stay in a chalet-style condo just a quick walk from the ski runs. Tucked into the Mount Hood National Forest, these high-end and high-altitude chalets will make you feel like you've stepped into a Bavarian winter wonderland. They sleep eight to ten guests and come equipped with luxurious amenities. Be sure to take advantage of the year-round heated pool. Like Meg, you can swim in the warm water or soak in the hot tub while snow showers rain down. A network of trails wind through the resort—perfect for snowshoeing in the winter or an easy walk in the summer.

Stop Three—Mt. Hood Brewing Co. Located in Government Camp right off Highway 26, this mountainside pub is a favorite pit stop of Meg's. She didn't get a chance to stop by for a pint in this adventure, thanks to worsening conditions at Timberline and a broken arm on the way back to sea level, but she'll certainly be back for a refresher the next time she finds herself on the slope. Mt. Hood Brewing Co. features hand-crafted microbrews, delicious pub food, and a relaxing space to kick back after a long day on the ski runs. Meg recommends their signature beer—Ice Axe IPA. It has plenty of hops to get your taste buds tingling with a clean, smooth finish. Mt. Hood Brewing Co. sells their beer exclusively in Oregon, so if you want a sample you'll have to brave the altitude.

Stop Four—Timberline Lodge. From Government Camp, follow Highway 26 east for about a mile and take the first exit onto Timberline Highway. The road takes you five and a half miles up the mountain to the lodge and the ski resort. Timberline Lodge should head the list of any Pacific Northwest travel itinerary. The lodge itself is a work of art and a testament to the resourcefulness and resolve of our American culture. Built timber by timber by workers seeking to gain a new trade during the Great Depression, the craftsmanship of this National Historic Landmark is truly a feat. You can wander through Timberline's hallways, where you'll discover hidden nooks and crannies showcasing gleaming handcrafted wood designs, and an alcove where you can catch a glimpse of Mount Jefferson on a clear day. The lodge offers free guided tours by U.S. Forest Service interpreters. It's a chance to get an insider's look at Timberline, and a history lesson to impress all of your friends when you return home. Timberline's guest rooms can book quickly during ski season, so plan ahead if you intend to stay overnight. The lodge's restaurants are open to the public. Meg likes to find a comfy spot in front of the fire to sip a hot chocolate and watch the skiers pass by outside.

Stop Five—The Silcox Hut. The Silcox Hut, also known as "Oregon's highest hotel room," is only accessible by ski lift, snowcat, or by trekking 1,000 vertical feet with the power of your quads. Regardless of how you get there, the remote high mountain hut is worth the trip. Before entering the Silcox Hut, be sure to stop and soak in the stunning view. The Cascade mountain range and forests stretch for miles from this vantage point. You'll feel like you're floating in the clouds, and gain a new perspective on the meaning of the Pacific Northwest's wild open spaces. The Silcox Hut is available for private events and overnight group rentals. It's the perfect ski weekend getaway. You and your guests will be treated to delectable meals by the hut's live-in host, and have the benefit of all of Timberline's amenities. Bring your skis, a bunch of your friends, and stay for the night. Or just swing by for a glimpse of the charming hut the next time you find yourself 7,000 feet above sea level.

ACKNOWLEDGEMENTS

To everyone at Storm who's been a part of this re-release: Vicky Blunden, Alexandra Begley, Oliver Rhodes, Becca Allen, the cover artists, page proofers—it's an absolute delight to work with you!

Printed in Dunstable, United Kingdom